'You're the perfect one to deal with Chelsea Whitmore, Scarlatta.'

Jake Scarlatta stared at the chief. There had to be a way to convince Talbot that moving Whitmore to his fire station was a bad idea. Damned if he could think of one, though. 'I wish you'd reconsider,' he said lamely. 'I run a really tight ship.'

'And Whitmore will rock the boat?'

More likely cause a major flood. But he knew she was a good firefighter. No matter what his personal feelings were, it wasn't fair to smudge her reputation. So she'd made one mistake—Jake knew all about making classic mistakes and having them haunt you. Now it looked like his penance was going to be dealing with her.

'Okay,' he told the chief. 'Do it, then. We'll manage. Somehow.'

Available in January 2004 from Silhouette Superromance

On Her Guard
by Beverly Barton
(The Protectors)

Lydia Lane
by Judith Bowen
(Girlfriends)

Code of Honour
by Kathryn Shay
(City Heat)

The Target
by Kay David
(The Guardians)

Code of Honour
KATHRYN SHAY

SILHOUETTE®
SUPERROMANCE™

To my daughter, April, as you enter into your first year
of university. May the values found in this book—hard work
and dedication to your profession, maintaining your code
of honour and devotion to those you love, no matter what
the circumstances—be ones you uphold throughout the
rest of your life.

*First published in Great Britain 2004
Silhouette Books, Eton House, 18-24 Paradise Road,
Richmond, Surrey TW9 1SR*

© Mary Catherine Shaefer 2000

ISBN 0 373 70882 3

38-0104

*Printed and bound in Spain
by Litografia Rosés S.A., Barcelona*

Dear Reader,

What made me want to write about firefighters? Initially, because it's an exciting profession. The strong, silent, heroic type of guy has always appealed to me, too, so I thought—wow, perfect heroes. And female firefighters intrigue me, mostly because I admire their desire to break into this traditionally male job.

Code of Honour, the third in my CITY HEAT series, deals with the everyday life of a career firefighter, and universal themes that affect us all. How important is integrity? Do we learn from our past mistakes? Is there a compromise between being honourable and getting our own needs met? Lieutenant Jake Scarlatta is forced to confront these issues when he does the unthinkable— falls in love with Chelsea Whitmore, a firefighter in his charge. At first he fights his feelings. When he realises she returns them, the battle between his particular code of honour and his intense love for this woman rages within him. Then, when things start to go wrong at the fire station for her, he is forced to decide if he'll stand by her or fulfil the requirements of an officer in the Rockford Fire Department.

I think this series is an accurate portrayal of a fire department in upstate New York. I hope I stayed true to the characters of these men and women who are truly America's bravest. They are utterly courageous, often funny, always interesting, even romantic people. I hope you find that the characters in my books are all these things, too.

Please write and let me know what you think. I answer all reader mail. Send letters to Kathryn Shay, PO Box 24288, Rochester, New York, 14624-0288, USA or e-mail me at Kshay1@AOL.com. Also visit my websites at http://home.eznet.net/~kshay and at http://www.superauthors.com

Sincerely,

Kathryn Shay

ACKNOWLEDGEMENT

There are many people to thank for their help and input in my CITY HEAT series.

The first group is the Gates Fire Department, particularly their chief and officers, who invited me to the fire stations and shared their experiences with me. Thanks, too, go to the many Gates line firefighters who let me wear their gear, taught me how to hold a hose, put out a fire with an extinguisher and observe several of their drills, including live burns.

Next, I had the privilege of working with the 542-person Rochester, New York Fire Department. My appreciation goes to many specific fire stations for allowing me to visit. With meals, tours of their fire stations and the recounting of many of their experiences, the men and women at Engine 16, Engine 17, Quint/Midi 5 and Quint/Midi 9 gave me my first feel for the professional life of a city firefighter. Specifically, my deep gratitude goes to Firefighter Lisa Beth White for sharing her insights into the life of a female in this predominately male department.

The Rochester Fire Academy personnel could not have been more welcoming. Battalion Chief Russ Valone, in charge of training, allowed me access to classes, training sessions, practicals and to observe recruits simulate life in a fire station and put out fires. Special appreciation goes to the 1997 Fall Recruit Class and their trainers.

My warmest gratitude and affection go to the Quint/Midi 8 firefighters. They were all gracious in letting me ride along on the rigs, wear old gear and eat several meals with them. These guys spent many afternoons and evenings sharing their experiences, answering my questions, giving advice on my story lines and suggesting possible improvements. From that group, Firefighter and Paramedic Joe Giorgione was the best 'consultant' an author could ask for.

Any 'real feel' these books have is due to all these brave men and women who told me their stories. Any errors are completely mine.

CHAPTER ONE

"YOU'RE the perfect one to deal with Chelsea Whitmore, Scarlatta. There's already a woman in your firehouse on another shift, so the setup is ideal. And you fought tooth and nail for Francey Cordaro's rights. Now that someone's retired, there's room in your group right now."

Jake Scarlatta stared at Chief Talbot, the Rockford Fire Department's top man, whom he'd always liked and respected, and tried to keep from objecting immediately. There had to be *some* way to convince the chief that moving Whitmore to his fire station wasn't wise. Damned if he could think of one, though. "I wish you'd reconsider," he said lamely.

Talbot stroked his graying mustache and studied Jake. "This have anything to do with that incident with DeLuca years ago?"

Jake kept himself from flinching at the mention of his one past, very public mistake. "In a way. I like to run a tight ship now."

"And Whitmore will rock the boat."

More like cause major flooding. But he knew she was a good firefighter, and no matter what his personal feelings were, it wasn't fair to smudge her reputation. "It won't be easy. My men aren't as...liberated as Ed Knight's group. Francey was an easy fit there."

In reality, when his crew got wind of Whitmore's possible transfer, they had grumbled to the point that Jake had to put his foot down and tell them to shape up and be professional. Their fire station, Quint/Midi Twelve was a good solid place to work, but sometimes it needed firm leadership.

Talbot said, "Well, Whitmore's not going to be an easy fit anywhere. I think you're our best choice. She didn't make a stink about what happened over at her last company, Engine Four, but she could sue the pants off us if she wanted to. We've got to be very careful this time."

Tales of what had happened to Chelsea Whitmore on her last assignment—she was one of the five females out of five hundred firefighters in the RFD, in upstate New York—had swept through the department quicker than brushfires. She'd made the classic mistake—dated a fellow firefighter in her group, broke his heart and then the guy went berserk and endangered himself and his entire crew. The woman would never live that down.

And since Jake knew all about making classic mistakes and having them haunt you, it looked like his penance was going to be dealing with Whitmore.

"When will she start?"

"Her leave was open-ended. She wants to come back as soon as possible."

Jake sighed heavily. "Do it, then. We'll manage. Somehow."

"I knew I could count on you. We really—"

Jake's pager beeped, startling him. He was on edge not only because of the topic of discussion, but because his good buddy's wife, Beth O'Roarke, was expecting their first child any time within the next month, and Jake had agreed to be ready to fill in for Dylan on his shift at the firehouse on a moment's notice.

He read the pager note and bolted out of his seat.

Talbot's bushy brows rose. "O'Roarke?"

"Yep. Beth's in labor. Gotta go." Jake was out the door

in seconds, and Chelsea Whitmore was the last thing on his mind.

CHELSEA WHITMORE gazed in the direction of the state-of-the-art birthing room where they'd taken her best friend Beth two hours before, and where the expectant father, Dylan, had flown to when he arrived at the hospital. Chelsea paced, worried. God, what an afternoon. The surprise, the confusion, the fear... And she hadn't slept well last night. Again.

She tried to calm herself by checking out the waiting room of Rockford Memorial Hospital's birthing unit. It was posh, with cushioned couches and chairs, plush carpet, a TV and even a small refrigerator. Late-afternoon May sun filtered through the large windows to the side.

Tired, she sank onto one of the couches, leaned back and closed her eyes. "It'll be all right," she told herself. "*They'll* be all right."

Though she was a certified EMT—Emergency Medical Technician—it was hard to block out her fear as she sped to the hospital, Beth belted into the front seat of her Camaro, in full labor almost a month early. Especially since Chelsea had just learned last year of Beth's traumatic past and all the loss she'd experienced at such a young age. Chelsea closed her eyes, silently praying. *Please, God, let them be all right.*

"Chelsea?"

Her eyes snapped open.

A man loomed over her—Jake Scarlatta, a lieutenant in the fire department, Dylan's friend and a surrogate brother to Chelsea's other best friend, Francey. His linebacker shoulders were tense, his gray eyes worried.

"Oh, hi." She cocked her head questioningly; she knew he was replacing Dylan on the shift when Dylan got their call. "What are you doing here?"

"It's four o'clock. Dylan's relief heard what happened and came in early, so I headed right over." He glanced at the door. "Is Beth... Is everything all right?"

"I don't know. She's been in there two hours."

He nodded solemnly, then studied her face. His expression softened. "Babies take a while, you know."

"I know. And the doctor told her last week it weighed at least seven pounds, maybe more."

"That's probably why the little rascal's coming early."

Chelsea shook her head. "Those two don't do anything the easy way, do they?"

The story of Lieutenant Dylan O'Roarke of the Rockford Fire Department and Beth Winters, his ex-EMS instructor, had become legend at the fire academy. Eight years of open animosity that rivaled that of the Hatfields and McCoys had ended last winter when they were forced to work together—and then had fallen in love.

But it hadn't been smooth going after that. Though Beth had kept it a secret for a long time, she'd lost her husband and child when she was twenty. She'd been almost unable to risk a relationship with Dylan, never mind having a baby with him. To make things even chancier, she was forty years old, not exactly prime childbearing age. But she'd done it, because of love.

Which Chelsea no longer believed in.

Jake cleared his throat, then asked, "Mind if I sit?" He was normally reticent and old-world polite, but today his carriage was stiff, his voice controlled.

Chelsea was pretty sure she knew why. "Go ahead."

The couch dipped with his considerable weight. As a fitness trainer as well as a firefighter, Chelsea appreciated good muscle tone and mass. Jake was a big man, but in dynamite shape.

"What happened?" he asked. "Ed Knight called me to

come in and sub like we planned, but Dylan had shot out of there like a rocket and nobody knew the details.''

Chelsea shook her head. ''I had lunch with Beth around noon, then we went to my place.''

''Dylan told me you and Francey were trying to keep Beth company when he was working.''

''Well, given what she went through in the past, we've all been extra careful.'' She smiled. ''It was nice of you to rearrange *your* life to be on call for Dylan this whole last month.''

''Not much to rearrange,'' he mumbled. Chelsea remembered Francey saying she worried about Jake's life revolving around the fire department. ''So, what happened?'' he repeated.

''About two, her water broke and contractions started.''

''Right away?''

''Yeah, it was scary, 'cause they were coming fast and furious. We got here in time, though.''

Jake nodded reassuringly at the birthing room. ''It'll be fine. This is a wonderful thing.'' The faraway look on Jake's face intrigued her.

Interested, she asked, ''You've got a kid, don't you?''

''A daughter.'' The corners of his mouth turned up. ''She's the light of my life.'' Then he frowned and cleared his throat. He stood and jammed his hands into the pockets of his light twill jacket.

Chelsea recognized the distancing maneuver—like a colonel who'd revealed too much to his troops and was embarrassed. Though she didn't know Jake very well, mostly just through Francey, she could tell he was more remote than usual.

She decided to address it. ''Jake, I know they've talked to you about my transfer.''

His face blanked as his lieutenant's mask closed over

it. "They're going to call you. It's official. You're coming to my group."

Though she wasn't at all surprised, the certainty of it unnerved her. Watching him, she couldn't read anything from his face. "Are you upset about getting me on your crew?"

He hesitated, then said, "Not upset. But having a woman on board is never easy." He would know this, Chelsea thought, from Francey, who worked on another group in his firehouse. Fire stations ran four shifts, scheduled for four days on, three days off, three nights on, three days off. "Don't get me wrong. Francey's like a sister to me. So I'm not prejudiced against female firefighters."

"But I come with extra baggage."

He nodded. "If it's any consolation, I think what the guys at Engine Four did to you is despicable. They deserved the official reprimand. And you deserved the public apology."

Chelsea cringed. The nightmare at her previous firehouse haunted her even in her waking hours, like a ghost from the Shakespearean plays she'd loved to read in high school. "Some people say I deserved the way they treated me. Because of what happened to Billy."

"We make our own lives. Nobody's responsible for the actions of another."

The look of sadness on his face surprised her. She wanted to ask him about it, but the door to the birthing room swung open.

Both of them turned to see Dylan, in green scrubs and hat, a white mask hanging around his neck. His cheeks were wet with tears. Chelsea bolted from the couch. Dylan crossed to her. "It's a boy. I have a—" choking on the last word, he grabbed her in an emotional hug "—a son."

Chelsea's eyes misted. She bit her lip to keep herself under control. "He's okay? Beth's fine?"

Dylan drew back. "They're just great. She's breastfeeding him now." His eyes shone. "It's unbelievable, Chels." His face sobered. "And thanks for your quick thinking. If you hadn't been with her...gotten her here..."

"Well, I was, and she's fine." Chelsea's voice betrayed none of the panic she'd felt when Beth's pains had come too close together, too fast.

Drawing in a breath, Dylan shook his head and glanced at Jake. Dylan smiled again, a goofy, I'm-a-father grin. Without a word, the men hugged. Chelsea hadn't seen that much emotion out of Jake even at Francey's wedding. "Congratulations, Dad."

Dylan grinned. "It's a miracle."

"I know." Jake's tone was dry.

The proud father glanced at the door. "You can see them in fifteen minutes." He scanned the area. "Where are France and Alex?"

"I called them as soon as Beth went in," Chelsea answered. "They'll be here by the time we can see her."

"Good." Another dumbstruck smile. "I'll come get you then."

With his usual flourish, Dylan headed to the door, still grinning like an idiot.

As Chelsea watched him go, a spark of jealousy ignited in her. She'd wanted all that once—marriage, children. Well, no more. That dream had vanished after what had happened with her boyfriend—her *ex*-boyfriend—Billy Milligan. Right now, the only male she wanted in her life was Hotstuff, one of her cats.

She turned to find Jake staring at her.

Chelsea stared back.

For two people who were going to be spending days and nights together, they had little to talk about.

JAKE HAD NEVER seen Beth Winters look quite so mussed, not even after the strenuous Confidence Walks at the academy. Stringy-haired, sweaty, lines of fatigue etched around her eyes and mouth, she beamed at the baby nestled in her arms, then at her visitors. Alex and Francey had arrived within minutes of Dylan's announcement and had come into the birthing room with Jake and Chelsea.

The room had been designed like a suburban home-owner's dream bedroom. A big double bed with a soft print comforter. Matching throw pillows. A couple of stuffed chairs. Thick carpet. Jake stood behind the others as they crowded around the new mom and baby; Dylan had taken a seat on the bed to Beth's right. Leaning over, he placed his index finger in the sleeping child's wrinkled hand. The baby, still mottled and red, grasped it reflexively.

"Hey, buddy," Dylan said softly. "Don't you wanna wake up and meet your family? Aunt Francey and Aunt Chelsea are here. So are Uncle Jake and Uncle Alex."

All four visitors were as quiet as fire hiding in walls, silenced by the aura of absolute joy that surrounded the trio. Jake remembered feeling as awestruck when his daughter, Jessica, was born, though the setting had been a sterile delivery room. It had been, in fact, the best moment in his life.

He glanced at Francey; she had a death grip on Alex's hand. He smiled warmly at the woman who was Beth's other close friend and practically a sister to him. It was good to see her happy. She and her husband, Alex, had had a rocky time of it, trying to reconcile Alex's constant worry about Francey's safety in her work as a dedicated firefighter. At lunch a few days ago, Francey had filled Jake in on how Alex was faring in his never-ending strug-gle to accept her job. He was coping better, she'd said, but some tension still remained.

Jake's gaze traveled to Chelsea Whitmore, off to the

side and breathing deeply; he suspected it was to calm herself. But her eyes glistened. Jake, too, was flooded by emotions he normally kept dammed up. Struggling to keep them at bay, he coughed and said, "What's his name?"

Beth looked up and smiled serenely. All signs of anxiety, prevalent during her and Dylan's tumultuous courtship, were gone. Absent, in fact, during her whole pregnancy. "Ask Dylan. I let him pick a name."

Dylan reached down and took the child from Beth. Holding up his son, Dylan said proudly, "Meet Timothy Dylan O'Roarke. Timmy for short."

The women gasped; Alex's eyebrows rose. Jake tried to contain evidence of his own surprise. The husband Beth had lost twenty years ago in a tragic accident was Tim Winters.

Beth reached up and touched Dylan's arm. The look that passed between them was so intimate that Jake opened his mouth to suggest they leave the new family alone.

But then Dylan turned to Chelsea with the devil in his eyes. "Now, how long before you can teach him to pitch?"

Chelsea laughed. It was a low, husky sound that curled through Jake like a shot of good bourbon. "A couple of years. He'll probably be able to strike out as many of you as I did Thursday night in the department softball game."

Francey said, "You're on *our* team starting next week when you come to our station house, Chels, so that's not an issue anymore."

The smile on Chelsea's lips died like fire under foam. Jake guessed she wasn't any happier about breaking into a new group than the group was to have her. But they'd all pull through, he'd see to it, mainly because the fire department couldn't afford any more fallout over her breakup with Milligan.

When the baby began to fuss, the group decided to leave

the O'Roarkes alone. After hugs and kisses, the four of them ended up in the waiting area.

Alex put his arm around his wife, who was beaming like a proud parent. "I envy them," Alex said.

Francey stared at him. "You do?"

"Of course."

"Well, that's news." She scowled. "I'll think about that later. Right now I'm starved."

"Surprise, surprise," Alex said dryly, dropping a kiss on top of her head.

"Want to come to dinner with us?" Francey looked from Jake to Chelsea.

Jake smiled, surprised at the envy he felt. So many happy people. Happy *couples*. At forty, he'd missed his chance for that kind of thing, but his emotions were running high today; the armor he kept in place buckled under such obvious devotion. "No, thanks. I've got plans."

Turning away, his gaze landed on Chelsea. He recognized the look on her face—it mirrored his. "I'll take a rain check," she said. "I've got to be at the gym in an hour." Chelsea owned the Weight Room, a health club about two blocks from his firehouse. Though he never worked out there, other firefighters did, and they had nothing but good to say about it.

As they all headed to the elevator, Jake ended up walking behind the Templetons, next to Chelsea. She was tall—about five-eight—and nicely toned. Though the cinnamon-colored dress she had on didn't reveal her form, he'd seen pictures Alex had taken of her and Francey working out.

At the door to the parking lot, the Templetons bade them goodbye and left. Chelsea looked at him. "I guess I'll see you in a couple of days."

"Yeah, Friday morning, right?" He stared at her. He'd never noticed what an unusual shade of brown her eyes were—light with flecks of gold. This afternoon they reflected a weariness that had nothing to do with fatigue. Absurdly moved, Jake wanted to reach out and squeeze her arm; he stuck his hands in his pockets to douse the urge. ''Well, have a nice night.''

She nodded and pushed on the bar on the glass door.

''Chelsea?''

She turned. The late-day sun behind her sparkled off the silvery gold of her hair as it swung softly around her shoulders. Unsmiling, standing tall, she looked lovely. And lonely.

''It'll work out at Quint Twelve.'' He winced at how inane he sounded.

Her expression was bleak. ''Will it?''

He nodded.

She gave him a half smile, opened the door, stepped out and let it swish shut behind her. Jake watched her until she was out of sight.

As soon as he crawled through the doorway, Jake could see flames licking the roof of the rickety three-story building. The biocarbons in the insulation created a whirlpool of black smoke, temporarily blinding him and his partner. Intense heat stilled his movements. Wondering why the ventilating crew hadn't cut the roof yet, Jake gripped the hose to spray the windowless attic bedroom. He levered the handle forward. No water spurted out the nozzle. He could feel the line buck, so he knew it was charged. Sensing his best friend, Danny DeLuca, behind him assisting with the hose, Jake started to turn.

Then it was there. *Flashover.* A bed, an old desk, several stacks of magazines and a full bookcase burst into flames of their own volition. The fire breathed in new life. It crouched in front of him, hovered above him, attacked from each side.

In that instant, Jake knew he wasn't getting out alive.

He pivoted to Danny; a glowing timber dropped—in seemingly slow motion—onto his buddy's head. Jake opened his mouth to warn Danny, but his breathing apparatus muffled the sound—

Jake bolted upright. His hands fisted in the light blanket that had fallen below his hips. His entire body was covered with sweat and as taut as a stretched lifeline. From the sliver of moonlight peeking in from the skylights, Jake could just make out the row of bookshelves, the oak desk that had been his father's, the stacks of magazines he'd been cleaning out the day before. He was home, on the third floor that he'd converted into living quarters for himself. Not in a fire with Danny. He forced his hands to unclench and his shoulders to relax. In a few minutes he was able to move.

He swung his feet onto the thick carpet, rose and crossed to the windows behind the desk. Outside, the street was deserted. A quick look at the clock over the bookcases told him the reason. Four a.m. His heart still pounding, he forced himself to think.

It wasn't the first time he'd had this dream, but he *had* gotten some help in analyzing it. From Reed Macauley, the department psychologist, whom Jake had gotten to know through Dylan and from his own brief stint at the academy. When Jake had recounted his dream to Reed, the psychologist had listened without speaking until Jake had finished.

"From what you tell me, this seems to come when something stressful is happening," Reed had said then. "Your mother's death. Your daughter's surgery. Ben Cordaro, who's been like a father to you, getting hurt...."

Well, the stressful event now was Chelsea Kay Whitmore's joining his crew. In fact, he'd see her at the fire station in about three hours.

He didn't need this. He didn't want it. He *wanted* the

status quo. He *wanted* his life left undisturbed. Dylan had
teasingly called him the Quiet Man, John Wayne's stoic
movie character, and Jake liked that just fine.

Reed had focused on that, too. "This nightmare is the
tip of the iceberg, isn't it, Jake?" he'd asked.

Jake had thought about lying, but only a fool sought
help and then didn't tell the truth. "Stuff's happened to
me."

Reed had waited.

"I was responsible for somebody hitting bottom. Somebody I...cared about."

The psychologist had been the one who'd said the words
he'd parroted to Chelsea last week. *We make our own
lives. Nobody's responsible for the actions of another.*

It didn't apply now.

"I believe that, only not in this case," he'd told Reed.

"Tell me about it," Reed had urged.

He hadn't been able to then, or the second or third time
he'd found himself in the psychologist's office. But after
successive bouts with his demon, insomnia, and frankly,
after seeing how Reed had helped Dylan and Beth, Jake
had finally been able to breach his staunchly erected de-
fenses.

"It was my buddy, Danny. We'd been friends since
high school. Played football together, best man at each
other's wedding, had a kid the same year. We got into the
academy at the same time, and after a couple years, wran-
gled being on the same group in the RFD. It was great
until I made lieutenant and Danny..." The pain had blindsided him, and he had to stop. He still felt guilty that his
career aspirations had triggered a rift between him and the
man who'd been closer to him than a brother.

After a moment Reed had asked, "Danny?"

"He started going downhill. First there was drinking.
Then some drugs. I hauled his ass when I found out. It

didn't interfere with work for a long time. Even when it did, I let it go because Danny always had trouble with my being a lieutenant. I didn't report his screwups for several months. By the time I did, it was too late—for him and for me.''

''What happened to him?''

''Before the brass could can him, he quit.''

''And?''

''He left town. Left his wife and son without a second thought.''

''And you.''

''Me?''

''He left you, too.''

''Yeah, after calling me every name in the book.''

''You said it was too late for you. What did you mean?''

''I, ah… Damn, this is hard to say.''

Reed had given him a grim smile. ''I know.''

''Before this happened with Danny, I'd wanted to be everything in the department—lieutenant, captain, battalion chief, hell, maybe even chief some day.''

''And now?''

Jake had pushed back the sadness welling inside him. ''How I handled Danny's downslide was a black mark on my record. I was formally reprimanded, and a letter was put in my file.''

''From what I hear, it's got company with a lot of commendations.''

''Some.''

''So you *could* move up the ladder. You could take the Captaincy exam this summer.''

''I guess. But I've lost the drive…the interest.''

''You've lost your dreams,'' Reed had said wistfully.

Yeah, thought Jake now, he'd lost the dreams. He turned from the window, disgusted with his ruminating, stalked to the spacious kitchen and bath alcove he'd carved from under the dormers and switched on the coffee.

Surveying the area, he thought of Ben Cordaro's remark. The man who had been like a father to him after his own dad had died had taken one look at the haven and recognized it for what it was. *Hell, Jake, you could live in this room and not come out for months.* It was true. He'd spent a whole year renovating the third floor of the house he'd grown up in. His mother had lived alone for years after Jake and his sisters had left home. When Jake's marriage had broken up, he'd taken over the mortgage, moved in with her and stayed after she died, which was five years ago. He'd modernized the other floors with help, but it was the top level he'd lovingly worked on solo.

He'd nailed in every tongue-and-groove oak board of the ceiling, cut through the roof for the two skylights, put up the Sheetrock and painted the walls a deep beige. He'd laid the expensive carpet and picked out the furniture with care. Its dark tan upholstery and brown plaid pillows accented the wall color and the warm wood. He'd chosen a sofa bed, telling himself it was for guests, but he knew in his heart he'd use it. No one else had ever slept here, and only Ben, Dylan, Francey and Jessica had been allowed up here.

When the coffee was done, he poured some into a huge mug labeled World's Hunkiest Dad—Jessie's sense of humor—and trekked to the leather recliner. On the low oak table was a manual he'd been reading the evening before—*Sexual Harassment in the Firehouse.* Damn.

Ignoring it, he twisted to gaze out one of the windows flanking the recliner at his backyard. He remembered playing there with the Cordaro kids, who'd been like brothers and a sister—

The phone shrilled in the darkness.

Firefighter instincts on alert, he bounded off the recliner

to the sofa bed and scooped up the receiver on its second ring. "Scarlatta"

"Jake, it's Barbara."

Danny DeLuca's wife. "What's wrong?"

"I'm sorry to phone so early, but Derek just got in."

"Just got in? It's five in the morning."

"I know."

"Why didn't you call me sooner?"

"I can't bother you every time my son does something he shouldn't. But…" She hesitated, then said, "He smells like pot. And he's obviously drunk."

"What did he say?"

Barbara hesitated again.

"Barb?"

"He asked me why I was surprised." Her voice filled with tears. "He said he's just like his old man."

Jake clenched his fist. "I'll be right over after I shower."

"I'm sorry to lay this on you."

"Don't talk like that. I'll be there soon."

After he hung up, he stared at the phone. Did he have time to do this? He was due at the station early, because of Chelsea Whitmore's arrival.

God, he hoped the rest of the day would go better than how it had started out.

As he headed for the bathroom, the memory of the nightmare hovering over him like a black cloud, he somehow doubted it would.

CHAPTER TWO

AT SEVEN O'CLOCK Chelsea dragged open the heavy steel door to Quint/Midi Twelve and entered the bay. This station would be her home for who knew how long.

Home.

The word had no meaning for her. She'd never really had a home, other than the years she'd spent at her mother's house raising her younger sister, Delaney, after her mother had died. It was one of the reasons she'd joined the fire department.

Now that's irony.

Chelsea stood just inside the cavernous bay, and studied the two rigs, both glistening with sunlight from the high windows on the garagelike doors. The large fire engine, the Quint, did almost everything—pumped water, carried ladders and an aerial bucket and stowed backup breathing tanks and a host of other equipment. Next to it stood the Midi, a small two-person truck, which housed medical supplies, the Hurst tools for car accidents and fire-suppression equipment; it also pumped water when needed. Often the Midi went alone on medical calls.

"Good morning." The husky baritone came from behind her. Turning, she found Jake Scarlatta standing in the doorway of the watch room. He looked bigger today, an odd impression for Chelsea, who was tall and in good shape but weighed what most women would consider too much. She was also used to working with big guys at her gym. But the breadth of Lieutenant Scarlatta's shoulders in his light blue shirt seemed greater, his legs longer in his navy pants, and his height more imposing than it had at the hospital or when she'd seen him at Francey's and Beth's weddings. Maybe because he was in his element.

"Good morning." As she crossed to him, she noticed lines of strain bracketing his mouth and eyes. He obviously hadn't slept well. She was intimately acquainted with the signs.

"Welcome to Quint Twelve, Firefighter Whitmore."

Ah, so that was how it was going to be.

"Thank you, Lieutenant."

He nodded at the turnout gear she had draped over one arm and the canvas gym bag she clutched. "Why don't you get your goods on the rig, then come into the watch room? I'll brief you about today's schedule and get you a locker for your things."

"Where am I?" she asked, referring to her position on one of the trucks. The officer on duty assigned each firefighter a job for the entire four-day shift.

"Driver of the Midi." She wasn't surprised. As an EMT, she had more training than regular firefighters, who were Certified First Responders and could perform only basic medical procedures.

After placing her gear on the truck, she joined Jake in the watch room. As in many station houses, the office area was long and narrow, with glass on three sides, facing the bay. It was furnished with large gray filing cabinets, two desks, a computer that hummed in the corner and a couple of chairs. A big bulletin board, covered with memos, hung from the one wall. Also displayed prominently was a small poster that read People say our standards are too high. Given what's at stake, that's impossible. Everyone in the fire department knew Lieutenant Scarlatta ran a tight ship. Which was fine with her.

Jake sank onto a chair and motioned for Chelsea to sit

on another. "Shouldn't I let somebody know his relief is here?" she asked.

"I just paged Kilmer, the night Midi driver."

She nodded.

He picked up a sheet of paper and scanned it. "I thought it'd be best to go low key today. No training or inspection. While the guys do first-day-in checks, I'll show you around. Before that, though, I'm, ah, cooking breakfast. Because you're here. Sort of a welcome."

Chelsea stiffened even as she recognized how stupid it was to be irritated by such a thoughtful gesture. Since her ordeal with Billy Milligan, she'd become as easily spooked as a nervous mare. Delaney had suggested she vent her feelings in her diary—something she'd been doing since she was thirteen. It had helped, but apparently not enough.

"Something wrong with breakfast?"

"No."

"You...bristled."

"It's very considerate of you to make breakfast. But I wish you'd just call it what it is."

Under furrowed brows, his smoky gray eyes darkened to charcoal. "And what's that?"

"Look, I don't imagine your crew is dying to have me here. So isn't breakfast sort of a bribe to smooth the way?" When he didn't answer, she angled her chin and consciously kept her hands from clenching. "I'd like to know what I'm up against. I was hoping you'd be straight with me—always."

Jake steepled his fingers and peered over them at her. She saw a muscle leap in his jaw. "I can understand why you're cautious. But, for the record, I find your attitude unnecessarily defensive. My team will treat you with cordiality and respect. I expect the same from you."

He was good, Chelsea thought. A real diplomat. Okay,

she'd go along. Taking a deep breath, she forced her shoulders to relax. "I apologize if I've offended you. You're right, I've reason to be cautious. But I'm sure your men will be Sunday-school polite. Breakfast would be nice."

He watched her for a moment, then said, "Well, let's go. Leave your bag here. I'll get you a locker later."

He gestured her out the door before him, and they headed to the refurbished kitchen in back. She'd been to this firehouse several times with Francey, but she hadn't seen the remodeling. Heavenly smells of cinnamon and baked bread assailed her nostrils. The kitchen was large— about thirty by thirty—and had white appliances, except for a clunker of a stove. The cupboards on the perimeter were painted a glossy teal, and the spanking-clean tile floor would have made Martha Stewart proud. In the middle stood a beautiful trestle table of carved oak.

At which sat two men. They looked up when she and Jake entered.

"Gentlemen, this is Firefighter Chelsea Whitmore. Chelsea, meet two of your crew." Jake sauntered over to stand behind a broad-shouldered blond man with street-wise blue eyes. The lieutenant casually placed his hands on the guy's shoulders and kneaded them as he spoke. "This is Peter Huff. He'll be riding shotgun with you on the Midi today—he's an EMT. Peter just joined our group about four months ago, but he's subbed off and on for years."

Huff smiled, but it was a thin one, without any warmth. "Whitmore."

Jake moved to the second man—wholesome-looking, probably in his early thirties, with kind brown eyes. He was smaller than Huff but sported the necessary muscles to be a "smoke eater," as firefighters called themselves.

Jake ruffled the guy's brown curly hair. "And this ugly schmuck is Mick Murphy."

Chelsea noted Jake's physical contact with the guys. She knew from subbing that, in some firehouses, the men were so close they were like one big family. Quint Twelve was obviously that kind of group—and she knew in her gut she'd never be part of it.

Mick shook off Jake's hand, stood and playfully socked his lieutenant in the stomach. Then he picked his way around the table toward Chelsea and gave her a grin that reminded her of a little boy anxious to make friends. "Welcome, Chelsea. I'm glad you're here." He stuck out his hand.

She took it, unable to keep her eyebrows from raising in surprise. "Thanks."

Leaning closer, he whispered conspiratorially, "My wife, Andrea, says a woman's presence will civilize us."

Chelsea smiled. "I can't wait to meet her."

"The feeling's mutual." As Mick turned, another firefighter entered the room.

His stocky form stiffened when he saw her. Dark Italian eyes smoldered with resentment. Even his hand, which had just raked black hair out of his eyes, fisted.

It was Joey Santori.

Billy Milligan's buddy since high school.

And Francey's ex-fiancé. Chelsea had met him a few times when he and her friend were still a couple, and she'd been witness to several unpleasant scenes between Francey and this hothead after they'd broken up.

Men scorned were all alike.

"Joe, you've met Chelsea, haven't you?" Jake's voice was carefully casual. As close to Francey as he was, Jake had to know Chelsea was aware of Joey's history.

Santori shrugged. "Yep." Giving them his back and crossing to the coffeepot, Joe missed Jake's scowl.

Jake's prediction about his men's cordiality had just been proved false. Chelsea caught his eye but kept her face blank. His cold expression revealed nothing of his feelings.

The air was charged. To defuse it, Jake said, "Have some coffee, Chelsea, while I put the finishing touches on breakfast."

Huff snorted from behind the newspaper he'd picked up.

"Peter is our gourmet chef." This came from Mick, who'd been leaning against the counter. He stepped toward Huff, circled his buddy's neck with one arm and hugged him. "Nobody cooks better than you, Petey, baby."

Shrugging, silent, Huff continued reading, but some of his reserve dissipated at Mick's open affection. Ludicrously feeling excluded, Chelsea spied the coffeepot and headed to it. Mick got there first and filled a mug for her. Grateful, she sat at the table. For something to do, she picked up a section of the paper and scanned it.

"Son of a bitch." The curse was accompanied by a loud, tinny thump.

Chelsea looked up, surprised at the normally stoic lieutenant's flash of temper.

Huff said, "Pilot light go out again?"

"Yeah. I was keeping the French toast warm. This damned stove's gonna kill us before the new one gets here."

"Wouldn't be taking so long if Huff hadn't insisted on a fancy German model." Mick's voice was teasing.

"Only the best for me, Murphy."

A man rushed into the kitchen buttoning his RFD shirt. "Sorry I'm late."

Jake glanced at the clock. "You've got a couple of minutes to spare, Diaz. Besides, Lanahan's still sleeping." Sometimes the night shift slept in after the morning crew arrived, especially if they'd had a lot of runs. "Everything okay?"

"We were up till dawn with the baby."

"Which one?" Huff asked.

"The littlest." Diaz rolled his eyes. "Jeez, no wonder my old man took off when I was young. Babies and jobs don't mix."

Mick clapped Diaz on the back. "This is our resident Daddy of the Year, Chelsea. He's got four, goin' on five, kids, and still countin'."

"You're just jealous, man." In a lightning quick move, Diaz pivoted and grabbed Mick in a headlock. Then the tall, muscular man smiled at Chelsea, his demeanor degrees warmer than Huff's or Santori's. "You must be Chelsea. Hi, I'm Don Diaz."

Chelsea nodded.

"Actually, I *am* jealous," Mick confessed when Diaz let him go. "I wish like hell Andrea'd have another kid."

Diaz joked, "Yeah, well, if you need instruction on how to get your peck—" He swallowed the rest of the word; everyone stilled.

Here it comes, Chelsea thought. *The watch-every-word-they-say syndrome.* In the past, she'd put her fellow firefighters at ease with some ice-breaker comment—like she knew all the words for the male anatomy and could teach *them* some—but no more.

"Chow's on," Jake said, breaking the silence.

Chairs scraped back. Santori was first in line. Huff followed. Mick moved behind them. "Come on, Chelsea."

She stood and crossed to them. Mick stepped aside, and she allowed the gesture. "Thanks." She reached the food. "Mmm, this smells wonderful." The aroma of French toast, Canadian bacon and home fries wafted up to her. Her stomach growled loudly. She put her hand to her waist. "Oops, sorry."

Jake, Peter, Mick and Don all chuckled. Joey did not.

There was little conversation over the meal, which the crew devoured with the gusto of lumberjacks. They made a few grudging compliments, intermittently remarked on the runs the night group had gotten. Jake told Joey his grandfather had called this morning to talk to him, and Huff asked about their training today. But that was the extent of it.

When they were done, Mick asked, "How much do we owe you, Jake?" Though some citizens thought their taxes paid for firefighters' food, the group members all pitched in for meals.

The lieutenant shook his head. "Nothing. My treat."

"Whoa..."

"Why?"

"To celebrate Chelsea's arrival."

"Hey, great."

"Thanks, buddy."

After each man scraped his plate, Jake made a few announcements and suggested the guys begin their chores— starting the rigs, checking the water tanks, washing any apparatus that was used in the night runs. And there was morning housework. He and Chelsea would finish cleaning up, then he'd show her around.

The men filed out, each slapping Jake on the back or punching his arm as they left. Except Joey Santori. He only stopped by Jake's chair long enough to toss a five-dollar bill on the table, then left the room in frosty silence.

Sighing deeply, Chelsea sank back in her seat. She got the message loud and clear, just as Santori had intended.

After a moment Jake stood. Chelsea did likewise, and silently they picked up their plates and crossed to the sink. "I—" Jake began when the tone sounded over the PA system, indicating an incoming call.

And the computer in the watch room clicked on.

It was a run for Quint/Midi Twelve.

"EMS call at Parker and Thornton."

"The Midi," Jake said.

Chelsea raced for the door.

When she reached it, she heard, "The Midi *and* Quint go into service."

Jake hurried down the hallway behind her, ducked into the watch room, ripped the work order out of the printer and scanned it.

"Damn it," he said.

The dispatcher announced, "Multiple gunshot wounds. Police are on their way."

SO MUCH for an easy day, Jake thought, as he checked the side mirror to see the smaller rig careering along behind him. He'd hoped for a couple of light calls to acclimate Chelsea—maybe one of the frequent stove fires that summoned them to Dutch Towers, the senior citizens' complex two blocks away. But this was serious. The sirens screeched, and Murphy sounded the horn as he drove the big truck to the scene. Jake occupied the officer's position next to him. Diaz and Santori were in the jump seats.

Jake listened for radio instructions. "Police are at the house now. Wait for scene clearance, Quint Twelve. Repeat, wait for scene clearance."

"Quint/Midi Twelve en route. We'll wait for scene clearance." Jake let out a low whistle when he clicked off. This could be dicey.

In less than two minutes, the trucks pulled up in front of a two-family dwelling with peeling paint and rickety porch steps. It was eerily quiet in this residential section of the city. The stillness reminded him of a room before backdraft hit. A female police officer stood guard in front of the house and spoke into a radio, probably alerting officers around back that the fire department had arrived.

The six Rockford firefighters exited the trucks with the precision of trained soldiers initiating an attack. As he approached the cop, Jake saw Whitmore and Huff opening their rig's back door and hefting equipment. Santori, Diaz and Murphy followed suit on the other truck.

"Quint/Midi Twelve is on the scene," Jake said calmly into the radio. "Approaching the police now."

The officer grimaced at him. "The scene is under control. Two people are down—a twenty-six-year-old-man and a woman about the same age. Proceed back but don't touch anything. This is a crime scene."

Jake nodded and turned to his crew. They were covered in goggles, face shields, protective sleeves and gloves. Chelsea held out a set for him; he slid them on. He saw Huff step up and speak to the officer. He caught up to them as they headed to a side yard littered with shards of glass, pieces of wood and broken concrete. The smell of garbage penetrated Jake's face shield.

Behind the house, they found what they were looking for.

Two police officers stood guard, one on each side of a handcuffed man. One cop was taking notes, the other carefully eyeing the suspect. Two bodies lay motionless on the ground in an increasing pool of blood.

Jake said, "Whitmore, Diaz and Santori, the man's yours. Huff and Murphy, the woman."

As he headed for the officers, his crew hurried to the victims.

"You hurt?" he asked a tall, thin cop with a mustache.

"No."

A younger one, pale but steady, said, "Me, neither."

Jake looked at the handcuffed shooter. "Are *you* hurt?"

"What are ya—dressed up for Halloween?"

"Are you hurt?" Jake asked again.

The guy shook his head, sending greasy locks of hair into his wild eyes. Drugs. Dilated pupils confirmed it.

Scanning him, Jake said, "What day is it?"

"Huh?"

"Answer the damn question." The older officer yanked on the cuffs.

"May twenty-second." The man's words were slurred.

Jake lifted the guy's arms, pushed back a grungy sleeve and took his pulse, all the while questioning him. "What's your name? Who's the president of the United States?"

When he finished with the vitals, and was sure the officers and the shooter were not in need of care, Jake turned to the firefighters attending to the victims. He heard the slurred words of the shooter behind him. "They deserve it. He was screwin' my old lady." The accusation was accompanied by several colorful obscenities.

Ignoring him, Jake crossed to the male patient and looked down. "Situation assessed?"

"Yes, sir," Chelsea said in a confident voice. "Airways open, breathing normal, but blood pressure is low. We've got to stop the bleeding."

"Need anything?"

"Not at this time."

He checked with Huff. The female victim had a superficial flesh wound, but she'd been rendered unconscious by an apparent blow to the head. Her stained pink housedress had splotches of blood on the chest, possibly the man's. Despite how often he saw this much blood, Jake still winced.

Turning to the male patient, who was in more serious condition, he observed his crew in action. Efficiently, Chelsea elevated the man's legs so blood would flow to the vital organs. Joey stripped off the guy's clothing as Diaz took another set of vitals.

"Pulse is fast, decreased bp. We need the oxygen?" Don asked.

Chelsea said, "Yeah, set it up." Jake helped Don assemble and crack the canister as Chelsea moved across from Joey. Blood oozed from the man's shoulder, and he moaned. "Santori, check for an exit wound on his back first, then get gauze pads from the bag and apply pressure."

She looked up and gasped. "Joe, there's a slit in your face shield."

Quickly Jake ripped off his own shield, moved to Joey and replaced his mask. Jake's pulse accelerated. Possibilities of contamination to the firefighters were endless at this kind of scene, given all the blood, which could be infected.

He'd just moved to get another shield when he heard Joey say, "No exit wound."

As Jake watched, Joey set the patient on his back again. The change of position sent spurts of blood onto him. Droplets spattered his glasses—and smeared his face shield. Right where the slit had been.

Joey packed the wound with heavy bandages, then took a quick glance at Chelsea. She was getting another set of vitals and didn't look at him. Jake saw the young firefighter's hands shake and his skin pale. Though only thirty-one, Joey was a seasoned firefighter and did not often have rookie-like reactions.

The injured man moaned.

"Sir?" Chelsea bent to listen to him.

"Son of a bitch—" heavy breathing "—shot me."

The older cop approached and leaned over. "That the man?" He pointed to the suspect.

"Yeah."

"Why'd he shoot you?" the officer asked.

"I was with his wife. Goddamned whore."

Chelsea noticed the inside of the man's arm. It looked like a pincushion. Jake saw it, too, and swallowed hard. HIV now topped the list for contamination.

"Are you on drugs?" Chelsea asked.

"Nah." His voice faded and his head lolled to the side.

The screech of the ambulance sounded in the background. Jake turned to check Peter's victim. Murphy and Huff had gotten her onto a backboard; Santori and Whitmore did the same for the man. By the time the ambulance crew made it around back, the victims were packaged and ready to go.

The firefighter EMTs gave their report to the paramedics as Jake glanced at his watch.

Only fifteen minutes had passed.

It seemed like hours.

THE MOOD WAS SOMBER when the Quint and Midi pulled into the firehouse bay. It always was after a serious call.

As they exited the trucks, Jake said, "Get rid of the contaminated material in the biohazard bags. Restock the rigs, then meet me in the kitchen for debriefing." His tone was neutral and his eyes were hooded; Chelsea couldn't tell what he was thinking. She helped restock the vehicles, feeling the tug of fatigue in her shoulders and the adrenaline drop in her bloodstream, similar to coming off a sugar high.

Ten minutes later, all six firefighters were seated around the table drinking coffee that by now tasted more like paint thinner.

"First, you did well," Jake said, warm approval in his tone. "You took universal precautions, you handled the patients efficiently and—" he paused significantly "—you worked like a team."

They nodded. Mick gave Chelsea a thumbs-up.

"So, let's hear what you think." Jake sipped his coffee and waited.

Huff raised cool blue eyes to Chelsea. "You did a good job, Whitmore."

She didn't say thanks, only nodded. She knew she had. "So did you."

"I second that, Chelsea." Jake's voice was strong, pleased. It felt like a warm bath on a cold February night.

Jake pinned Joey with a purposeful stare, and the younger man coughed nervously. Though his eyes were narrowed, his pallor affirmed that he realized the danger he'd been in. "Thanks, Whitmore."

Jake let the situation sink in. Then he said calmly, "Let's talk about how that slit in your face shield happened."

Huff leaned forward, sparks of animation in his formerly stony face. It made him look younger, more approachable. "Sometimes defective equipment gets by us. Once, when I was still on the police force, a bulletproof vest was missing a whole section of padding. Nobody spotted it right away."

Chelsea cocked her head. Huff caught the gesture and explained, "I retired from the police force two years ago."

She wondered what made him choose firefighting, wanted to ask, but this wasn't the time. If firefighters were notoriously reticent, cops were even worse. She nodded again.

"All right." Jake straightened. "We'll assume it came that way from the factory. Joe, report this to the battalion chief. Tell him I want something in writing to the company. In the meantime, I'll call them and ream them out."

Santori nodded. "What're the chances the guy's—" he cleared his throat "—HIV positive?"

Jake didn't respond, so Chelsea answered. "Pretty high, if he's a drug user—and he appears to be." She waited a beat. "We were protected, Joe. There's almost no chance of your being infected with the new face shield Jake put on you."

"Except from the lieutenant's germs," Mick joked. "Who you been kissin' lately, Jake?"

Huff and Diaz chuckled, but Joey remained dead sober. He held her gaze. "Thanks again."

She gave him a weak smile and felt the vise in her chest—which had been here since she arrived at the station this morning—ease a bit.

"Good job, all of you," Jake said. "I'm gonna go file the report." He gave Chelsea a sidelong glance. "I think you can probably find your way around here." He didn't smile, but his voice sounded slightly amused. "After your performance this morning, I don't think you need coddling."

As compliments went, it was mild, but then, they usually were from the officers. She was thankful to get it.

The rest of the day progressed without drama—a call to pump out a flooded basement, a "fire" that resulted from burned food and even a run to get a cat out of a tree. There was also an EMS trip to Dutch Towers, where Jake resignedly replaced Huff on the Midi and accompanied Chelsea.

She knew that Dutch Towers was a staple of the Rockford Fire Department calls. What she didn't know, and what Jake explained on the way over, was that years ago he had brought one of the residents back to life with mouth-to-mouth resuscitation. Since then, old Mrs. Lowe had viewed Jake as the son she never had; he tried to go to Dutch Towers whenever he could. Chelsea was amazed at how gentle and concerned he was about the woman's heart palpitations this time, which had turned out to be nothing.

Between calls Chelsea explored the common area,

which had huge recliners around the TV, the bunk room in the back—nothing new there—and a workout area with updated equipment. She knew this was Dylan's station, too; he'd been reassigned to Group Four as a lieutenant. For years he'd been conducting a firefighter trivia game, the proceeds of which went to charity and to buy furnishings for the firehouse—like a new large-screen TV. She'd have to remember to get in on the game next week.

Huff cooked his ''gourmet'' hamburgers for lunch. Chelsea got in line and listened and laughed as Mick told her horrible firefighter jokes. She dished up her food and didn't mention that she generally avoided eating red meat; she'd wait until another time to drop that bomb. She managed to get half the burger down, then ate the salad and dessert with relish.

From the tension of the day and little sleep last night, Chelsea was whipped by four o'clock when her relief arrived. Her muscles felt as if she'd hauled hose up three flights of stairs. She'd just opened her locker outside the coed bathroom and was dragging out her bag when she heard someone come up behind her. She knew who it was just by his smell, a woodsy scent noticeable even after a long day.

Lieutenant Scarlatta had removed his dress shirt and was clad only in the RFD's navy T-shirt the firefighters all wore and blue trousers. She remembered telling Francey one time, ''God, I love men in T-shirts. Is there anything sexier?'' Of course, that had been in her naive days, when she'd loved the sight and smell and feel of men in general.

''You leaving?'' he asked, raising his arm to lean against the lockers. The T-shirt outlined his impressive pecs.

She nodded and dragged her eyes to her gear.

''The day went all right, didn't it?''

''More than all right.'' She peered at him, acutely aware of his physical presence. ''Jake, I'm sorry about spouting off this morning. I guess I was more wired than I realized about starting here."

"It's okay." His lips quirked. "I'll remember to give you the straight skinny from now on—always."

She grinned. His gaze focused on her mouth, then he pushed away from the locker and straightened. "You were valuable to us today, Whitmore."

"Thanks."

He nodded, jammed his hands in his pockets and strode off.

The old Chelsea, who still surfaced from time to time, would have noticed his nice gluts in addition to his pecs. But that Chelsea had gotten into trouble. The new Chelsea didn't want her around anymore.

THE MAN LAY ON HIS BED in his cold, empty bedroom, staring into the darkness. The stillness of the night let his other side surface, the one he sometimes couldn't control. Like Jekyll and Hyde. He should get up and turn off the air-conditioning. But the coolness helped him think better. At the station house, he only felt confused.

There was something about her being there that wasn't right. Chauvinism aside, old grudges notwithstanding, women didn't belong in the fire department. Okay, so she was in good shape. And she was a capable firefighter. Today showed she could handle herself in an emergency. Jekyll had liked that.

Still, it went against the laws of nature. And God knew what this women's lib stuff had brought to society. His own mother had been involved in the movement. His hands fisted as he remembered her dragging him to hear Gloria Steinem speak in downtown Rockford. It had wreaked havoc with his blue-collar father, and nothing had gone right after that.

No, she didn't belong there. Nobody really wanted her there. Well, she'd no doubt slip up, like she did at the other place. If not…who knew what could happen?

CHAPTER THREE

"NO, NO, JEEZ, you guys, *catch* the ball!" Seventeen-year-old Jessica Scarlatta jumped up and screamed at the Rockford Raiders as a ball sailed over the heads of the shortstop and the left fielder for a home run in Frontier Field, the brand-new baseball stadium. Jake's daughter was heedless of the spectacle she made in the throng of fans amidst the smell of hot dogs, beer and popcorn.

Jake lounged in the seat and watched her fondly, not commenting. It was one of the reasons she was so open and uninhibited—he'd been careful to let her do her thing for years. Her mother, Nancy, had grudgingly gone along, even after the divorce, while trying to instill proper manners and behavior in her. Between the two of them, Jessica had turned out just fine.

"A grand slam." Jess shook her head in disgust as she finally sat.

Jake tugged the bill of her Raiders cap down. "They're gonna lose, sweetheart. You'll owe me."

She shook her head again, her dark blond ponytail swinging jauntily out of the back of the cap. "You really want that Tommy Hilfiger shirt?"

His laughter felt good after the day he'd had. "Yep. The striped one. Fifty bucks."

She peered at him with innocent gray eyes the color of his. She had his nose and the exact stubborn set of his jaw. "Dad-dy."

"Don't daddy me, babe. You lost fair and square." He

glanced at the scoreboard. "Or at least you will in two innings. Now get rid of that little-girl look and let's go get hot dogs."

Her eyes brightened. "Cool." She glanced mournfully at the field. "They won't catch up."

"We'll come back for the last at-bat, anyway."

As Jake followed his daughter up the steps of the stadium, he noticed more than one guy ogling her. He stifled the urge to shield her from view, feeling his heart twist more each time he was faced with the fact that his baby had grown up. She was the only thing that meant more to him than the fire department. That she was going off to college in a few months almost killed him. He was having trouble with that and everything else about her maturity. Not the least of which was that she'd turned out to be a beauty. And she had style. Her blue shorts and striped top were pretty ordinary, but on her they looked like designer togs.

Just like you, Dad, she'd told him recently.

Clothes. His one indulgence. Fairly innocuous, though. Putting on the slate-gray T-shirt and matching shorts after work had made him feel good; nice clothes always did.

They reached the Three Dog Night stand and waited their turn. He put his hand on the nape of Jessica's neck and kneaded gently. "Seen Derek lately?" Danny and Barb's son was a friend of Jess's.

She looked at him over her shoulder. "No. He's not in any of my classes this year and he hasn't called in a while." She watched him. "You've got that Scarlatta scowl on your face. What happened?"

"He's causing his mother trouble again."

Jessica patted his hand, suddenly older and wiser than her years. "He needs help, Dad."

"Yeah, I know. I'm taking him to dinner tomorrow night. We're gonna talk about it."

She scowled and turned to face him.

"What?" Jake asked.

"Last time I saw Derek, he said something about going to Key West to live with his dad."

Jake dropped the ten-dollar bill he was holding. After retrieving it, he asked, "Has he heard from Danny?"

"I don't think so." Jess turned to move up in the line.

Sighing, Jake shook his head, and decided to distract himself from this unpleasant news. He didn't get enough time with Jessica and he didn't want to ruin the upbeat mood. He scanned the area. The stadium was new and housed a food and gift area that ran about a third of its perimeter. It always amazed Jake how he could get prime rib sandwiches, rotisserie chicken, sweaters and bracelets at a baseball field. He remembered going with Danny to see the Raiders play at the old Silver Stadium, which had one concession stand. They'd wolfed down hot dogs and let the cotton candy melt on their tongues, just glad to be at a minor league game.

After getting food and drinks, Jake looked for a table in the center court seating area, which was filled with other ball fans who'd given up on the Raiders turning the game around. When Jake was about to suggest they go back to their seats, he heard a voice. "Hello, Jake."

He glanced to his left. At a big table sat Chelsea Whitmore with a beautiful younger woman.

"Hi."

"I saw you and Jessica looking for a table." She shifted a bit, then said with the reluctance of a patient succumbing to a root canal, "You can sit here if you like. There's room."

"Great." Jessica plopped down next to Chelsea's companion. "I'm Jessica Scarlatta."

Jake took a seat next to Chelsea as she grinned at his daughter. He got a glimpse of long legs encased in baby pink shorts to match the T-shirt she wore. He thought she even had pink sneakers on. Quite a contrast to the masculine standard blues she wore all day. "Hi, Jessica, nice to see you. This is my sister, Delaney."

Jake's brows rose. The women couldn't have looked less alike. Delaney was petite and slender and dark-haired. Chelsea was solid and tall and blond. He glanced at her hair, loose around her shoulders. It certainly didn't look dyed, for there was no sign of dark roots.

He flushed when he realized everyone was staring at him. "Jake Scarlatta," he said, and shook Delaney's outstretched hand.

It was quick, but he saw the look Delaney sent her sister. They'd talked about him. He wondered what Chelsea had said.

"So, you're the new female firefighter on Dad's group," Jessica commented.

Sometimes Jake wished he *had* curtailed his daughter's tongue.

"Yes, I am."

"He said you did great today with the gunshot victims."

Chelsea shot him an uncensored sunny smile. "Thanks," she said. Jake took a sip of beer to hide his flash of pleasure at her reaction.

"Initiation by fire, so to speak," Delaney said.

Jess looked at her blankly.

"Don't mind my sister. She's a psychologist. She has to classify everything."

Jake wondered how Delaney could be old enough to have a degree in psychology.

"I'm going to be a doctor," Jess blurted. "I'm going into premed at Cornell next year."

"I went to Cornell." Delaney smiled wistfully. "Thanks to Chels."

"Delaney," Chelsea said warningly.

"I was fourteen when our mother died," Delaney went on blithely. "Only six years younger than Chels, but she saw that I finished high school and put me through college and grad school."

It was hard to mistake the pride in her voice and the love in her smile. Jake had a thousand questions, yet he smothered them all. But he did glance at Chelsea. Her face was red, the flush beginning at the vee of her shirt. Nestled there was a delicate gold chain, kissing the barely visible indentation between her collarbones. He took a long swig of beer.

"So, you two like the Raiders?" Jessica asked.

"We have season tickets," Delaney said.

"So do we," Jess told her.

"Chelsea's father was a minor league baseball player." When Jess looked confused, she explained, "We had different fathers. My last name is Shaw. My dad was a sax player."

Jake glanced at Chelsea, who was smiling at her sister the way he smiled at Jess. His gaze dropped to her plate, quickly bypassing the chain. "What are you eating?"

"Uh…"

Delaney filled him in. "A veggie burger. Chelsea doesn't eat red meat."

He narrowed his eyes. "You ate Huff's burger today."

"I, um, didn't want to cause any waves right away. I felt like I was holding back the dam all day as it was."

Before he could comment, a man swaggered to their table. "Well, well, well, if it isn't Wonder Woman."

Billy Milligan, Chelsea's ex-boyfriend, hovered over them. His hair was disheveled, and his eyes were bloodshot. He'd clearly drunk more than the beer he held in his hand.

"Heard you saved the day today, Whitmore."

From the corner of his eye, Jake saw Chelsea's hand fist around the napkin in her lap. He said, "Chelsea did great today. Who you here with, Billy?"

"The crew from my old station at Engine Four." He took a gulp of beer and wiped his mouth with the back of a not quite clean hand. It showed scars from his burns.

"Why don't you go find them, Milligan." Delaney's voice was ages older than it had been earlier. "Maybe *they* want your company."

"Why, you little cu—"

"Watch your mouth, buddy," Jake interjected. He stood and deftly eased himself between the table and Billy. "Three ladies are present, and one of them is my daughter."

Milligan, short, stocky and already weaving, stepped back from Jake's imposing form. Two other guys from Engine Four approached.

"Jake," one said, his baseball cap obscuring his eyes.

"TJ, get Billy out of here. The department doesn't need this."

Chelsea noted his choice of words through the cloud of embarrassment the scene had caused her. He was concerned about the fire department. She also noted that Jake's shoulders were backboard-stiff as he sat. He frowned and didn't look at her. The easy camaraderie was gone, doused by Billy Milligan's appearance.

"You about done, Jess?" Jake asked.

Jessica looked surprised, but nodded. She obviously knew her dad's signals. They got to their feet.

"Well, enjoy the rest of the game," Jake said to Chelsea and Delaney, his voice neutral.

Delaney tried to lighten the moment. "The Raiders are behind by ten. But you, too."

When they were gone, Chelsea wrapped the remains of her burger and tossed it into a nearby can. She sipped her beer, trying not to be affected, tamping down the hurt and fury kindling inside her.

"Milligan's a jerk, Chels."

"I know. I just wish he hadn't felt the need to prove it in front of my new lieutenant."

Delaney was serious. Only thirty, she often seemed older and wiser than Chelsea. "Just how much decency does Scarlatta have?"

"I don't know. Why?"

"Will he tell your new group about tonight's little scene with Milligan?"

"Oh, God." Chelsea was sickened by the thought.

"Well, if you'd just quit the fire department, you wouldn't have to deal with any of those Neanderthals."

"Jake's not a Neanderthal."

"Yeah, but he's pretty macho. Even if he is yummy."

"Yummy? You've been spending too much time with your teenage patients."

Chelsea didn't tell her sister she agreed. Delaney's description of Jake in that damn T-shirt was apt. And the way his shorts molded to his thighs... She cut off the thought. She was done with men, especially firefighters.

"Doesn't matter how yummy he is," Delaney continued as if reading her thoughts. "We both know playing with firefighters causes third-degree burns."

Chelsea sobered. "And scars." Her beer followed her burger into the trash, and she stood. "Let's go finish watching the massacre."

Delaney rose. "Chels, you don't have to put up with this stress. Think about it. You can support yourself with the gym."

"I know. But I love the work, and besides, I'm not letting anybody drive me out of the fire department."

"Better than letting them drive you crazy."

Hooking her arm around her sister's neck, Chelsea said,

"Then it's a good thing I've got a shrink for a sister, isn't it?"

Chelsea didn't feel quite as blasé as she pretended to be. And she was afraid the scene tonight would be back around three in the morning to haunt her. And maybe even tomorrow at work.

Oh, God, she hoped Jake didn't tell the crew about this. She didn't want to deal with a whole new round of gossip. Delaney's question surfaced in her mind.

Just how much decency *did* Scarlatta have?

FROM INSIDE the locker room, Peter Huff's deep voice was crystal clear; it stopped Chelsea as she reached the doorway. "It was typical female stuff—act three, scene four, from what he said."

Diaz chuckled. "My wife's into that kind of drama, too."

Huff continued in a smarmy tone. "Heard he really put her in her place. And we all know what that is."

"Right where women belong," Diaz added.

Oh, fine, Chelsea thought. *I'm the butt of sexual innuendo already.*

"After screwing up Milligan's life like she did, she deserves whatever she gets." Joey Santori sounded vicious.

The sudden slam of a locker was like a gunshot, then Mick said, "I don't think that's fair."

"All right you guys, let's move it." So Jake was there, too. In on this little discussion of her.

Easing down the hallway, though she hated creeping away like a cowed puppy, Chelsea thought, *Of course, Jake's in on it, you jerk. He obviously told them about last night.*

Feeling the familiar hurt well inside her, she tamped it down ruthlessly. No, she'd get mad, instead. She was done with being jerked around by male firefighters who were so entrenched in the old boy's network that they didn't care who they hurt. She stomped to the rig and threw her bag on the cement floor.

Damn them. She yanked open a side door and pulled out her air tank. She checked the gauge, saw that it was full and shoved the breathing pack inside. *She* hadn't done anything but end a relationship. *He* couldn't handle it. *He* made a scene everywhere she went. And then he set out to destroy his career.

She retrieved her gear from the hooks along the wall, then stowed it in the alcove, which the night crew had emptied of their goods. Forcefully she stuffed bunker boots, pants and an air tank into the small space.

"Got a problem, Whitmore?"

Chelsea looked into the impassive face of Peter Huff. The guy who'd just been slandering her. "No problem, Huff. You?"

"Me? Nope." Giving her his back, he put his goods on the truck. They worked in silence, though it was far from companionable. Chelsea was reminded of some of the girls in high school who'd been forced to play on the same team but in the cliquishness of teenagehood never spoke to each other.

Well, who cared?

When Peter left, she leaned against the rig and couldn't keep back a sigh. *She* did. *She* cared. Because she was hoping she'd have some respite here. That these guys wouldn't trample her, wouldn't shut her out. Especially Jake.

So much for hope.

She made her way to the kitchen, where the shift met for coffee and discussed the upcoming day. As she entered, Mick's smiling face greeted her like a ray of sunshine peeking though dark clouds.

I don't think that's fair, he'd said. He'd stood up for

her. She smiled back. Huff came in behind her, got coffee and took a seat. Then the lieutenant entered.

"Morning, Chelsea." Jake addressed only her. Of course, he'd already had a powwow with the others.

She nodded, but didn't speak. Those gray eyes had warmed up yesterday. They were filled with humor and goodwill last night. Today he was Benedict Arnold. One of the boys.

Small talk was made over coffee. Chelsea refused to join in; as it was only her second day, her silence wouldn't be noticed.

After about twenty minutes, Jake stood. "All right. Housework assignments are on the bulletin board. When you're done, let's meet in the bay. We're doing confined-space training today." The men groaned when he referred to the newest form of rescue the fire department had taken on—crawling into dark, smelly, tight places that no one in his right mind would willingly go.

Jake chuckled. "That's right, time to show your stuff." Facing Chelsea, he said, "Could you stay back a minute? I want to catch up on how much of this training you've had." Something like a grin curved his lips. "We're going through the pipe today for the first time." The city had provided the department with big water pipes the firefighters could use to prepare for the psychological aspects of being confined.

She kept her face impassive and gave him a haughty nod. When everyone left, he studied her. "Something wrong?"

"No, why?"

"You're quiet."

"I'm always quiet."

"Sure it's not something I should know about?"

She shook her head. "No, Lieutenant, I have nothing to tell you that you don't already know." She held his gaze, and he shifted uncomfortably. "The confined-space training?"

He studied her for a moment longer, then said, "Our group's gone over the basics and seen the videos on claustrophobia. We're ready for our first shot through the hole."

"I've been through it."

His brows rose. "You have?"

She nodded.

"Well, good. You can help us. None of us has yet."

"Fine."

When she started out ahead of him, he said, "Whitmore?"

She turned.

"You sure nothing's wrong?"

"Nope. Nothing." She walked out the door.

THE HELL THERE ISN'T, Jake thought half an hour later out in the bay. They'd reviewed the basics on breaching a confined space and were ready to crawl through the thirty-foot-long, two-foot-diameter iron pipe laid ominously on the cement floor of the huge garage. To make it even more difficult, the ends were blocked once the firefighter entered the pipe. Done frequently enough, the drill would acclimate the rescuers to dark, tight spaces. So far, Chelsea hadn't been any help at all. She'd been more like a kid pouting at not getting her way.

"All right, who wants to go first?"

No response.

Not even Chelsea, who'd done it.

He shrugged. "Okay, I'll go." Dropping to his knees, Jake stuck his head inside; the faint scent of disinfectant couldn't mask the iron smell. His shoulders just managed to clear the opening. Inside, it was tunnel-dark. Smothering. He drew in a deep breath, which filled his lungs with heavy air and made his mouth taste coppery. Closing his eyes, he inched in. He could feel his breathing escalate. Sweat popped out on his brow. His stomach muscles clenched. Jeez, this was tougher than eating his first smoke.

"Come on, Lieutenant, you're halfway there." Murphy's voice from somewhere outside calmed him. Slowly, he crept along. When he reached the end, he pushed aside the plywood, shimmied out and came to his feet.

"It wasn't pretty," he said as he wiped his face with a towel Mick tossed to him. Whitmore was barely looking his way. "My physical reactions were acute." He gave them a rundown of his body's responses. Chelsea offered not a speck of support.

Mick went next. He ducked his head in, his shoulders, and crawled about a foot; then he backed out. "Can't do it. Not today." His expression was sheepish, but they'd been told most people took more than one try to master the pipe and not to proceed if they felt they couldn't.

Jake smiled and patted his shoulder. "That's okay. Your reaction's not uncommon."

Santori looked at him. His gaze slid to the hole. Stepping back, he crossed his arms over his chest and shook his head. "I'm not gonna even try."

"I will." Diaz got a foot farther than Mick.

When Peter took his turn, he got a third of the way through.

"Listen," Jake said soothingly, "this isn't unusual. It's a tough exercise. We'll keep doing it till we all get it."

Filled with winter frost, Santori's eyes narrowed. "What about Whitmore?"

Jake's gaze slid to her. He could tell she was enjoying this. Pushing herself away from the truck she'd been leaning against, she headed to the pipe. Dropping to her knees, then her stomach, she inched in. Her shoulders disappeared. Her fanny scraped the top, but she fit better than the guys. The soles of her boots disappeared.

After a minute Jake bent down at the other end. "Halfway, Whitmore, you can do it."

In almost no time the plywood block slammed back, and her head popped out. Gracefully, she eased her body onto the cement floor of the bay and got to her feet. Though some strands had escaped the knot she habitually tied her hair into and her face was flushed, she was breathing easy. Staring down her nose at the guys, she offered no explanation that she'd done it before. No confession that it was hard for her the first time. She glared at them, hitting them all square on their masculine egos. Then she turned and left the bay.

Jake was angry. *Really* angry.

Twenty minutes later, he found her at the rig, fiddling with the water gauges. She was driver today, but he suspected her actions were perfunctory.

"Whitmore, I wanna talk to you."

She kept her back to him as she unscrewed and replaced the covers. Sweat made a line down the back of her T-shirt, which clung to her, outlining solid deltoid muscles. "So talk."

He clamped his lips for a minute to get control of his temper. Damn it, he'd done his best to ease her way in here. He didn't deserve this shit. He wouldn't tolerate it. "Look at me, Whitmore." As it was a direct summons from an officer, she had no choice.

She turned, her eyes brandy-colored and mutinous. "Yes, sir."

"What the hell's going on?"

"Going on?"

Feeling his temperature rise like heated mercury, he straightened to his full height and counted to ten. Then he said, "Yesterday you were part of the team. Today you did your best to make the guys feel like shit. You know how tough it is to go through that pipe the first time.''

She arched an arrogant brow. ''*You* did it.''

Purposefully ignoring the comment, he closed the distance between them. It surprised him that he was almost a head taller than she was. ''Why didn't you tell them you'd done it before? Why didn't you encourage them through it?''

''Why should I?''

''Because you're part of this crew. And crew members support each other.''

She straightened, too, which brought her face close to his chin. ''Well, I didn't *feel* like part of the crew this morning when you all were trashing me in the locker room.''

Jake froze. His mouth gaped. ''You heard that?''

''Yeah, I heard that.'' She stared him down, the emotion in her eyes reaching flashover. ''Thanks a lot for sharing last night's drama with them, Lieutenant.''

He drew a blank. Then it dawned on him. His thumb hit his chest with a thud. ''You think *I* told them about Billy's shenanigans?''

''Oh, spare me.'' She turned her back on him again.

Without thinking, he spun her around. Sexual harassment training had taught him that uninvited touching was taboo, but by the time he remembered it was too late. Still, he didn't let her go. ''I didn't tell the guys anything.''

Her look was pure disbelief.

''I didn't.''

She stepped back and crossed her arms.

He jammed his hands in his pockets. ''Joey and Peter ran into Billy at Pumpers after the game. Milligan filled them in.''

Chelsea's shoulders lost some of their starch. *Good.*

''You know, Whitmore, try giving some of us the benefit of the doubt. What would I have to gain by spreading gossip about you? I'm tryin' to make it easier here for you. For us all.''

Eyes rounded with surprise, she stared at him. ''I thought—''

''Yeah, it's obvious what you thought. Cut me some slack, will you?''

She didn't respond. Even, white teeth came out over her bottom lip, instead.

''And the guys, too. They shouldn't have been trashing you. I would've stopped it if I'd caught it in time. But you could have either risen above it or confronted them this morning, instead of sulking about it all day.''

With one last glare, he turned and left her alone with the rig.

CHAPTER FOUR

STROBE LIGHTS flashed in sync with the pounding rhythm of a group named Death Face. Its predecessor, Skull, hadn't been much better. Jake closed his eyes to block out the lights hammering the black walls of Beelzebub's Den, Derek's favorite club; wearily, he rubbed his temples. His head was throbbing from another night with not enough sleep and a very long day with Firefighter Whitmore.

Jake could picture her proud carriage and tilted head as she challenged him. *Well, I didn't feel like part of the crew this morning when you all were trashing me in the locker room.* She hadn't backed down, and he admired her grit.

"That sound is *so* awesome. Don'tcha think, Jake?"

Dragging his mind away from his latest problem, Jake smiled at one of his perennial ones. "Sounds like a lot of noise to me, buddy."

Derek grimaced, then, as usual, smiled at Jake. The boy loved him as much as he loved Derek. It was one thing Jake was certain of. But he was not at all certain about how to help the young James Dean who sat before him. Derek wore the collar of his black shirt turned up, and had perfected the practiced sneer of a rebel.

Death Face wrapped up their set just as the waitress approached.

"Ready to order, handsome?" She only had eyes for Derek.

Derek nodded. "Yep." He looked at Jake. "You?"

"Sure."

"What'll ya have?" She'd edged close to Derek, her hip brushing his arm.

Derek gave her Danny's grin. "Two hamburgers with the works. Some of those big French fries. And two more Dr. Peppers."

Actually Jake would have preferred a cold beer and some hot sex, but he'd settle for... Damn, where had that come from? Must be the erotic lyrics of the music. He wasn't dating anybody, and it had been a while since he'd had a good, long night of lovemaking.

The waitress grinned, snapped her gum and took their menus.

As he watched her leave, Derek said, "Man I love that waitress. She's hot."

Jake was transported to another time....

Hey, buddy. Let's go to Georgie's. They got these hot waitresses that wear little black French-maid outfits.

He'd gone with Danny; the waitresses had been as hot as Danny had said. He and Danny had been eighteen, a year older than Derek.

Jake experienced nostalgic feelings similar to those he'd had about Jess at the game last night. He remembered Derek as a little boy. Found himself wishing things didn't have to change.

"Derek, let's get this out of the way before we eat."

The boy blew bubbles into his soda. "Yeah, yeah, I know. Ma's pissed off at me because of yesterday."

"I'm pissed off, too."

Mutiny rose in Derek's almost black eyes. That same mutiny had been in Danny's the last time Jake had seen or spoken to him.

You sold me down the river, just like I was afraid you'd do when you got to be an officer. You turned me in. It'll never be square between us again, man. Never.

"Drinking and drugs are unacceptable, Derek. Why are you fooling around with them?"

"Somethin' to do."

"Something dangerous."

The boy shrugged. "Maybe it's in my genes."

Jake felt his shoulders tighten. He rubbed the muscles of one while gathering his thoughts. "This is about your dad, isn't it?"

The boy made a conscious study of his glass. "Whaddaya mean?"

"I miss him, too, Derek."

"*I* don't miss him. He walked out on Ma, me *and* you."

"Yes, he did. It doesn't mean we don't still care about him."

"Speak for yourself." Derek's tone held disgust and anger, but Jake could detect the underlying hurt. The boy sighed and asked, "Listen, are you gonna rag on me all night, or is this gonna be fun?"

"One more point. Then we'll enjoy the music." Begrudgingly Derek smiled at Jake's dry tone. "I want you to talk to a counselor."

"A shrink?"

"Yes."

"No way!"

So much like Danny. *Get help? Like from a shrink? You gotta be kiddin' me.*

With fatherly concern, Jake leaned over and grasped Derek's arm. He'd spent ten years building trust with this boy. He rarely called on that bond, but now was the time. "I want you to think about it." Derek watched him with owl eyes. "For me."

Derek's Adam's apple bobbed. His surly teenage-boy mask slipped, and he was all kid for a few seconds. "Okay, I'll think about it."

Jake sighed. *Thank God*. He didn't know what he'd do if he lost Derek. Losing Danny had been bad enough.

As the screech of an electric guitar split the air, Jake vowed never to let that happen. He decided he'd talk to Reed about it.

THE WEIGHT ROOM, a huge complex with three main workout areas and side rooms for specialties like aerobic kick boxing and gymnastics, was hopping. Trainer Spike Lammon towered over Chelsea as she raised the barbell from flat on her back on the padded bench. Spike was dressed in gray pants and shirt with the club's snazzy logo, and his fit body was worth a thousand dollars of advertising for the gym. His forehead furrowed as he checked off her routine on the clipboard.

"Come on, babe, this is the last of the weights." He grinned like a little boy with a frog behind his back. "Think about all those *younger* women you'll be competing with."

She tried for a scathing look, but sweat poured into her eyes despite her hot pink headband, and her limbs, encased in flashy hot pink shorts and crop top, were close to muscle burnout. Nevertheless she bench-pressed two hundred pounds of iron one more time.

"Great job," Spike said when she was done. "That's it for tonight."

She sat up and scowled. "Let's go in the back and work on my floor exercises."

He shook his head. "You're pushing too hard."

Playfully she socked him in the arm. "Remember all those younger women breathing down my neck."

"Still, I think you should stop."

"She at it again, Spike?"

Chelsea turned to see Francey Templeton behind her. She took in Francey's outfit—black nylon shorts and a plain white T-shirt. She couldn't get that girl to dress right. Exiting the locker room was her husband, Alex; now *he* knew what to wear. Garbed in hunter green workout clothes, he could have walked off the pages of *GQ*.

Spike shook his head at Francey. "She's working too hard." His voice was ripe with affection.

"At what?" Alex asked as he came up to them, his hand sneaking familiarly to his wife's neck. She leaned into it. Chelsea turned her gaze away. Sometimes their closeness was hard to watch.

"Chelsea's competing in the Fitness Triathlon at the Dome Arena here in Rockford."

Alex cocked his head. "I've never heard of it."

"It's a woman's fitness contest." Spike ruffled Chelsea's hair. "They compete in muscle strength and tone, running endurance and speed and a dance and gymnastics routine."

Francey brightened. "Sounds like fun."

Groaning, Alex said, "Don't get any ideas. Men look at you more than I like already." He dropped a kiss on the top of her head. "I'm off to warm up."

Francey trailed her fingers down his arm. "Remember, if I beat you in weights again, you cook all week."

"You won't," he called over his shoulder as he left.

Spike faced Francey. "I've got to get back to the desk. Don't let Chelsea do the gymnastics routine tonight."

As if figuring out a jigsaw puzzle, Francey stared after the trainer. "Are all men alike?"

"Too protective? Some." Chelsea glanced over her shoulder at Spike. "He's a godsend, though. He runs the gym. Overseeing my training is an extra bonus."

"And he's yummy to look at."

Delaney's comment about Jake came back to her—*even if he is yummy*. Well, her lieutenant wasn't very yummy two days ago when he was spitting nails at her.

"Wanna come to the back room with me?" she asked Francey.

"No. Why don't you keep me company on the treadmill and fill me in on what's been happening at the station. That way you can cool down."

"I want to work out some more."

Francey squeezed her arm. "You look exhausted."

Sighing, Chelsea rolled her shoulders. "I slept better last night. I took a pill and it helped. But okay, I'll stay here."

As the women headed to the machines, Francey said, "You haven't been sleeping well since the thing with Billy. Beth thinks you should see a doctor."

"How is she?"

"Great. All three of them are. We just came from visiting them." The women mounted treadmills. Francey set her speed low and glanced at her friend. "Jake was there, too."

"Was he?"

"Yeah. Timmy threw one of his early evening tantrums, and Dylan and Beth couldn't do anything with him. Jake was the only one who could calm him."

"Jake's good at that kind of thing."

Francey frowned. "He looked as tired as you."

"Well, we're off for three days before we go on nights, so he can rest up." When Francey didn't respond, Chelsea asked, "Did he say anything about the crew?"

"Nope. I even got him alone a minute, and he told me to mind my own business." Francey chuckled. "He always was the most closemouthed of all of us."

"You talk about him as if he's part of your family."

"He is. Just not by blood. In a lot of ways, he understands me better than my brothers."

After a moment Chelsea asked, "Why *is* Jake so quiet, France?"

''Personality. Life. His father—my dad's best friend—died when Jake was ten. Dad tried to fill in, but Jake became the man of the house for his mother and three younger sisters.''

Chelsea thought about what had happened with her and Delaney after their mother's death.

''Then there's all that stuff with his best friend, Danny DeLuca, just before you and I got into the RFD. Jake doesn't talk about it—all I know is Danny got in trouble and Jake was his lieutenant. I do know DeLuca quit and left town.'' She hesitated. ''I don't like to gossip about Jake.''

When Chelsea nodded, she changed the subject. ''So, how has it been with your new group?'' Francey speeded up on her treadmill, but Chelsea didn't. She would cool down and go home.

''Not so hot,'' she replied.

''Really? Don't tell me Jake's done something to make it that way.''

''Well, kind of.''

''I don't believe it. Even though he's reserved, he's the kindest, gentlest man I know. Excluding his big-brother teasing when he beats me at arm wrestling.''

Chelsea related the details of overhearing the crew talk about her confrontation with Billy the night of the ball game.

Francey didn't say anything for a moment. ''If Jake tells you he wasn't a part of it, he wasn't.''

''You trust him that much?''

''With my life.'' She glanced at Chelsea. ''Don't get upset at me for saying this, Chels, but maybe you're looking for trouble where none exists.''

Chelsea stepped off her machine and wiped her face with a towel, then sat wearily on the edge of the treadmill. Suddenly she felt like she'd been battling a blaze for hours. "That's what Jake said. Maybe I *am* overreacting. He's gone out of his way, otherwise, to make me feel accepted."

Francey zipped her machine a little higher. She wasn't even breathing hard. "I know all those guys pretty well. Except for Joey, they're nice men. And Joey's problem is that he associates you with me. Since I got married, he's been even more hostile."

"I don't know how to act there, France. I tried showing them up in the confined-space exercise, and that backfired." She filled Francey in on her performance. "I didn't tell them I already did it."

Francey gave a low whistle. "I'll bet they were mad. Anybody make it through on the first time?"

"Superman did." At Francey's questioning look, Chelsea shrugged. "Jake."

"Of course. He's so cool, he would."

An image of her lieutenant in a sweaty T-shirt assaulted her. He'd looked pretty yummy.

Chelsea shook off the memory. She picked up her gray and pink Weight Room warmup jacket and got to her feet. "Well, I'm done. I'm going home and curl up with my cats. If you need anything, Spike will be here till closing."

"Chels?"

"Yeah?"

"Cut them some slack. Maybe you'll sleep better."

She shot Francey a weak smile and headed for the locker room. God, she *had* to start sleeping better. In two days she'd have all of group three at Quint Twelve as company for the night.

JAKE LOOKED FORWARD to the first night shift with Chelsea Whitmore on board about as much as he'd relished getting third degree burns on his back. Since she'd shown up the guys on her second day here, things had been tense.

They'd known, of course, what she was doing. And they didn't like it one bit. Hell, neither did he.

"Ah, I miss that Scarlatta scowl."

Jake was surprised to see Dylan coming through the door to the kitchen. "What're you doing here? You're on furlough for a few more days."

Dylan nodded. "I just brought in the weekly trivia game questions." He tossed a sheet of printed paper on the table. "Read 'em and weep."

Jake fingered the sheet absently. "Beth looked great the other night. And the baby..." He paused. "I envy you, buddy."

Dylan studied him a moment. "Wanna talk?"

"No, why?"

"No reason. Stop over tomorrow if you feel like it. Beth and the baby nap in the afternoon, and I get to clean the house."

"Maybe."

Dylan sniffed. "What smells so good?"

"It's probably tofu."

"What?"

"Nothing. Whitmore's cooking."

"I see. Is—"

A light knock sounded on the door. Jake glanced over to see a tiny, white-haired lady carrying a huge plate of cookies.

Dylan grinned. "Mrs. Lowe. How are ya, darlin'?"

Sharp, knowing eyes narrowed on him. "Don't get fresh, young man." She turned to Jake. "Haven't you taught him any manners yet?"

"I'm tryin', Mrs. Lowe." He sniffed with marked exaggeration. "Are those my favorite *pizzelles* I smell?"

"Of course they are." She moved into the room and set the plate on the table.

Like a little boy behind his mother's back, Dylan

sneaked a cookie; Mrs. Lowe slapped his hand away. "It'll ruin your supper."

"I'm cookin' for my wife and new baby tonight." He winked. "I got pictures in the car, Mrs. L. Wanna see?"

The old woman's face lit from within. She looped an arm through Dylan's and said to Jake, "Enjoy the cookies, boy, but bring the plate back next time you come to the nuthouse."

Jake stood, smiling. "I will. I'll walk you out to the bay. We're doing training before supper."

When they reached the huge garage, Dylan and Mrs. Lowe said goodbye and detoured to the left. Jake found his group waiting by the confined-space pipe. Chelsea leaned against the rig, her face impassive. Mick sat on the floor next to Joey and Don. Peter had taken a straight chair and was leafing though a magazine.

"Hi, guys." Jake held up a clipboard. "Let's go over a few procedures for the CSP before we try it again. This is a technically complex rescue."

Groans all around.

Except from Whitmore. He didn't look at her because he didn't want to see her smirk.

Briefly Jake reviewed the equipment they might need for a confined-space rescue, along with some of the physics involved in the maneuvers. Though it was a complicated task, he was really giving them time to prepare for another stab at the pipe. After twenty minutes, he couldn't delay any longer.

"Anybody have any suggestions for making this easier?" Don Diaz asked. "I sure as hell hate not bein' able to do somethin'."

Jake started to give a piece of advice he'd read in *Firehouse* magazine, when Chelsea pushed away from the rig. She cleared her throat. "Over at Engine Four, when we did it the first time, the captain suggested we use visual imagery. Think about something pleasant, at least to get inside. After the second or third time through, you won't need to do that."

Huff caught on first. "You done this before, Whitmore?"

She faced him squarely. "Yes."

"Why didn't you tell us?" Joey asked, despite his previous desire to give her the deep freeze.

"Yeah, why didn't you help last time?" This from Mick.

She swept them all with a level gaze. "Because when I came in that morning, I heard you guys in the locker room trashing me about Milligan."

Silence. They all stared at her.

Then Huff said, "Hurt your feelings, Whitmore?"

No firefighter in his right mind would admit that. Jake hoped she wouldn't.

"Not on your life," she said. "I was just mad. I don't like to be talked about."

Good girl, he thought. She could hold her own with these guys.

Huff shrugged. "Fair enough."

When nobody else jumped in, Jake said, "Let's remember that, then." He nodded to the pipe. "Now, let's try it again."

With his encouragement and Chelsea's suggestions, two of them made it through the pipe.

An hour later Chelsea was putting the finishing touches on dinner when Jake entered the kitchen. "Smells great."

She kept her back to him as she stirred tomato sauce. He came up beside her and leaned against the counter. *He* smelled great, too, she thought.

He frowned at *The Healthy Firehouse Cookbook* on the counter. "What is it?"

"Bean sprout steak."

"What?"

She looked up, her eyes dancing with devilment.

"You jerkin' my chain, Whitmore?"

"Who, me?"

Crossing his arms, he said, "It feels good, doesn't it."

"What does?"

"Having the ice broken."

She nodded.

"Thanks for helping with the drill."

Poking green beans with a fork, she didn't look at him. "I should have done it last time."

In her peripheral vision she saw him watching her. Then he pushed away and sat at the table.

"It's Italian grilled chicken with pasta," she said. "They'll like it as long as they don't know it's got only three grams of fat per serving."

"You eat chicken?" he asked.

"Yeah, especially when I'm training."

He turned around. "Training?"

"I, um, compete sometimes in fitness contests. There's a women's triathalon coming up, and I'm in it." She explained the events as she kept vigil over the food.

"Is it fun?"

"Yeah. As long as you're in shape."

After she put the fettuccine noodles into boiling water, she edged to the sink to wash her hands.

"Hell, I only know two out of three," she heard Jake complain.

"Of what?"

"Dylan's trivia." He chuckled. "He's something else. This week the subject's famous sons."

Chelsea laughed, too. "Read me the questions."

"Who is the Boston firefighter whose son almost died of congestive heart failure two years ago, but was saved by another firefighter who lived in his apartment building?''

''Search me.''

''You gonna play?''

''Obviously not this week.''

''It's Leo Stapleton. His son Garrett was saved in a dramatic rescue in 1998. It was profiled in *Firehouse*.''

''Wow.''

''Whose son made a fortune by patenting and printing the phone labels for fire and police numbers? This was before nine-one-one.''

''You can't possibly know that.''

''Yep, I do. His last name is Conway. Fred, I think. The guy who wrote *Fire Fighting Lore*.''

Chelsea asked, ''Is there anything you haven't read about the fire department?''

Shrugging, Jake said, ''Well, I don't know the last one.'' His brow furrowed. ''What book did Firefighter Joseph Bonanno dedicate to his mother, Audrey, who died from critical burns sustained at home?''

The name sounded familiar. Chelsea glanced at the counter. And smiled.

''Damn, nobody's gonna get that,'' Jake said. ''Dylan's crazy.''

Chelsea came up behind him and dropped the cookbook on the table in front of him.

Jake laughed, deep and from his belly. It made her insides flutter like the heroine in a Victorian novel. ''Hey, thanks, Whitmore.''

Turning back to the stove, she tried to ignore the warmth spreading though her. ''You're welcome. Chow's almost ready. Set the table and call the boys.''

''Yes, ma'am.''

She stole a quick peek at him. His gray eyes flashed

with humor. He was grinning a curl-your-toes grin. Man, this guy was lethal when he turned on the charm.

Good thing she was immune.

AT TEN THAT NIGHT Chelsea sat at the oak kitchen table waiting to take the apple pie she'd baked out of the oven. Absently she rubbed the table's polished surface, wondering where the station had gotten such a quality piece of furniture. The Quint, to which she'd been assigned tonight, had had one call after dinner; the Midi was out on its second now. Besides playing Betty Crocker, she'd gone over some schedules, then come in here with a new procedural manual to skim. Outside the calls, she hadn't seen much of the crew since dinner; she'd heard them in the bunk room and then in the back office, but they weren't around now.

The bay door went up, and in minutes, Jake entered the kitchen. His hair was messy from the wind that had picked up earlier; he went to the sink and drew a glass of water. Taking a sideways glance, she saw his throat work as he swallowed. She shifted uncomfortably.

"Whitmore, you baking?"

"Who me?"

She kept her eyes focused on the procedural manual.

Mick Murphy strode into the room. "Oh, my God, what's that smell?"

From the table, she didn't look up. "What smell?"

"It's apple pie, isn't it?"

"Is it?"

Huff tromped in after writing his report; he'd affected his usual lazy demeanor, but sniffed loudly. "My firstborn for some of that, Whitmore."

Finally, a smile aimed at all three of them broke through. "That won't be necessary. It was covered in your six dollars for dinner."

At the bing of the stove buzzer, she got up and removed the bubbling, steaming confection from the oven. Mick got a wooden cutting board and placed it in the center of the table. "Don't wanna hurt Jake's baby."

At her quizzical look, Mick said, "Jake made this table."

"Really? It's beautiful."

"Yeah, you should see some of the stuff he's done."

Her lieutenant grunted and eyed the pie. "Don't suppose you thought to get vanilla ice cream."

Cockily, she crossed to the fridge and opened the door to reveal two half gallons. She knew the Mount Everest appetite of firefighters.

The guys sank into chairs like little boys waiting for birthday cake. When she told them the pie had to cool for a few minutes, they pouted.

"How'd the run to Dutch Towers go?" she asked Jake.

"Fine."

Chelsea smiled. "Which were they—scared or lonely?"

"Both." Peter snorted. "Mr. Steed was with Mr. Olivo when he had trouble breathing. 'Course, Mrs. Lowe came out to see Jake when she heard the truck."

Mick said, "She's sweet on Jake. Keeps track of his schedule."

Jake chuckled. "She's just lonely. Look, Whitmore, I'm dyin' here. Cut the pie."

Just as she finished dishing out the pieces—à la mode—Joey strolled into the room. He scowled at them all gathered around the table like a family at Thanksgiving. Then he sauntered to the coffeepot. Joey had first watch tonight, from ten to two, so he'd want to stay awake.

Chelsea caught Jake's look. His gaze slid to Joey, then back to her.

Okay, why not?

She got up and fished out another plate, then served the

last slice of her masterpiece. She sat down, handed it to Mick, who gave it to Huff, who passed it across to Joey.

The surprise on his face was almost comical. After recovering, he said, "Ice cream?" She passed him the container and the scoop. "Thanks." He took a bite. "It's good."

When Chelsea looked up, she saw a smile flirting with Jake's lips, and the approval in his eyes warmed her a like cozy fire for two.

After a moment Jake said, "I saw your grandparents at the Towers, Joey."

Joey grunted.

"Moses said you never called them back. Josephine misses you."

"I forgot."

Diaz said, "If I had family, I wouldn't ignore 'em."

"I'll call them in the morning." Joey sounded chagrined.

Huff and Diaz cleaned up the dessert plates. It was almost eleven when Chelsea said, "I, um, assume you guys have specific bunks. Anybody want to tell me which is mine?"

Almost imperceptibly, Mick hesitated in his movements. Huff turned his face away—to hide a snicker? Diaz shifted in his seat and coughed. Jeez, where did they expect her to sleep?

Jake stood. "Come on, I'll show you."

Miffed, she rose and followed Jake to the bunk room. With these guys, it was three steps forward, two back. From the hallway, she could see the bunk room was dark. Jake stepped aside so she could go in first, which was odd. She felt for the wall switch, then flicked on the light.

And gave a start of surprise.

Very male chuckles came from behind her, and she turned to see the guys, except Santori, lined up at the doorway. She faced the bunks again, which were pushed together. Five beds nestled up to one in the middle, all six touching.

"Somethin' wrong, Whitmore?" Jake asked, amusement deepening his voice.

"Look, I know you guys are close, but this is ridiculous."

Diaz said, "Don't they sleep this way over at Four? It makes us all feel safer."

She bit back a chuckle. "I guess I don't have to ask which bunk is mine."

The one in the middle had a pink lacy bedspread, white ribbons around the headboard and a teddy bear propped against the pillow.

Diaz said, "The bedspread used to be my daughter's. She loaned it to you."

"*I* brought in the ribbons," Mick told her.

"Whose is the teddy bear?"

Jake grinned. "It's an old one of Jessie's."

She looked at the guys again. Though Huff leaned against the wall, not participating, he was there, with a grin breaching his lips. Jake, Mick and Don could hardly keep a straight face.

Chelsea started to laugh. "If it's short-sheeted, you guys, you're gonna pay."

The men laughed good-naturedly, and began rearranging the bunks. Hers was shoved against a far wall, like theirs, with plenty of space, though no real privacy. Mick, Don and Peter went to shower. She removed Mick's daughter's bedspread and the ribbons and folded them neatly. Out of the corner of her eye, she could see Jake unbutton his blue shirt. He threw it on the bunk closest to hers where some RFD sweats rested. She sank down on her bed, hugging the teddy bear to her chest the way she cuddled her cats at night.

He grinned at her. "I'd check the sheets if I were you."

AT THREE Jake wasn't grinning. He was sitting up straight in bed, shaking. He'd had the dream again—Danny and the flashover. Only this time Chelsea Whitmore was in the middle of the inferno.

Flinging off the covers, he grabbed his sweat suit from the bottom of the bed. They all slept in gym shorts and T-shirts, but it would be cold in the kitchen, or the watch room if he decided to keep Mick company. He knew he wouldn't go back to sleep after being out cold for four solid hours and with the remnants of the dream lingering like stale smoke in his head.

He left the pitch-black bunk room silently. Diaz, Santori and Huff slept like the dead, but he didn't know about Whitmore, and he didn't want to wake anybody and explain his sleeplessness.

He was thinking about what Chelsea looked like laughing at the guys' prank when he entered the kitchen. A small light was on over the stove, casting the room in an eerie glow. A figure sat curled up on a chair, sipping from a mug. The feminine slope of the shoulders told him it was her.

"Chelsea?"

She jumped.

"Sorry, I didn't mean to scare you."

"It's okay."

Her voice was raspy. She cleared her throat. "What are you doing up?"

"I could ask you the same." Farther into the room, closer, the dark circles under her eyes told him the story. "Can't sleep?"

She nodded, the action sending her hair cascading around her shoulders like a golden waterfall. Though she wore it up in some kind of knot all day, she obviously took it out when she went to bed. It was mussed and a little wild. Sexy.

Uncomfortable with the direction of his thoughts, he crossed to the coffeepot, poured a mugful. "Want some?"

"No, mine's fine."

He joined her at the table. After a silence he asked, "You fall asleep?"

"Uh-huh. But I woke up and couldn't settle down again."

"Hmm."

"You, too?"

"Yeah."

She sipped her drink, then said, "Depression."

"What?"

"Delaney told me that when you can't fall asleep, psychologists say it's anxiety. When you wake up and can't get back, it's depression."

After another pause he asked, "Happen to you often?"

"Lately."

"'Cause of Billy?"

She nodded.

He watched her for a minute, curled up on the chair, her knees drawn to her chest. "Chelsea, what really happened with him? All I heard was bits and pieces. I didn't ask Francey or Beth for details because I thought it'd be prying."

"What do you think it is now?"

His shoulders stiffened. Though she had reason to be prickly, he had little patience at this time of the night. He started to rise. "Forget it."

She grabbed at his arm. "Don't go. That's the worst thing about insomnia. Being alone. At least at home I've got my cats."

He sat down. "I know." He thought about his dog, a gray mixed breed named Smoky, that Danny had given to him as a pup. She'd died two years ago, but she'd been good company during Jake's sleeplessness.

"I'll tell you if you really want to hear it," she finally said.

"It'll go no further, I promise."

"I know." Again she sipped her coffee. The RFD sweats she wore were big, the sleeves reached her knuckles. "I knew it was stupid to get involved with a firefighter. Half the world thinks females in the department are lesbians, and the other half thinks we sleep with the crew. But he was so nice at first. So funny and fun loving." She glanced around the kitchen. "You know how intimate firehouse living is. We were together all the time. We saved lives together, covered each other's back."

Jake thought about Danny.

"The attraction was mutual, and it was only natural to grow close." She sighed. "But I never really knew him."

"What do you mean?"

"As soon as we got serious, he changed. Became possessive. Demanding. He was critical of everything I did that didn't include him. He particularly hated the gym. I think because of all the guys there."

Jake nodded. "Go on."

She bit her lip. "He started making scenes whenever I wanted to do anything without him. I knew then I should end the relationship. But I'd waited too long. He'd gotten maniacally jealous. He insulted all my friends, their husbands, even some of the guys at work."

"So you finally ended it."

She waited a long time, then whispered, "Not until he hit me."

Jake was stunned.

"He'd been drinking one night when my gym manager gave me a ride to Billy's house from the club," she went on. "Billy went into a rage when I walked through the door. He knocked me around the living room until I finally hit him with a big metal vase and stopped him.''

"Chelsea, I'm sorry. I didn't know, wouldn't have guessed.''

"Nobody knows that part. I've never told a soul.''

He wondered why she'd told him. Probably sleep deprivation and the solitude of early morning; both could loosen your tongue like you'd drunk hundred-proof vodka.

"That's not all, though, is it?''

"Nope. When I refused to see him anymore, he had these fits of anger until he finally got it through his thick skull it was over. By then, the guys at Four were sick of it from both sides. Then he pulled the rest of his tricks.''

Jake knew about Billy's performance at work. He'd started taking chances, putting himself in situations that a rookie would know better than to risk. As Chelsea detailed them, Jake cringed. "He went into a fire without his gloves or Nomex hood,'' she said. "He took a staircase without a charged hose. He disobeyed orders more than once.''

"God.''

"And then he got burned.''

Jake had heard about that, too. Billy had been told to come out of a fire and refused. The building became fully involved, and his captain risked his neck to find him and drag him out.

Chelsea said, "The Cap told him that if he was going to kill himself over some broad, it'd have to be on his own time. He was suspended on some kind of emotional disability. Reed Macauley's working with him.'' When she looked at Jake, her eyes were misty. "Doesn't look like he's made much progress.''

"No, it doesn't,'' Jake said.

"Anyway, the guys blamed me. I became a pariah. I'd been there eight years. He'd been there twelve. Still…''

"It hurt.''

"Yeah." She stared into space as if she was seeing ghosts. "I'd eaten at their houses, had them to mine. I talked to more than one of them through the night about personal problems. Went to their kids' first communions." She sniffled. "Once, Connors got trapped on a roof. I saw it when no one else did. Another time, I pulled Jones out of the way of a falling girder. None of it mattered in the end." She shook her head sadly. "Male bonds, I guess."

He wanted to reach out and touch her. Hell, he wanted to hold her, to insulate her with his body and stop the shivers that came when she related the worst of it. Instead, he said softly, "Not all men are like that, Chelsea."

"Aren't they?"

"No."

"Well, you couldn't prove it by me."

"I'm sorry."

"Yeah, so am I." She fiddled with her coffee cup, then looked at him again. "So, Lieutenant, wanna tell me what monkey's on your back that wakes you in the middle of the night?" She indicated the room, still encased in an inky cloak except for one beacon of light coming from the stove.

He returned her gaze. Ordinarily, he wouldn't even consider sharing the sadness he lived with, never willingly reveal his inadequacies and fears. Or the dashed dreams he'd had of a big family and rising in the ranks of the fire department.

But there was something about the intimacy of their surroundings, while the firehouse slept around them. Something about her uncensored confession of her demons that made him want to share his. And then there were some uncanny similarities to his own situation with Danny—someone you loved and trusted turning on you,

public censure from other firefighters, daily reminders of
what had happened.

Just as he opened his mouth to speak, the lights went
on in the kitchen and the tone sounded over the PA system.

CHAPTER FIVE

WITH ORDERS to ready the hoses and prepare for entry, Jake bounded off the truck as it came to a halt on a crowded side street in downtown Rockford. They were first in, and the corner of the two-story house blazed with angry flames. As she hauled hose, Chelsea watched Jake approach the spectators.

Though it was four in the morning, several people had gathered under a street lamp outside the burning house. An old woman with snow-white hair and parchment skin gripped the lapels of her tattered chenille bathrobe.

''Ma'am, do you know if the house is occupied?''

''Y-yes.'' Her voice shook. ''Damned fool Edward. Eighty years old. His daughter begged him to move in with her, but she's allergic to cats, and he wouldn't hear of leaving Hester.''

''Hester?''

''Hester Prynne, his cat.''

''So you think he's inside?''

''Yes.''

''Where's his room?''

She pointed to the second floor on a side of the house where no flames were visible.

Abruptly Jake turned from the woman and faced his group. Already they had the lines out, the ladders down and their breathing tanks on. Over the blare of Engine Sixteen's arrival, Jake said, ''Santori and I will attack the fire. We'll take the hose to the second floor.'' He turned to Chelsea. "You and Huff come in behind us with a second line. You're search-and-rescue. Go up and to the left and start at the farthest bedroom. The woman says there's an eighty-year-old man in there somewhere."

She and Huff nodded.

Mick and Don knew to stay with the trucks to oversee the water. "Mick, position the aerial closest to the flames in case it bites us in the ass."

Jake faced Sixteen's officer, who rushed up to him. "Tom. We're ready to go in. Make sure there's a ladder at every window. And you need to ventilate. Top right-hand corner." Jake scanned his crew again and nodded as the battalion chief, who'd just arrived, strode to them. After briefly filling him in—the chief would take command—Jake said to Chelsea and Huff, "Stay in touch on the radios."

Now that the plan was set, motion and speed increased like a film on fast forward. As she yanked the hose and raced after Jake and Joey, Chelsea could see the firefighters dragging ladders to the side and back of the house. They were for access in case the staircase went up after they climbed it. Chelsea had been trapped once before like that; her officer hadn't taken precautions with the ladders, and the group had been in real danger.

Jake tried the door and found it unlocked. Chelsea shook her head as he pushed it open.

A volcanic blast of heat forced him and Joey back. Chelsea bumped into Peter, who steadied her. All four dropped to their knees. The house was smoky, but not the thick, black smoke that made visibility impossible. A tiny living room was off to the left, a hallway straight ahead. She adjusted her face mask; slippery with perspiration, the heat made her sweat bullets. They edged their way to the staircase on the right—slow going with their heavy bunker boots and the weight of equally heavy pants and thick turnout coats. They could see the origin of the fire as soon as they hit the steps. Top right bedroom. Jake spoke into the radio as they inched up the stairs. Sweat trickled down Chelsea's back and legs. She started to breathe faster. Knowing she had to conserve air, she forced herself to be calm. Jake opened the bedroom door and activated the hose. Before she turned to the left, Chelsea caught sight of stacks of something outside the bedroom and down the hallway. Newspapers. Hundreds of them.

"Lieutenant," she barked into the radio. "There're piles of newspapers right outside your location and down the hall."

"Understood," Jake replied.

She and Peter reached the last bedroom. A curtain of thick gray smoke whipped into their faces when they opened the door. She could see the faint outline of a bed; as she headed for it, Peter behind her, she heard coughing.

Dropping the hose, she reached for the victim. He began thrashing. Damn. Why did he have to be so big? Not much taller than she was. But stocky and overweight. She held his hands to his sides. "Sir, we'll get you out of here if you cooperate." Her Darth Vader voice stilled him—a common reaction to the sound coming out of the self-contained breathing apparatus. She repeated herself more loudly. He began struggling again. She held on tight.

He mumbled something that sounded like "Helen."

The thrashing stopped, and she released him. But when she dragged him up and tried to turn him, he yanked away from her and grabbed for the pictures on his nightstand. Peter lunged for him, pulled him back. A fit of coughing quieted the old guy, and he sank into Peter's arms, overcome by smoke.

Chelsea grabbed the man's feet, and together, she and Peter dragged him to the doorway. When they reached the end of the hall, she heard Peter swear. She turned and saw that the fire had caught on the newspapers, devouring them, and eaten its way down the stairs—which were blocked. She felt a brief moment of panic for Jake and Joey until she remembered the aerial was right outside the window of the front room.

And there was a ladder at the end of her hall. Peter must have realized the same thing. They began dragging the man back. At the window Peter dropped the guy and reached for the halligan strapped to his waist. The axlike staple of firefighting made quick work of the window, and in minutes a gaping hole greeted them. It also created an inferno behind them, the oxygen feeding the beast.

Huff looked at her, no doubt wondering if she could do it. And if she couldn't, which was the best place for him— getting the victim out the window or carrying him to the stairs and down. Finally he picked up the man by the arm-pits and began to swivel him. Chelsea raced to the window and climbed onto the first rung of the ladder. ''Somebody come and heel the ladder,'' she barked into her radio. In seconds Diaz was at the bottom, feet spread, bracing the ends with his toes on each of the beams, holding on with his hands.

Feet appeared first, and the back of the man's legs. He wore pajamas, hiked up to reveal bare calves. Chelsea grabbed hold as Huff slid the guy out a little at a time, giving her leeway to anchor him in front of her. First she spread his legs to either side so they weren't in the way; then she inserted her hands beneath his armpits to grab the ladder beams; with her knee beneath his groin to brace his weight, she started down. One step. Almost immedi-ately, her muscles flexed with the weight. Her chest heaved. She descended another step, hanging on tight, pic-turing her footing. Bump. Bump. Three more rungs. The man stirred. *Please, God, don't let him thrash again.* They'd break both their necks if he went wild. But he sank into the ladder instead, became a dead weight. Another rung. And another. By the time she reached the bottom, her arms were screaming with pain, sweat dripped into her eyes, and her breathing was race-car fast.

She felt someone brace her from behind and steady her as she hit bottom. Then another person—Mick—came around front and relieved her of her burden. She inched to the side as Diaz resumed his post, holding the ladder until Huff descended.

Mick handed the guy over to the paramedics, who'd hustled around the corner. Chelsea yanked off her mask, helmet and hood. "Jake and Joey?" she asked immediately.

"Got out on the aerial. The house is gone, though. It's fully involved."

"The newspapers," she said. "There were hundreds of them. I saw them stacked in the hall, but they could be all over the house."

A few minutes later Jake came up behind Mick. Chelsea's heart gave a little lurch. From a generator behind him, a light cast him into plain sight despite the darkness. His face was blackened, and his navy coat was covered with a thin layer of grime. But he wasn't hurt. He crossed to her, grasped both her arms and looked intently at her. "You all right?"

She nodded. His touch felt good; firm and safe. He held her gaze another few seconds, then squeezed her arms and stepped away. He turned to Peter. Clapping him on the back, he said, "Okay, buddy?"

In an unusual show of affection, Huff raised his arm and wrapped it around Jake's shoulder. "Fine, but too close for me."

Huff faced Chelsea. "You must be strong as a bull to carry that guy down."

"I am."

"Nice to know." He didn't touch her, but he did smile. She chided herself for what it meant to her. Along with Jake's attention, she warmed as much inside as out.

Maybe being on Quint Twelve was going to work out, after all.

JAKE STUDIED his troops like a proud general who'd just directed a successful maneuver. They'd handled the routine fire gone bad like the pros they were. Though right now, grimy and exhausted, they didn't look too professional. As dawn broke, they gathered around the table in the dim light of the firehouse kitchen. The strong smell of the coffee they sipped permeated the air as they hashed over the events of the night.

"I almost flipped when I saw the size of that guy." Huff's face flushed with emotion.

"Those ladders sure came in handy," Diaz said. "So much for the other guys raggin' on us about bein' too careful." He flicked his fingers out from under his chin— the ultimate Italian insult.

Mick clapped everybody on the back several times as he prowled the kitchen.

At the far corner of the table, Joey reminded Jake of a little boy who wanted to sulk but couldn't contain his excitement. "I figured we'd bought it when we looked out and the staircase was on fire."

Jake pushed away from the counter where he'd been leaning and sat down. It was time for a little official debriefing. "Let's start with that."

Casually he faced Whitmore, who'd exchanged a few comments with the guys but had stayed pretty quiet. "Nice job keeping your eyes open, Whitmore. At least we were prepared for the newspaper thing." She nodded. He liked her calm acceptance of the praise due her as much as her quickness in detecting the fire hazard. Jake addressed them all. "Turns out the entire place was a firetrap. The old man had copies of the *Sentinel*—" Rockford's daily newspaper "—dating back thirty years."

Huff gave a low whistle. His gaze flicked to Chelsea. "Good thing you noticed. *I* didn't."

Shrugging, she said, "It was easy to miss."

Mick stopped pacing. "You know, it's a female thing— women clean the house so they notice junk around more than we do."

Everyone's mouth dropped open at his politically incorrect statement. Mick stared at them blankly, then cocked his finger and thumb like a gun. "Gotcha."

The levity lessened the tension. Jake let them enjoy it before continuing.

"Mick and Don, good job covering the ladder situation from the ground and assisting with the victim." He jotted some notes. "Anything else we should discuss about that?"

"Yeah, and I'll say it." Huff's knowing blue eyes pinned Chelsea. Jake saw her brace her hands on the seat of the chair. "You know why men feared women coming into the fire department more than onto the police force?"

Chelsea shook her head.

"Female officers carry guns just like men. Most of their backup is with a weapon—it isn't dependent on physical strength." Chelsea watched him, poker-faced. "I've heard dozens of firefighters say they worry about a broad—their term—carrying them out of the dragon's mouth if they go down."

Awareness dawning, Chelsea slowly nodded. But Huff wasn't through. "How much do you weigh, Mick?"

"One ninety-five."

"Diaz?"

"One eighty, give or take a few."

Santori confessed to one seventy-five, Jake to two hundred.

"I weigh one ninety," Huff said.

Jake picked up on Huff's point. "How much do you think our victim weighs, Whitmore?"

"Easily two hundred. He was short but fat."

Huff said, "Guess that dispels that worry. I told you at the scene it was good to know you could handle him. I meant it."

Quiet for a moment, as if she was deciding how to handle the point, Chelsea finally said, "I guess it's normal that you'd question my ability. For the record, I was a competitive weightlifter for years, and I still compete in some strength contests. I can carry my weight, so to speak."

"Maybe you can beat Scarlatta at arm wrestling," Mick teased. "Nobody else can."

Arching an impish brow, she glanced at Jake. "Probably."

The guys razzed Jake with whistles and catcalls until he quieted them.

"Anybody else have a comment about the night?"

Chelsea said, "I do."

Jake scowled. He hoped she didn't blow the good mood.

"The old guy was tough to handle. It got me thinking about dealing with elderly victims and patients. Since we're so near Dutch Towers and since they seem to need us so often—" she nodded in Jake's direction "—I wondered if we should have some training on rescuing the elderly."

Her insight impressed Jake. Her interest in the Dutch Towers clientele—his own special cause—warmed him like aged brandy going down smooth. When everyone agreed, he said he'd talk to Reed about setting up some training.

Soon the morning shift sauntered in and buzzed about the fire. With the requisite embellishments, the night crew held court with the day shift. Jake excused himself to shower and take care of paperwork.

An hour later, exhausted and ready for bed, Chelsea crossed the parking lot and unlocked the door to her candy-apple red Camaro just as Jake exited the firehouse. As he came toward her in the bright morning sunlight, birds chirping cheerfully around them, she noticed he'd exchanged his uniform for jeans and a blue-and-black checked shirt, the sleeves rolled up his forearms. His feet were clad in Docksiders and no socks. "Just leaving?" he asked when he reached her. Briefly he scanned her denims and oversize top. Suddenly the sun felt midsummer hot.

"Uh, yeah. I got cleaned up, then talked with Mick for a while in the bay. He's been great to me."

"Everybody loves Mick. He's our resident peace-maker."

Studying the lines of fatigue in his face, Chelsea thought about his role in the events of the night. "And *you're* a good leader."

He gave her a show-stopper smile. "Hey, thanks."

"I've worked with a lot of officers. Insisting on the ladders was wise."

"I've taken guff about it from other companies."

"You're right to do it." She looked over his shoulder, remembering his calm reactions. They'd made *her* feel confident. "And you were so cool, even when things went wrong."

"Can't panic in a fire. It'll kill you."

"Just the same, I admired what you did."

He held up his hand. "Stop. I'll get a big head, as my father used to say."

Watching him for minute, she wondered what sort of

father he had. What sort of father he *was.* "We never got a chance to finish our conversation this morning."

"No, we didn't."

"Maybe some other time."

His expression became shuttered. "Maybe."

She felt the chill form between them like a newly built wall. One *he* erected. She started to turn away.

He grasped her arm, tugging her around. "You did good, Whitmore." His hand was big and muscular on her bare skin.

"Thanks."

"I told you it was gonna work out here."

"It's not over till it's over," she said, but she smiled at the familiar quip. Before he let go, he squeezed her arm gently.

With a quick smile of her own, she opened her door and slid into the front seat. She reached for the handle, but he grasped the top of the door, holding it ajar, and peered at her. The sunlight glistened off his hair, highlighting chestnut strands sprinkled here and there with a few gray ones. His eyes were warm with amusement as he patted the hood. "Nice car."

"My baby."

"It suits you."

"It does? How?"

He ran a hand over the roof. "Sleek on the outside." He swept the entire chassis with his eyes. "Strong enough to hold up on the road." He perused the interior. "Kind of cushy on the inside."

"You think?" she asked, struggling to conceal how rattled his assessment made her. There was something about the tone of his voice....

"Yeah, I think." Giving her a half smile, he slammed the door shut. "Have a nice day."

"You, too." She started the car and pulled away.

In the rearview mirror, she could see him give her a mock salute and told herself not to make too much out of his...friendliness. His interest was purely professional, as his goodbye gesture indicated.

There was, and never would be, anything personal between them.

JAKE STROLLED into the firehouse two nights later, their third on the night shift, satisfied with the way things had gone on Chelsea's first stint with them at night. Despite the initial tension, and because of her firefighting ability, her sense of humor and her refusal to take any guff from them, Chelsea had made strides with the guys.

And with me, too, he thought as he approached the office. It wasn't so bad having her around. She was even kind of fun.

And real easy on the eyes.

He thought about how vulnerable she looked curled up in her sweats on the kitchen chair that first night before the fire call came, like a little china doll who needed to be handled gently.

Yeah, right. An hour later that china doll hefted two hundred pounds of dead weight down a fourteen-foot ladder.

There hadn't been a repeat of that early-morning encounter, for the next night, she'd been on watch when he awakened at four. He often went out and kept the person who'd drawn the late watch company, but this time, he'd read in the common room. He was avoiding the intimacy.

His foot connected with something on the floor, and he bent down to pick it up. It was a stuffed animal. A cat.

Diaz. The guy was always buying his kids things and bringing them in to show the rest of them. They razzed him mercilessly but knew Diaz had had a rotten childhood and craved stability and family like a junkie. He must have dropped his most recent purchase. Thinking briefly about Chelsea's comments about her cats, he put it on the desk and looked at the bulletin board. Staring him square in the face was an eleven-by-fourteen blowup of…Jeez, was that Cat Woman? Yep, it was Julie Newmar, from the old TV show. He remembered drooling over the scantily clad half-feline. Who the hell had done this, and why?

"Jake?" Group Two's lieutenant, Ken Casey, stood at the doorway. A small, wiry man with body-builder muscles, he had a face that was a road map of lines.

"Hi, Ken. Tough day?"

"Yeah. Here's a list of the runs." He handed Jake a clipboard. "I'm outta here. I gotta take my kid to little-guy soccer tonight."

"Ken, what's with the poster?"

Group Two's lieutenant eyed Cat Woman like any good twelve-year-old boy might. "Don't know. Pretty hot stuff, though." As he headed for the door, he was smiling.

Jake made his way down the hall to the kitchen. When he walked through the doorway, he stopped abruptly. Chelsea was in the corner fixing salad. Diaz was at the table drinking coffee with Santori, and Mick was fiddling with a boom box in the corner.

And all around the room were computer-generated cat things—pictures of cats, cat food, cat toys.

"What's goin' on?" Jake asked.

Peter stood at the stove and shrugged. "Don't know. Somebody in Group Two must have done it."

"Funny, Casey didn't seem to know about Cat Woman."

Everyone turned at once. They were as straight-faced as funeral directors. Finally Chelsea folded her arms and said, deadpan, "I guess the cat's got our tongues."

Suspicion curled inside him. He narrowed his eyes.

"I don't know," Huff put in. "Maybe we should let the cat out of the bag."

All five of them chuckled. Then Diaz held out the morning paper. It was folded open to Letters to the Editor, and one of them was circled with a red magic marker. Jake glanced at the signature but didn't recognize it. "Edward P. Parker, former city school English teacher." He read the letter.

Dear Sir,
It is with both sadness and pleasure that I write this letter from my hospital bed to commend our city firefighters. On May 28, my house caught on fire and unfortunately my beloved feline friend, Hester Prynne, succumbed in the flames. I would be left with no memories of the cat who has shared my life for many years except for the efforts of the officer—and gentleman—on duty who saved several pictures of her, and in the aftermath secured the jeweled collar I had given her last Christmas. As yet, I don't know the officer's name, but his sensitivity and concern for an old man's idiosyncrasies are greatly appreciated.

Jake's face flushed. He knew he'd never live this one down. Though any one of them sitting here would have automatically done the same thing if they'd had the opportunity, firefighter humor insisted that they razz the daylights out of him about it.

Cavalierly he tossed the paper onto the table, swept his group with a disinterested gaze and, deciding to ignore their antics, went to get coffee.

It seemed to work, as they discussed training for the night, then dispersed and went about their chores. Six o'clock came, and there had been no runs.

Hungry, Jake entered the kitchen and found Chelsea setting the table and humming a little off-key. When she put a jar full of pussy willows on the table, he threw her a scathing look. She shrugged. Apparently he wasn't out of the woods yet.

"Chow's on," Peter called out minutes later. He held back a smile. "I think the officer and gentleman should go first."

Jake said, "Bite me, Huff."

"What's the matter, Jakey baby, don't you know we think you're the cat's meow?" Mick teased, giving Jake a hearty slap on the back as he walked by to take his seat.

Jake shook his head and briefly closed his eyes. When he opened them, he caught Chelsea looking at him. "Sure you want to join forces with Brutus and his gang, Whitmore?"

"Me? I haven't done anything." Her Huck Finn grin said, *Yet*.

Well, at least her presence kept the guys from tossing out some tasteless sexist remarks.

After dinner, they took some training off the computer, then Jake headed to the weight room to work out with Don and Mick. Chelsea strode by just as Jake arrived and started to stretch. Stopping in the archway to the hall, she watched them for a minute.

"What's wrong?" Diaz asked from the Universal machine in the corner.

"Nothing."

Mick snorted. "Sounds like my wife when she's mad at me."

"Mine, too." Diaz exchanged a male-fraternity look with Murphy. Jake rolled his eyes, headed for the weight bench and picked up a barbell.

Crossing her arms, Chelsea leaned against the doorway.

"You run a gym, don'tcha, Whitmore?" Diaz asked.

"Yes."

"Okay, Coach, tell us."

"I was just wondering what kind of warm-up you guys do."

"Just what Jake did."

She shook her head. "Jake stretched—he didn't warm up. There's a difference. Actually, stretching should be done after the exercising warm-ups because warm muscles stretch easier—cold ones tear."

Diaz winced.

Jake asked, "What should we be doing?"

"You really wanna know?"

All three nodded.

She approached Jake. "Proper warm-ups prevent injury, but you already know that." She angled her head to the treadmill. "Get on that thing." When he jumped on, she set it at a low speed.

"Your ability to do physical work increases at elevated body temperatures, which you need to do heavy exercising like weight training."

Jake nodded as he trekked slowly on the machine.

"An elevated body temperature allows more oxygen to be freed from the hemoglobin in your red blood cells. It also reduces the internal viscosity of the skeletal muscles."

"In plain English?" Mick leaned against the weight bench.

"It makes them move easier. Then the nervous system benefits, too. And it improves your range of motion—"

"Okay, okay, we buy it," Diaz said, straightening. "Just tell us what to do."

"First you want to reach as many muscle groups as you can in a general warm-up. So use the treadmill or the bike." She indicated the stationary bicycle in the corner.

"I hate those things."

"Then jump rope."

Mick and Diaz liked that better, picked up two ropes in the corner and skipped as they listened.

"Do a little stretching after you're through. But the most important thing is, do a specific warm-up for your next activity."

"Meaning?"

"I'll show you." After another couple of minutes, she said, "Get on the bench, Jake."

"Yes, ma'am." He stepped off the treadmill, then did as she asked.

Chelsea crossed to the bench and towered over him, giving him an interesting view of her upper torso. "What do you usually lift?"

"Two-fifty." She leaned over him. He swallowed hard, feeling his temperature elevate some already.

Like toys, she picked up two twenty-five-pound weights and put them on the barbell. "Okay, these first. Ten reps."

Easily Jake followed instructions. Then she doubled the weights. "Do ten more." She addressed all of them. "This will warm up your pecs—" she swept a soft hand over his chest, and Jake's grip faltered a bit "—the rotator cuff—" she fingered the joint on his shoulder, and he shifted on the bench "—and the delts and triceps—" she slid her hand over his shoulder and slipped it between him and the bench. Jake's back arched involuntarily at her brief, firm touch. "It'll also stretch your wrist and elbow."

"Working out will take forever that way." Mick voiced the typical layperson's complaint, but he kept jumping.

"If you don't do it, you're at greater risk for injury," Chelsea warned.

Jake cleared his throat. "Physical injuries take you out of firefighting. I think it might be worth the extra time."

Chelsea stopped him and gave him heavier weights. She got him to two-fifty in about four minutes. Gently she swiped his forehead. "He's broken out into a sweat. That shows he's ready." She glanced at her watch. "Ten minutes."

The guys scowled.

She shrugged. "Take it or leave it."

Mick grinned at her. "All right. Wanna come back and show us how to cool down?"

"Sure, I'll bring the ice packs for the back of your neck."

When all mouths fell open in surprise, she left the room laughing.

At about eleven, after showering, Jake headed for the bunk room. Huff was on watch, and the others had gone to bed half an hour ago. Which was early for Diaz and Mick. He chuckled. Must be the extra time in the weight room tired them out. Dressed in gym shorts and T-shirt, he opened the door. He could hear Santori snoring lightly and stepped quietly inside. He crossed through the unrelieved darkness to his bed by the window and pulled down the covers. His head hit the pillow—and connected with something hard.

"What the hell?" he sputtered.

The lights flew on. Confused, since he hadn't heard the tone that usually preceded the bunk room lights turning on automatically for a call, he looked around.

Huff was by the switch, and all four of the group in the bunk room were sitting up in bed looking at him.

His gaze shot to the pillow. There was a deep cardboard box on it. He peered inside. A tiny kitten, maybe seven or eight weeks old, stared at him with marble-green eyes. It was heather gray with white markings on its throat and paws; around its neck was a pink bow. When he lifted it out, the tag on the bow caught his eye. "Hester Two."

"We thought an officer and a gentleman should have only the best to sleep with," Huff commented.

The kitten licked Jake's fingers. Her whole puffball body fit in the palm of his hand. "Whose is she?"

"Yours," Chelsea said casually.

Jake's head snapped up. "You're kiddin' me."

"She's to remind you of what a hero you are," Joey told him.

Unconsciously Jake stroked the kitten's fur. It was as soft as Jess's hair had been as a baby. "Lay off."

The green eyes stared at him again. Pleadingly, he thought. So he stood, still holding the kitten, grabbed the box and walked out of the room. To the great pleasure of the team, he was sure, judging by the laughter he could hear as he moved down the hall.

In the kitchen he ran some water in a bowl. After a few swipes with a tiny red tongue, the kitten mewed until Jake picked her up again. He sat at the table, holding her in his cupped hands. "What do you want, sweetheart?" The kitten angled her head and rubbed against his palm. He obliged her and curved his finger down her back.

"She likes you."

Jake looked up. Chelsea stood before him in a long tailored shirt over her shorts and T-shirt. He wondered if the garment was hers or a man's.

Jake focused on the cat. "She's a cutie."

Chelsea smiled. "She looks just like her mother."

"Her mother?"

"The guys don't want me to tell you and spoil the joke, but we don't expect you to keep her. She's from a litter my cat Blaze had two months ago. I'll take her home tomorrow." She stared at him meaningfully. "For what it's worth, Jake, I think what you did for the old man was touching. We're teasing you, but any one of us would have done it."

Jake smiled. "I know. It's part of the mentality." He looked at the kitten. "Blaze, huh?" His tone was amused as the kitten climbed out of his hands and edged her little white paws up his chest. He chuckled as she reached his neck and rubbed a wet nose there.

His glance strayed to Chelsea. She was staring at the cat, at his neck, as if... He refused to finish the thought. It was stupid. Jake plucked the kitten off his neck and stood up. "A gift's a gift. I'm keepin' her."

"You are?" The pleasure that shone in Chelsea's eyes forced him to turn away. He wished he'd put on his pants—hell, armor might be better—to hide his reaction to her.

Placing the kitten in the box, he kept his back to her. "Yeah, I am." Without turning, he said, "Good night, Whitmore. Thanks for the kitten," and made a beeline for the dark anonymity of the bunk room.

AGAIN THE DARKNESS enveloped him. The man needed it—to let the other side come out.

It wasn't going according to plan. Not only had she done all right in the calls, but some of the guys actually seemed to like her. Hell, even *he* liked her sometimes, when he was himself. Not a good thing. *Concentrate on the bad,* he told himself. *Let it out.*

He couldn't get used to sleeping with her there. For one thing, she paraded around in shorts and a T-shirt, bringing out the animal part of a guy that would make Hyde look like a puppy. What the hell had the brass been thinking when they let broads into the department? They were men. They *knew* men. Living with women like this was unnatural. This whole thing was against nature.

Had he been good at hiding his feelings—this dark side of him? Usually he was. But sometimes it slipped out at the firehouse. She couldn't know. And the rest of them, too. Scarlatta, especially. He couldn't know. The lieutenant was too nice. An easy mark. He'd already been taken in by her. He'd heard them talking at night. Suddenly he wondered if Jake had the hots for her. Nah. Jake was a cold fish where women were concerned. Unlike *him*, who, when the mood struck, was hot and liked his women hot. Blazing hot.

Hyde wondered briefly what it would be like to have Whitmore underneath him.

CHAPTER SIX

PUMPERS WAS HOPPING. The long mahogany bar was three deep with people, mostly firefighters, and all the tables were full. It was the Friday night following the night shift, and Jake was sitting at a table in one of the back areas.

"I'll have a Corona, Cordaro. Don't forget the lime."

Francey Cordaro Templeton threw him a look of disgust. "I *almost* won."

"Almost doesn't count, kid." He winked at Alex. "Now go. I've worked up a thirst."

Rising, she stuck out her tongue at him. "Come with me, Dylan. There are a lot of people at the bar. We can talk while I'm waiting."

O'Roarke smiled at his wife, Beth, as he rose, slid his hand to her neck and squeezed. "Don't let anybody pick you up while I'm gone."

"As if someone would." She glanced at her pretty green blouse and jeans. "I'm not exactly pick-up material right now."

"You kiddin'?" Dylan's shock—and cow-eyed reaction to Beth—made everybody chuckle.

When he left, Beth turned to Diana Cordaro, Francey's mother, who sat across the table. "These jeans are two sizes bigger than what I usually wear. He's nuts."

There was wisdom in Diana's smile. "For some reason the aftermath of pregnancy fascinates some men." She leaned into her husband, Battalion Chief Ben Cordaro, and squeezed his arm.

Ben held her there. "You're damn right. I loved the way Diana looked right after she had our babies." He grinned. "During, too."

Jake felt a stab of envy. For a brief minute he wanted what it was the Cordaros and O'Roarkes had. Ruthlessly suppressing the unexpected—and unwanted—emotion, he asked Beth, "Who's with Timmy tonight?"

The smile on her face was sunshine bright. "Connie Cleary and Sandy Frank. You remember them?"

"Yeah. Last year's recruit class. 'I Am Woman' from karaoke."

Beth looked as if a genie had granted all her wishes. "Connie's especially sweet on him. She's going to help care for him when I go back to work and Dylan's on days."

"When will that be?" Ben asked. Jake saw the twinkle in his eyes. The man who had been a surrogate father to him had some of the devil in him.

"Not for a while. Isn't my replacement working out?"

"Hell, no. We need you back next week."

Beth caught on. "Sorry, boss. No way."

"They grow up so fast." Diana's voice trembled. "You don't want to miss it." A poignant look passed between her and Ben. They'd gotten divorced when their children were young, and Diana had missed much of their childhood.

Which reminded Jake to call Jess.

And Derek.

When Alex prodded Diana to talk about what she *did* remember of Francey's childhood, and Diana obliged, Jake recalled going to see Reed about Danny's son.

"The kid's headed for trouble, Reed," he'd said. "We're not even sure he's going to graduate from high school."

"From what you told me, the sooner he gets help, the

better. I don't have experience with teenagers, but I can give you some names.'' He'd swiveled to his computer and called up a file. "This is from a local organization I belong to. The psychologists in it keep a list of people outside their specialty that they can personally recommend.'' Reed had ripped the sheet out of the printer and handed it to Jake.

Jake had scanned it, and his eyes skidded to a halt near the bottom. "Delaney Shaw? Do you know her?''

Reed's scowl was totally out of character. It made him look little-boyish, less world-weary. He pulled off his reading glasses and rubbed his eyes. "Afraid so.''

"What do you mean?''

"I took a couple of workshops with her at the University of Rockford recently. She's a pain in the ass.''

"Yeah? Why?''

"Well, first she looks about fifteen, so it's hard to take her seriously. Probably because of that, she's like a pit bull in making her points. I disagreed with her a couple of times in discussion and became her target. But in all honesty, other psychologists say she works miracles with adolescents.''

Jake thought for a minute. "Did she know your connection with the fire department?''

"Yeah. We had to introduce ourselves, and where we worked inevitably came up.''

"She's Chelsea Whitmore's sister.''

"Ah.'' Reed, who'd been seeing Billy, had understood right away why Delaney might have a grudge against him. "I didn't connect them because of the name difference,'' he said.

"Look who we found!''

Jake was pulled back to the present by the return of Francey and Dylan—with Chelsea Whitmore in tow.

And a guy.

"Hi." Chelsea's gaze rested briefly on Jake. Then she reached for and clasped the tall, muscular man's arm. "This is Spike Lammon. Spike, you know Dylan's wife, Beth, and Alex and Ben from the gym. This is Diana, Ben's wife." She zeroed in on Jake. Her tone changed almost imperceptibly. "And this is my lieutenant, Jake Scarlatta."

"The cat man," Dylan teased as he yanked out the chair next to his wife.

"Don't start."

Jake stood and gave Spike a firm handshake.

Spike. Interesting name. Jake had known a guy in high school who'd been called Spike apparently for his sexual performance. He shook off the thought and averted his eyes from Chelsea and her friend as they sat down and began to chat with Diana and Ben.

"He runs the gym for me when I'm working at the firehouse."

Spike smiled at her with eyes that simmered with all-male interest. They were sleeping together, Jake bet. He remembered the oversize shirt she'd thrown on the other night.

Chelsea's voice oozed like warm honey as she praised Spike. "I'm lucky to get him. Spike was an Olympic contender for the U.S. volleyball team a few years ago."

Alex gave a low whistle. "Did you make it?"

"I wrecked my knee after the second day of tryouts. I never knew how far I'd have gone."

"He would have made the team."

Spike slid his arm around Whitmore's chair and squeezed her shoulder. "My biggest fan."

"That's because you're helping her get in shape for the triathlon," Beth said.

From what Jake could tell, Chelsea didn't need any help getting into shape. Tonight she wore a long flowing navy skirt with white flowers; in deference to the early-June warm weather, she'd donned a gauzy sleeveless top. For the first time, Jake was treated to an unobstructed view of her arms. Beautifully sculpted and no bulges. They'd been firm when he'd touched her. In a spurt of sexual curiosity, he wondered what the rest of her would feel like, sleek and bare, under his hands.

Jake turned away and smothered the vivid image; it was as dangerous as sparks near gasoline.

"I wonder where Reed is," Dylan said.

"Reed's coming to Pumpers?" Surprised, Jake switched his focus fast.

"Yeah, Beth talked him into it." Dylan ruffled his wife's hair. "She's a regular meddler in his life these days."

"Reed's a good friend to us. I want to see him happy."

"Speak of the devil." Ben stood and clapped Reed Macauley on the back.

"Hi, guys." The fire department psychologist scanned the group, was introduced to Spike—who still had his arm draped on Whitmore's chair—then sat down next to Jake. He made small talk with Beth and Dylan as he sipped a draft.

After a moment Chelsea stood and murmured to Spike, "I'm going to make a phone call. I'll be right back."

Chelsea hoped her leaving hadn't signaled to anybody that something was wrong. But the truth was, Reed Macauley's presence made her uncomfortable. He was seeing Billy regularly, she knew, and by now, he'd be privy to all their dirty laundry. Private things that should have stayed between them. And it made her cringe to think the man knew only Billy's skewed view of their relationship. After sneaking into the long, narrow alcove where the phones and coatroom were, she rested her head against the wall and closed her eyes, scolding herself for being such a wimp.

She didn't know how many minutes had passed when she heard a voice, "The phone's not being used."

Oh, great. Of all the people to notice her retreat. She opened her eyes. "Jake."

"You okay?"

She bit her lip. "I'm fine."

He studied her implacably. "You look upset."

She didn't reply.

"It's Reed, isn't it."

Damn. Why did he have to understand? "It's stupid. But it makes me uncomfortable to see him."

Jake shoved his hands in the pockets of his navy blue cotton pants. The action made his open-at-the-throat white linen shirt pull across his pecs. She remembered how hard they'd felt under her fingers the other night in the weight room. He said, "Not stupid. Human."

"I shudder to think what he knows about me. Or *thinks* he knows."

"If it's any help, Reed never passes judgment. And he's as ethical as the Pope."

"It's dumb anyway," she said. "I'm a grown woman. I should be able to handle this." She shook her head. "Still, it's worse than his reading my diary. At least that way he'd get the truth."

The corners of Jake's mouth turned up in a mischievous grin. "Firefighter Whitmore keeps a diary? Now *that* I'd like to see."

"It was just a figure of speech."

He didn't believe her, she could tell. God, how embarrassing. She thought of those little fancy blank books she'd filled up nightly for as long as she could remember.

Finally he said, "Well, I'm sorry you're upset."

"Did you come out here just to—"

"Jake, there you are!"

Chelsea pivoted to see a petite woman approaching them. She looked familiar.

"Barb," Jake said in greeting.

Shapely, auburn-haired Barb stood on tiptoe to hug him. Chelsea couldn't remember the last time she'd had to do that to hug anybody. Jake's return embrace was brief but warm and familiar. When Barb pulled back, she smiled at him—like Bergman had at Bogart in *Casablanca*. Her gaze dipped below his chin. "The shirt looks nice on you."

"You've got great taste."

So Barb had given him the sexy shirt. Chelsea felt a sinking sensation in her chest.

"I'm sorry I'm late. I got tied up at the restaurant."

Restaurant. Chelsea *had* seen the woman before.

Grasping Barb's arm, Jake faced Chelsea. "Chelsea Whitmore. Barb DeLuca."

Chelsea smiled. "From DeLuca's Diner. I eat there a lot."

Delicate eyebrows arched. "I hope it's been good."

"Very."

Barb turned to Jake. "Look, if you're busy…"

"No, I want to talk to you," he said, "and we keep missing each other. This can't wait any longer." He glanced over her head at the bar. "But it's a zoo in here. Let's go out to my Bronco."

Chelsea straightened. "Well, I'll get back to the group."

"Tell Francey that Barb and I are going to talk for a while. Otherwise, she'll come looking for me like a mother hen."

"Sure." Chelsea nodded to Barb. "Nice to meet you." She gave Jake a weak grin and started to the table.

After she took two steps, he caught her arm. "Chelsea?" She turned. "You all right to go back there?"

Emotion welled in her throat, but she battled it. Talk about stupid. "Sure."

As Chelsea headed to the group, she saw Jake and his friend start for the exit.

To his car.

To talk.

And what else?

Like a good firefighter, used to suppressing unpleasant images, she didn't let herself think about it.

JOEY SANTORI blared the horn of the truck for the fifth time to signal their arrival at the high school. He grinned at Jake, who rolled his eyes at the unnecessary drama. Though Jake knew Joey was a highly competent firefighter, right now he looked like a kid with a big toy.

Things were a lot more relaxed at the station house these days. Chelsea had been on board for almost a month. The guys seemed to have accepted her; she'd given them no choice, really, with her competence, her guts in standing up to them and all the things she'd added to their lives—fitness expertise, medical and fire-suppression knowledge, even a willingness to go in on their jokes.

When Joey blew the horn again and Jake frowned, Joey said, "Hey, old man, you forget what it was like to be in high school?"

"When I was in high school, kids didn't need these kinds of assemblies."

"You were an angel, right?"

Hardly, Jake thought, remembering how he and his then girlfriend and soon-to-be wife, Nancy, and Danny and Barbara had skipped out of their last assembly of the year. They'd gone to a cabin owned by Danny's grandfather and spent the sizzling hot day screwing their brains out and skinny-dipping in the lake. Jake found it hard to believe he'd ever been that young.

"Of course I was an angel. You know me, straight-as-an-arrow Scarlatta."

The trucks took the turn fast onto the bus-loop blacktop of Jackson High School. Two hundred seniors filled the bleachers that had been set up outside for the special Stay Sober assembly planned for the day of their senior prom. Jessica was somewhere in the midst of the hormone-driven mass.

"All right, gang, time to impress the kiddies," Joey said.

Though they might joke about this activity, they knew it could save lives. All six tumbled out of the trucks, in full turnout gear, and rushed to the scene of a staged critical car accident.

A Rockford deputy police chief stood to the side of the blacktop, speaking into a microphone. The kids were attentive and somber-faced. The same reaction they had every year. "Usually the first to arrive at an accident scene is the fire department. Our city station houses are located so that they can reach any place in their jurisdiction in three minutes."

Jake led his crew to the car that had crashed into an abutment erected for the demonstration. He knew that the vehicle, donated by a local Kiwanis Club, had two victims pinned inside; one was hysterical and one was near death, hypothetically speaking, of course. The inebriated driver stumbled around the blacktop. The roles were played by students.

"Now watch as the firefighters go into action." The police chief's voice was grave.

As arranged, Jake confronted the driver while Chelsea and Huff hurried to the right side of the vehicle, Mick and Joey to the left. Diaz stayed with the small rig. All of them but Chelsea had participated in this yearly drill. Not surprising, she was doing well in this activity, too.

"Son, are you hurt?" Jake asked with just the right combination of concern and authority.

The boy's head lolled back and forth. "Juss fiiii…"

Quickly Jake checked his pupils, took his pulse. He angled his head to the vehicle. "Who's in the car?"

"Girlfriend…her buddy."

Jake yelled, "Two victims."

Joey yelled back, but was drowned out by a police car swerving onto the scene. The officer at the mike said, "The police will now take care of the legalities." Another siren split the air. "And although the ambulance will arrive in seconds, the firefighters are in charge of the scene. While they extricate the victims, Lieutenant Jake Scarlatta of the Rockford Fire Department will talk you through what's happening." He waited a beat, then said, "And don't lose sight of the drama off to the side." In his peripheral vision, Jake could see the police approach the drunk driver.

Jake took the mike. "First the firefighters will stabilize the wheels to prevent movement of the car." Diaz and Santori, who'd gotten the material from the Midi, chocked the wheels.

"Now, two of them, who happen to be EMTs, will assess the victims."

Chelsea and Huff stuck their heads in the car.

"Weak pulse on one," Chelsea called. She tried the door. "Door's stuck."

"This one looks okay, but she's hysterical." Huff yanked at the door, too, and Jake bit back a smile at Peter Huff's bit of drama. "Stuck, too."

"Quint Twelve firefighters will now retrieve the Hurst tools from the smaller truck. Most familiar to you is the Jaws of Life, but there are two others that'll help us to extricate your classmates.'' Jake personalized the statement intentionally. The thought of Jess on the road with a drunk boyfriend or a car full of drinking kids made his current nightmares pale in comparison. ''Notice the firefighters donning goggles and leather gloves. This is for protection from the tools and flying metal and glass, as well as the blood, which in a crash this serious is plentiful.''

As planned, Chelsea carried the generator to the car. ''Firefighter Chelsea Whitmore is starting the generator.'' The unpleasant, ear-popping, lawnmower-like sound split the air. Huff and Whitmore approached the car, tools in hand.

''Help, help!'' one of the victims screamed. Joey poked his head in the door.

''Firefighter Santori will calm the victims and cover them with blankets.'' Joey accepted the blankets from Mick.

Jake continued, his voice level and grave. ''What we'll do now is remove the car from around the victims, instead of removing the victims from the car.''

First Joey stuck a small ram inside the posts of the car and popped the door. He disappeared inside. Then Huff taped the front side window.

''In order to get the window out we need to keep it from shattering all over your friends. Lifelong injuries to eyes and skin can occur in rescue work.'' Again, a little heavy-handed, but Jake knew that some scare tactics were needed.

Huff cut the window like it was cheesecake, then removed it. Chelsea vaulted to the hood of the car along with Huff. Jake had specifically asked Chelsea to do the heavy work, though she didn't know why. Lifting the shears as easily as she did gym weights, she cut through the hood and worked the shears through the metal. The grating sound made his teeth hurt. "Now they'll pull it back." Huff joined Chelsea on top and curled the metal back. The entire car had been removed, like a cardboard box from around a new kitchen appliance.

"Our job is done. The medical crew takes over now."

With that, the female ambulance attendant replaced Joey and they began to "package" their victims. The ambulance director narrated as Jake and his crew stood to the side.

"First we'll stabilize the spinal cord. Spinal cord injuries…"

Jake nudged Chelsea. He whispered, "Chelsea, take off your helmet."

She cocked her head.

"I want the kids to see you're a woman."

Mick joked, "You're a flamin' women's libber."

"She's a good role model for high school students," Jake explained.

"Should I fluff out my hair, too, Lieutenant? And take off my coat?"

When he saw she was smiling, he quipped, "No, we don't want the boys to go into cardiac arrest."

Chelsea tried to stop the warm feeling spiraling inside her at his compliment. He was razzing her. But she appreciated the fact that he felt comfortable enough with her to tease. She looked around the school campus. This whole faked rescue was one of the most unusual things she'd ever done in conjunction with school safety. Mostly the fire department went into elementary schools to teach fire safety. As the ambulance attendant placed the patient on the backboard, Chelsea said, "This is great. It feels so real."

"Some of the teachers cry every year." Mick proudly pointed to a group of faculty. Sure enough, Chelsea watched a few wipe their eyes.

Purposefully the attendant wheeled the backboard in front of the group and secured the victim so that she looked like a moon walker. The other victim, on a stretcher, too, was wheeled in front of the seniors. The girl shouted to the driver, "I told you not to drink. You wouldn't listen."

Jake touched Chelsea's shoulder. "Look over here." Chelsea turned to see the driver with the police. He was instructed to walk a line; he weaved off it four times. The officer produced handcuffs and manacled the kid's hands behind his back. Pretending to sober up, the boy said, "I didn't do nothin'." He was prodded into a police car, which promptly left the bus loop.

"I don't like to think about the number of times I've had to go to homes and tell parents about a scene like this," the police chief said into the mike. "It's no easier to tell the drunk driver's family than it is the victim's. Everybody loses in an incident like this." He paused. "Think about it tonight when you go to take that first drink. Do you really want to be one of these kids?"

Chelsea checked her watch. "It only took forty minutes."

"One class period," Jake told her. "These kinds of assemblies are given at all the high schools in the city by off-duty firefighters like us before the senior proms."

"You guys got this down pretty good."

He grinned at her. "You fit right in."

Surreptitiously, Chelsea scanned the group. In the past few weeks, she'd begun to feel like she really *did* fit in. It had happened slowly, and at times she still felt some discomfort, some lack of trust. But mostly she felt accepted. Even Joey's blatant animosity had lessened. Her gaze fell on her lieutenant, who was joking with Huff. It was due, she knew, to his leadership. He'd coaxed all of them along, and she found herself appreciating him and liking him more each day.

"Don't you think, Whitmore?"

"I—"

A blur of pink sped past Chelsea as a tall bundle threw herself at Jake. "Oh, Daddy, you were wonderful!"

Jake hugged his daughter. Chelsea was moved by the emotion on his face. He couldn't help but be thinking about her in one of those cars.

"Yeah, well, just remember this. If... What's his name again? Your date?"

"Eric."

"If Eric so much as looks at a beer, I'll—"

Jess placed a hand on his chest. "Dad, give me a break. I'm not dumb. Besides, we can't go to Prime Time if we drink."

"Prime Time?" Chelsea asked.

Jessica faced her. "Chelsea, hi. You were great. The guys couldn't believe you were a girl the way you tore into that metal."

"Thanks. What's Prime Time?"

"An after-the-prom chemical-free activity held at the school. Teachers and students have been working all year on providing an all-night party. Food, games, sports, karaoke, you name it."

"But you have to stay chemical-free to get in." Jake smoothed Jess's hair. "It's one of the best activities in the state for keeping kids clean." He turned to Jessica. "Is Derek here?"

"Nope. And he's not going to the prom or Prime Time. Jeez, Dad, *nobody* misses them."

Jake scowled.

"Oops, I gotta go."

Jake kissed her. "What time will you be at the house?"

Thanks to Francey, Chelsea knew that Jessica lived with her mother, but spent a lot of time at Jake's.

"Four. See you then." She glanced at Chelsea. "I'd like to have muscles like yours. Think I could come to your gym sometime?"

"Sure."

"Okay. Bye."

Jake watched his daughter until she disappeared into the school. When he turned away, his face was rigid. "I wish I could wrap her up in a blanket and keep her safe like I used to when she was a baby."

Chelsea reached out and touched his arm. "You've done a great job with her. She's got a good head on her shoulders. She'll be fine."

"It's not her I worry about. It's all those testosterone-crazed boys in her class that keep me up at night."

"Delaney says parenting a teenager is the devil's payback." Chelsea smiled. "But she gives the devil a run for his money. She's great with kids."

"Chelsea," Jake said, his eyes like gray clouds, "the Derek I mentioned..."

"Yeah."

"He's the son of a friend of mine. He's not doing well. I..." He hesitated.

"Yes?"

"Actually, your sister's name was given to me as a possible therapist. I wondered if—"

"Hey, Scarlatta, get the lead out."

Jake turned to see the guys had boarded the trucks and were waiting for them. "Damn. We'd better get back. We shouldn't be talking about this now, anyway. I don't want it public knowledge." He looked at the school. "But I didn't want to wait until our next shift."

Chelsea said, "Why don't you call me tonight? I'll be home about seven. We can talk then."

His smile chased the clouds out of his eyes. "All right, I'll do that. Thanks."

JAKE PUNCHED OUT Chelsea's number at seven-thirty. His stomach churned, and he couldn't figure out why. This wasn't a personal call. It was about Derek getting hooked up with Delaney.

As the phone rang on Chelsea's end, Jake wasn't sure what had made him inquire about Delaney Shaw as a possible therapist for Derek. Maybe it had something to do with Chelsea herself. Her competence, her good-heartedness, her—

"H-hello."

Hmm. She sounded anything but competent now.

"Chelsea, this is Jake."

She cleared her throat. "Jake?"

He heard pounding in the background. "Chelsea, is this a bad time? You said to call at seven."

"Uh, bad time… No, it's not—"

"Hell… Let me in now!"

"What was that?" Maybe the TV was on.

"Uh, nothing."

"Goddamned bitch!"

Jake realized that was no TV. Someone was there with her. Someone violent. "Chelsea, are you all right?"

"N-no."

"Listen, hang up and call nine-one-one."

"I can't call nine-one-one. It's…Billy's at the back window of the kitchen."

"Is it locked?"

"No, I left the side windows open because it's hot. He's standing so I can't close them. But they have screens." Glass smashed in the background. "Oh, my God—"

"Chelsea?" No answer. *"Chelsea?"*

When he still got no answer, Jake hung up his cordless

phone and punched out nine-one-one. He spoke into the receiver as he sought his shoes. "Somebody has just broken into the back of a house at eight hundred Lake Terrace." Grabbing his keys from the desk, he bounded down the stairs. "I was talking to the homeowner. Send the police right away."

Jake was out the door before he disconnected the phone.

CHAPTER SEVEN

FOR A MOMENT, Chelsea stood openmouthed staring at the hole in the kitchen's plate-glass window. When she saw a booted foot kick in the remaining jagged glass, she dropped the phone and dashed for the front door. She could hear Billy swearing as he crawled through the window. She undid the chain, twisted the dead bolt and reached for the doorknob.

He grabbed her from behind. His sinewy arms, which she'd seen carry a four-year-old boy out of a fire and cradle an old man who'd been badly hurt in a car accident, banded around her chest and cinched her rib cage. "Goin' somewhere, babe?" Her heartbeat escalated, and a cold knot of fear pulsed in her stomach.

Stay calm. "Let me go, Billy."

"No way. I already did that, and look where it got me." His grip tightened, became viselike and painful.

"All right, we'll talk. Let's go into the living room and discuss this rationally."

"Promise you won't run."

"I promise."

When he let go of her, she darted away from him to the kitchen. But Billy was quicker than fire eating through walls. He caught up to her, yanked her around and slammed her against the wall. She yelped as her shoulder, which she'd wrenched earlier at the gym, hit the phone.

"Lying bitch." Without warning he raised his arm and backhanded her across the cheek. Pain jolted through her, vibrating to each nerve ending in her neck and skull. Her eyes watered. She shook her head to clear it and got her first good look at him.

He was her height, so she stared into bloodshot eyes with dilated pupils. He smelled like booze. His mouth had frozen in a sneer. Just as he was about to deliver another blow, she dropped to the floor. His fist connected with the phone, and he howled like a bear caught in a trap. He turned as she crawled around him and stumbled to her feet. Viciously he grabbed the back of her sweatshirt and whirled her around. His face was a mask of rage.

She brought up her knee and rammed it into his groin. When he doubled over, she twined her hands and hammered them on his neck. He slumped to the ground.

Her entire body shuddered with feverlike chills as she stared down at him.

Muffled shouting preceded the appearance of two uniformed policemen in the doorway to the kitchen. Another called from outside the broken kitchen window.

"Are you all right, ma'am?"

For a moment they wavered before her as if she was seeing them through heavy rainfall. She closed her eyes, swallowing the sob that rose in her throat. A young policeman reached for her arm to steady her. "Sit down." He eased her into a chair. When Billy moaned and stirred, she trembled in panic.

The older cop said, "We've got him." He bent, dragged Billy to his feet and handcuffed him in seconds.

Billy straightened, and his eyes found her unerringly. He assumed a petulant, little-boy expression. "Come on, honey, this was just a lovers' spat. Tell 'em to let me go."

Chelsea hesitated. She thought of the scandal in the fire department. She thought of the ground she'd gained with her new group, which could be lost. Then the pain in her face registered and the black fright she'd felt when he hit her resurfaced. "Take him away," she said.

AS THE COPS were hauling a handcuffed Billy to the car, Jake tore into the driveway of Chelsea's split-level house. He was out of the Bronco in a shot. As he reached the officers, his heart was hammering in his chest.

The cops faced him. "You her husband?"

"No."

Billy seemed to shake off his lethargy. "Jake, tell these clowns to let me go. I ain't done nothin'"

For a moment Jake remembered the code of brotherhood in the fire department. He remembered the isolation of having Danny's buddies turn on him. But then he remembered Chelsea saying, *No, not until he hit me,* and her shaky voice on the phone only minutes ago; cold fury overcame his wavering.

"Go to hell, Milligan." His shoulders tight with tension, Jake headed for the front door. He found another cop in the living room off the foyer. The broad-shouldered man blocked his view of Chelsea.

"I guess that's all for now. You'll need to come down to the station tomorrow morning to make a statement, but this is enough to hold him." The officer hesitated. "You need anything?"

"No." Her voice was hoarse, but controlled. Too controlled.

When the cop turned to leave, Jake got his first glimpse of her. Dressed in gray-and-pink sweats, she was curled up on a pristine white leather sofa, its huge pillows swallowing her like a giant cloud. On her lap was a gray-and-white cat. Her hand was buried in its thick coat; a second cat lay at her feet.

"Chelsea?"

Her head snapped up. She held an ice pack to her cheek.

"You know this man, ma'am?" asked the officer.

"Yes."

"I called nine-one-one." Jake explained the phone call and subsequent events.

When the officer was satisfied, he left, closing the door with a jarring thud. For a moment, the silence hung like heavy smoke in the room.

Then Jake crossed to her. Slowly he reached over and lowered her hand. A purple bruise ran the length of her cheekbone, tapering off by her chin.

"Goddamned son of a bitch," Jake said.

A weak grin claimed her lips. "My sentiments exactly."

He raised the hand holding the ice pack back to her face. "Keep this on it."

She winced when the cold compress connected with the bruise. Her eyes watered, and she sniffled. She averted her gaze.

Jake sat next to her, close but not touching. He didn't know what would spook her.

"You know," she said, "I've done everything I can to show him it's over." She trailed a shaking hand over the cat. "I've tried being nice, being mean, talking to him, ignoring him. Nothing's worked."

"This will."

She gave him a quizzical look.

"You can get a court order to keep him away from you. You've got grounds now."

Big brown eyes rounded with disbelief. "Oh, that'll go over big with his buddies in the RFD."

"Chelsea, you don't really have a choice. He beat you up."

Anger flared for a minute on her stark white face. "It's easy for you to tell me what to do. You don't know what it's like to put up with shit from the guys for hurting a brother."

He waited a beat, then said, "Yes, I do."

She stared at him. "What do you mean?"

"I'll tell you later."

She shook her head. "I've heard that before."

"No, this time, I promise I'll tell you."

Need burned in her eyes—for comfort, for understanding, for affirmation that she wasn't wrong. He could give her all three, and suddenly he wanted very badly to do that.

First the physical. Rising, he dragged over a leather footstool and gently propped her feet on it. "Lean back." She moaned. "Did he hit you somewhere else?"

"No. But he threw me against the wall...." Her voice trailed off, but not before he caught a trace of remembered fear in it. She rubbed her shoulder and said, "I slammed into the phone. Even that wouldn't be so bad, but I already wrenched my shoulder working out earlier."

Despite his abhorrence of violence against women, he smiled. "You're pretty tough, you know that?"

Gingerly she lay back and closed her eyes. Her face was ashen. "Of course I am."

He sat down on the couch and watched her. "Wanna talk?"

She shook her head.

"How about a good cry?"

Visibly she choked back the emotion. "No."

"What can I do for you, Chelsea?"

"Nothing." He could see her struggle to stay calm. "Thanks for calling nine-one-one. You can leave now."

A little stung, he said, "I just got here."

She shrugged. "Sorry, I didn't mean to be rude. I just don't like to put anybody out."

"Hey, you're saving me from panic on prom night."

She smiled weakly.

"Talk to me about it."

A heavy sigh escaped her lips. She leaned against the cushions. "Did you see the movie *Pretty Woman*?"

"Yeah."

"Remember that scene where Richard Gere's lawyer hits Julia Roberts?"

"Uh-huh."

"Billy hit me like that. *Do* guys learn how to do that in school?"

Jake remembered Roberts asking Gere that. In spite of the gravity of the situation, he was a little flattered to be compared to the movie star. He leaned over and ran his knuckles down her good cheek. "Like Gere told Roberts, not all men hit, Chels."

Her eyes filled, but she battled back the tears. Still, she leaned into his touch, wanting comfort.

"What can I do?" he repeated.

"Can you stay?" she whispered. "Just for a little while?"

"I'm not going anywhere." He dropped his hand to her shoulder and squeezed it. "Did you take a painkiller?"

"No."

"Do you have any?"

"Yeah. Upstairs in the bathroom."

Jake crossed the room and took the stairs by the door two at a time. At the top, a long hall stretched before him. The first door on his left was the bathroom.

He was surprised by its size. About twelve by twelve, it was painted completely white with slate-blue fixtures; matching blinds covered two long windows. As he rummaged through an oak medicine chest, he could see the sky beginning to darken through the skylight. His eyes dropped to the long, wide vanity. On it were dozens of jars. Intrigued at this glimpse of Firefighter Whitmore, he picked one up. Bubble bath. Another was bath gel. A third, body wash. There had to be ten jars altogether.

Hmm.

Pivoting, he faced the huge blue tub that sat gleaming in the corner.

Even that wouldn't be so bad, but I already wrenched my shoulder working out earlier.

He flicked the silver knobs on the faucets; then retrieved some Sinful Nights bath bubbles and opened the jar. The scent made him think of good sex, and lots of it; he poured in a generous amount. Letting the water run, he smiled. Who would have thought tough-girl Whitmore would harbor geisha-girl sensuality? Suppressing the images conjured up by *that,* he rose and headed downstairs. He detoured to the kitchen to get a glass of water. Anger came back big-time when he caught sight of the shattered window. Damn Milligan. Jake would board it up before he left.

Armed with water and a renewed dose of resolve, he entered the living room; she was lying back, eyes closed. "Chelsea?"

She stirred. "I'm dozing."

"I started a bath for you."

"How did you know....?"

"Your collection of bath soap's a dead giveaway. Here, take this."

She looked at the pill. "Percocet?"

"Yeah, your cheek has to be throbbing."

"It is. But these put me to sleep."

"Good."

"I want to hear your story."

"Later. Take it." She swallowed the pill with water. He noticed that her hands were still trembling when she returned the glass. "Come on, up."

The cat on her lap scampered off as she moved, and the other darted from the room. She groaned painfully. Jake bent and clasped her arm, helped her stand. He saw her bite her lip, watched her struggle for equilibrium. He slid a hand around her waist. It felt firm even through the fleece of her sweat suit. She leaned heavily on him as he guided her up the stairs to the bathroom door.

"You're pretty shaky," he said. "Need some help in there?"

She gave him a weak grin. "No, I'm fine."

"You're not fine. Look, I'll wait right out here."

"That's silly."

"Then I'll be silly."

"At least go into the sitting room back there." She angled her head to the end of the hall.

"I will when you're settled." He waited, not wanting to upset her. "Chels?" She turned. "Do you have any wood around here? I'll board up the window for you."

Whatever color she'd regained drained from her face. The bruise stood out like a neon sign, advertising Milligan's aggressive fist. Taking a deep breath, she said, "There's some plywood in the basement. I think there's a hammer and stuff there, too." She gave him a wrenchingly grateful look. "Thanks for doing that. I don't know if I could—"

"You don't have to. I'll take care of it."

But he didn't. Not right away. After she closed the door behind her, he leaned against the wall outside the room until he heard the toilet flush, then the faucets go off. He turned to head downstairs to fix the window when he heard the sound of breaking glass. He circled to the bathroom door.

"Chelsea?" No answer. "Chels?" Still silence.

He pushed open the door.

She was against the wall across from the mirror; a broken cup lay in the sink. She'd stripped off her sweats and was clothed only in a long T-shirt and underwear. She stood openmouthed, staring at her reflection. Then, like a rag doll, she slid down the wall to the tile floor and buried her face in her hands.

He dropped to his knees. Forgoing any platitudes—she *did* look like hell—he soothed his hand down her silky hair. "It's okay, Chelsea. Let it out."

She shook her head, but he could see her shoulders shake. Firefighters were notorious for keeping their emotions inside, especially in front of somebody else. And he knew from Francey that female firefighters were even more determined to be stoic. He thought that as a colleague, he should probably let her get it out in private.

But as a man, he couldn't leave.

"Chels?"

Slowly she raised her head. Her eyes were dark with pain. He sank down next to her and pulled her onto his lap. She didn't resist, which was testament to how raw she was. Gently he enfolded her in his arms; her face nestled in his neck as she cried with quiet restraint. It was all the more heartbreaking for its reserve.

Chelsea was mortified by her weakness. She'd been holding on to her composure like a rookie to a life rope, but lost her grip when she was finally alone, when she saw the hideous bruise on her face. The fear of Billy violating her safety engulfed her all over again. Her control shattered, her resistance vanished, and she turned to Jake. She couldn't remember the last time she'd sat in anybody's lap, let alone cried like a child.

But after a moment sanity dribbled into her brain. This was her lieutenant. She was half-dressed. They were on the floor of her bathroom. She tried to pull away. He held her to him. She tried again.

His words stopped her retreat. "I never told anybody before, but I cried like this once when somebody I cared about turned on me."

Startled by his stark confession, she drew back to look

at him. She hadn't realized her hands were gripping his shirt collar. "A woman?"

"No, my best friend." Jake nudged her face to his chest, as if he wanted anonymity to tell the story. She felt him swallow against her cheek. "He got into drugs, booze. Eventually it affected his work. I covered for him. Made excuses. When I realized I couldn't protect him any longer, I reported him to the chief."

"Oh, Jake."

"Then he turned on me. After he told me off for betraying him, he walked out of the firehouse, and out of my life, forever. We'd been friends since we were five years old."

"I'm sorry."

"Some of the guys hated me for ratting on him. Others condemned me for not doing it sooner. I lost stature in the department and gave up my dreams to go further. But what hurt most was that those guys were my buddies, too." His hand locked on her neck. His lips were in her hair as he whispered, "So, see, I know how it feels."

She nodded.

For a long minute they sat on the floor of the dim bathroom, silent, sharing a kindred pain.

Chelsea stirred first. She drew back. Sniffled. Wiped her eyes. "Thanks for telling me." She nodded at his chest. "And for that. I feel better."

"A good cry'll do it every time."

She angled her head to the tub. "Now get out of here while I take a bath."

"Okay. I'll go fix the window."

She sank onto the floor away from him. He stood and stared at her. His eyes twinkled with masculine mischief. "Sure you don't need some help in here?"

Glad for the lightened mood, she shook her head. "No."

He turned to the door. When he reached it she called, "Hey, Lieutenant?"

He looked back. "Yeah?"

"You're a nice guy, you know that?"

"Remember that on our next training stint."

It only took about fifteen minutes to board up the window until a repairman could get to it. Then he bounded up the stairs and put his ear to the door. The sound of a woman taking a bath had been absent from his life for a long time, and he'd forgotten how sexy it was. For a minute he let the sensual feelings wash over him, then he headed for the sitting room. At the end of the hall, she'd said.

Flicking on the lights, his gaze swept the room. It was shaped like an L, the longer section a living area that opened up through a curved archway into the bedroom proper.

Its colors matched the bathroom: white walls, slate carpeting. A white wicker couch with thick blue cushions and throw pillows was flanked with floor-to-ceiling bookcases. A matching rocker, lamp and footstool were across from the door, an oak desk in the corner. Various lamps in white wicker or wood graced the room. An unusual piece, a white cradle, housed magazines in the corner. Four huge plants grew in wild profusion, one in each corner.

He crossed to the archway. On the other side of it sat a big white wrought-iron bed with a blue-and-white floral-print comforter; windows flanked it. Two large dressers, then another door, probably access to the bathroom. Surrounded by such blatant femininity, he stared at the paneled door, swamped by images of Chelsea in the bath. Her long legs all soapy, water trickling between her breasts, down to...

Forcefully he shook off the vision and headed to the sitting area. To distract himself, he checked out the contents of the bookcases. A row of history texts. Bestsellers. He grinned. Two whole shelves of romance novels. At the bottom were rows of books with no titles on the spines. He pulled one out. It was a diary. He chuckled. So she *did* keep them. He'd wait until the right time to jab her about those.

To the left of the bookcases was an embroidered framed poem, "A Fireman's Prayer." It reflected what he asked for every time he walked into a burning building—to be brave and skillful enough to save others, and that God would guide him to the right places. On the chair below it was an embroidered pillow. He picked it up. It read Men, Coffee, Chocolate. The richer the better. Hmm. That didn't sound like Chelsea. As a matter of fact, he had trouble picturing Chelsea doing—what was this called, needle-point?—at all. Then he saw the signature in the corner. Delaney. It figured.

He heard a rustle behind him. Turning, he froze and briefly closed his eyes to block out the vision of Chelsea standing in the archway. The dull ache he'd felt all night for what she'd gone through turned into an ache of a totally different kind.

Unsuccessfully he tried to keep his eyes off her hair, washed and dried, just a bit damp and curly around her face. His gaze dropped to her breasts. They were covered in ice-blue satin; the gown was scalloped at the neck and hung in soft folds past her waist to her feet. His body responded with sharp need. At least he was dressed to cover it this time, he thought dryly.

"You're staring at me."

His grin came straight from his libido. "I…you…" He drew a deep breath. "You look like you just stepped out of the pages of a fairy tale."

"Why, Lieutenant, how poetic." Suddenly she weaved slightly and grabbed the door frame.

He crossed to her and clasped her upper arms. "Steady." The satin slid seductively beneath his fingers.

"I'm woozy from the pill."

"Let's get you into bed." His voice was raw. Sexy.

Pure feminine reaction lit her eyes.

Ignoring it, he crossed behind her and turned down the covers. He swallowed hard at the satin sheets. Could she recreate a man's fantasy any more accurately? he thought with grim humor. "Get in," he said gruffly.

"Yes, sir." Her sass was diluted by a big yawn.

Dutifully she climbed in; he tucked the covers beneath her chin, letting his fingers linger on her skin.

Her eyes were already closing. "You can leave now," she said trustingly. "And you can lock up with the key by the back door."

"Oh, I can, huh?"

"Yeah."

But he stood over her and watched her until her breathing evened. Then, without censoring his reaction, he leaned down and kissed her forehead. She smiled in her sleep.

CHAPTER EIGHT

THREE DAYS LATER, on her last day off before starting a new shift, Chelsea marched into the Rockford Fire Academy. Though her stomach still churned from seeing her face in the mirror this morning—her cheek looked like a modern art painting with its obscene mixture of yellows, blues and reds—she wasn't going to hide out. She'd done nothing wrong.

But she sighed as she opened the academy's front door. If only she didn't have to face her new group from Quint Twelve *and* her old crew from Engine Four, who'd also been Billy's group. They were all scheduled for a training session together. To top it off, she and Jake were meeting her sister at noon about Derek DeLuca. Delaney had been out of town at a conference for three days, and although Chelsea had filled her in on the basics over the phone, her sister hadn't seen her face yet.

Actually, since the assault, Chelsea had seen only Jake and the police officers. She smiled as she remembered opening the door to her lieutenant the morning after.

"Hi," she'd said with not a little surprise—and something else she didn't want to name.

Dressed in wheat-colored jeans and a plain forest green T-shirt, he'd looked like a model for L.L. Bean.

"Hi." His jaw was tight as his eyes narrowed on her face.

"Please, come in. Want some coffee?"

Jake stepped inside. "Yeah, if we have time."

"Time?" she asked as he followed her to the dining room.

"I want to go with you to the police station."

A warmth worthy of Jamaican nights spread through her. "Really?"

He nodded. "If it's okay." He gave her an assuring grin. "I thought you might not want to go down alone."

"I don't." She reached out to touch his forearm. Felt muscles tense beneath her fingers. "Thanks for being so considerate."

His eyes had twinkled. "Wouldn't want you to write bad things about me in your diary."

"Oh, God, did you see them?"

"Mmm." He took a seat at the light oak table as she veered into the kitchen.

After pouring coffee for both of them, she returned and set a mug in front of him.

She remembered what she'd said about him in the re- vealing little books. "Did you read them?"

"What, a Boy Scout like me?"

She'd stared him down.

"No, of course not." He'd sipped from his mug, then glanced at the saying on it. It was Delaney's gift and read Firefighters Like It Hot. His laugh had been male and hearty.

Thinking about the luscious masculine sound, Chelsea headed to the first-floor arena, where the off-duty firefight- ers who were being paid overtime to do special training on the elderly were having coffee. About two dozen RFD personnel milled around the cavernous gym. She scanned the crowd; her heart hammered in her chest when she saw some of her old crew standing to the left where the kitchen jutted off the arena—Captain TJ McManis, Miller, Con- nors and Donatelli.

When Donatelli caught sight of her in the doorway, he

nudged the others, and they all turned to look at her. Their grim expressions changed to surprise at her battered appearance. Pinning them with a stare that said, *This is why I pressed charges,* she strode, head held high, to her new group, who were by the stage. As she made her way through the crowd, she could hear the whispered murmurs.

Jake noticed her first. He winked, and she felt her stomach contract. Things had changed between them. She'd seen him twice since the other night, and both times, like now, she'd felt a connection with him, an intimacy she didn't feel with the others. He seemed to feel it, too. She'd been unable to forget how she'd sat on his lap, how he'd soothed her and told her of his demons.

Mick's head snapped around when she reached them. She was shocked by the expletives that poured from his mouth. He ended with, "The bastard."

She shrugged. "Needless to say, he's not my favorite person."

"Are you all right?" Diaz asked, his brow furrowed.

"Yeah, it looks worse than it is."

Jake's grim expression told her he did not agree.

Huff grasped her arm and tilted her chin. With EMT thoroughness, he examined her cheek. "Man, what the hell's the matter with the guy?"

Warmed by their sympathy, she was beginning to relax when Joey came up behind Jake. He looked hard at her, then shook his head and said, "You okay?"

"Yeah, Joe, I'm okay."

Over the mike, Reed Macauley defused the moment. "Time for your lessons, ladies and gentlemen. We'll meet in the EMS classroom on this floor." Though the main offices at the academy were upstairs, the EMS office and a large airy classroom were attached to the gym.

At his announcement, everyone began to file out of the arena. Jake lagged behind, but caught up to his crew and handed her a cup of coffee. His fingers brushed hers. She nodded at his thoughtfulness.

Inside the classroom, the firefighters she'd worked with from Engine Four were lined up in front of a row of windows that faced the parking lot. Waiting for her? She stopped abruptly, but Jake nudged her on, grasping her elbow gently. "It's okay. We're here."

He hooked Huff's gaze, flicked his to the side; Huff frowned as he glanced over. Mick caught the signal, too.

They flanked her. Edging close, they steered her to one of the empty lablike tables down front. Jake dragged out the middle chair, and as she sat down, Billy's buddies filled in the table in front of her. Intentionally? To intimidate her? Don, Mick and Joey quickly grabbed the chairs behind them. She gave them a grateful smile.

Firefighters protected their own, Chelsea knew; she just hadn't been sure where she belonged until now.

From a podium in front, Reed called for everyone's attention. A huge chalkboard, a projector and a screen were behind him. "As you know, we're here today to do some training on dealing with elderly patients on EMS calls and as victims in fires. Since Dutch Towers is so close to both your stations, we're starting with your groups. But all RFD personnel will receive this training." He smiled. "First, I'd like a show of hands. How many of you are in your twenties?"

Seven guys stuck up their hands.

"Thirties?"

Fifteen. As Chelsea lifted her arm, she glanced at Jake and raised her brows.

"Forties?"

Jake and Reed waved.

"Hey, Scarlatta," a guy in the back called, "not long before you get your own place at the Towers."

"Over the hill, Jakey boy," somebody else said.

Over the hill? Hardly. Chelsea's eyes were drawn to the gunmetal gray thermal top that stretched across Jake's linebacker shoulders; it was tucked into black jeans. Beltless black jeans. Tight, beltless black jeans. When she raised her eyes, he was watching her with a heated look. Mortified, she flushed and faced Reed.

"All right, on the front of the card, write your age and your strongest physical and emotional assets."

"That means your good points, Santori," a firefighter next to them taunted.

Joey said, "Too bad you don't have any, Mack."

Reed continued. "Now turn the card over, add forty years to your age and write down what your biggest physical and emotional liability might be."

No one joked this time. Chelsea squirmed like a kid in the principal's office. It wasn't pleasant to picture yourself failing; in her case, top physical condition had always been a given. To think about not having it was chilling. She wrote that the lack of strength and endurance would be difficult for her to handle.

"Now that you've put yourself in their places, let's talk about our roles in the care of older people. In the next two hours we'll list the disabilities they might have that would impede our helping them or saving their lives. Then we'll brainstorm ways to compensate for that. You'll be out by noon, I promise." Reed scanned the group. "Jake, since you're the closest to their age except for me, how about starting us off?"

"Thanks, buddy." Chelsea smiled at his dry tone. "How about loss of hearing and sight?"

Reed wrote it on the board. "Johnson, what do you think?"

"Slowed movements."

The board quickly filled with brittle bones, loss of bladder or bowel control, aggravated fearfulness and senility.

"Good job. Now, each table will work with the one behind it or across from it. For fifteen minutes, brainstorm the problems in EMS calls and fire rescue that result from these impairments. After that, we'll hammer out our role in dealing with them."

In unison the three Engine Four firefighters pivoted to face Chelsea. They were trying to intimidate her, she was certain.

Jake said easily, "Why don't you guys work with the table across from you?"

"Why?" Miller asked.

Before Jake could answer, Mick stood up and said, "The lieutenant asked you to leave, guys."

But the Engine Four firefighters stayed where they were, looking as innocent as choirboys.

Crossing his arms, Joey lounged in his chair, but Chelsea, who'd turned in her seat, caught a hint of the tension in the set of his jaw. "I saw Billy this morning, guys," Joey said. "Not a mark on *him.*"

Donatelli's face darkened. "Hey, all we wanna do is work with your group. Nobody said nothin' about Billy."

Jake stood, too, as Reed reached for the captain's shoulder. "TJ," Reed said, "table four doesn't have anybody to work with. Why don't you take your guys over there?" When the captain hesitated, Reed said, "Now." His tone was stern, commanding, contrary to the Clark Kent manner he usually assumed.

Once everybody settled down, the five male Quint Twelve firefighters regrouped, moving their chairs so they surrounded Chelsea.

She said, "I feel like the wagon trains are circling."

Diaz quipped, "Yep, warding off the Indian attack." He paused. "They have any Puerto Rican cowboys back then?"

"Nope, you'd a been the cook," Joey told him.

"Shut up, guinea."

Jake laughed. Huff grinned. And Chelsea felt her eyes mist.

"Thanks, guys."

"You aren't gonna go all female on us and cry, are you, Whitmore?" Huff teased.

"Nah," she said. "I can't remember the last time anybody made me cry."

Jake caught her eye. His gaze burned hotly. It said, *I can remember. You were half-dressed and on my lap.*

His look also revealed how much he'd liked it.

"WANNA COME to DeLuca's with us, Chelsea?" Mick asked after the morning's training was over.

"I'd love to," she said, glancing at Jake. "But I'm meeting my sister here. We're, uh, gonna have lunch."

Jake thought, *After she meets with me.*

"Next time." She watched them with turbulent eyes. "Thanks again."

Mick squeezed her arm. Huff patted her shoulder. Diaz ruffled her hair. And Joey said, "Maybe you'll bake us another pie."

"Maybe."

When they filed out, she faced Jake. "I don't know what to say."

"I told you, Chels, all men aren't alike."

The look she gave him melted his insides like candle wax. "Maybe."

For a moment Jake was flooded by a resurgence of the feelings he'd had in her bedroom the other night. He took in a deep breath. "Thanks for volunteering to do some physical fitness classes at the Towers. You sure you want to take that on?"

"I want to help them out," she said simply. "Anyway, I won't be doing it alone. People volunteered to help."

"Well, *that* was interesting." They turned to find Reed behind them. "I don't mind refereeing, but I wish I'd known what I'd been in for. I feel like we just went the full nine rounds."

Chelsea bit her lip. "I'm sorry, Reed."

He frowned. "Chelsea, none of this is your fault." He gave Jake a playful punch in the arm. "But this guy could've warned me."

"I should've. Sorry."

"No, I—"

"Oh, my God, look at you!"

Jake whipped his head around and saw Chelsea's sister standing in the doorway of the EMS classroom. Staring at Chelsea, Delaney hesitated a second, then rushed in, dropped her briefcase onto a desk, grasped Chelsea's chin, examined her cheek and swore like a sailor.

Chelsea's tone was dry. "Delaney, we're in mixed company."

Delaney glared at Jake. Her eyes rounded when they landed on Reed. "Yes, well, one of their pals did this to you."

"Do you always go off half-cocked like this?" Reed asked in annoyance.

"Pardon me?"

"I asked if you're always so rash."

She tossed her head haughtily, making her long, dark curly hair bounce. "Just because you take life at a snail's pace, doesn't mean the rest of us should."

He crossed his arms. "Being judgmental is not a positive quality in a therapist."

She snorted. "You'd know, wouldn't you, sitting up here in your ivory tower, not having contact with the real world?"

The amused scorn on Reed's face died like the flame of a match caught in the wind.

"The real world leaves something to be desired, Dr. Shaw." He turned to Jake. "Stop by and see me before you leave, Jake." He faced Chelsea. "Hope things work out for you, Chelsea. If you need me for anything, I'm here."

Possessively Delaney placed her hands on Chelsea's shoulders. "She has me if she needs help."

Reed pinned her with a gaze that was a mixture of disdain and fascination. "We can't always help the ones we're close to." He nodded and left.

"Sit down, Delaney," Chelsea said, "before you alienate *everybody* here."

Delaney rested troubled eyes on her sister. "Sorry. I wasn't prepared for how you look." She glanced out the door. "And that guy manages to push all my buttons."

Jake chuckled. "Reed?"

Delaney swung her gaze to him. "He's the most infuriating man I've ever met."

"Well," Jake said, "your experience sure is different from anybody else's."

Furrows marred her high forehead. "Seriously?"

"Yeah."

She shrugged.

"And he recommended you to me."

Her mouth gaped. "You're kidding me. He went after me in that workshop every chance he got."

"Funny, he said the same thing about you."

Delaney shook her head and sank onto a chair. "Well, it's all water under the bridge, since the workshop's over. We'll probably never see each other again." She straightened and, just like at the baseball game, assumed a different persona—more professional, less emotional. "Chelsea said you need some help. For one of your children?"

"More like an adopted child." Jake explained Derek's situation to Delaney.

"I'm sorry," she said with genuine feeling. "Abandonment at such a young age can be so painful." Her gaze flicked to Chelsea. The look the sisters shared told Jake they knew something about youthful neglect.

"Which is why I need to get him some therapy."

Delaney hesitated. "Well, I'd like to help. I've been interested in the children of emergency rescue people. But—"

Chelsea said, "I know you're not taking new patients, Delaney. I thought you could do this as a favor to me."

"It's not that."

"What, then?" Chelsea asked.

Delaney's face was serious as she turned to Jake. "Listen, I know you were there for Chelsea when she was attacked the other night, and I appreciate it. But my feelings about the fire department right now are not very positive." She nodded to her sister. "Chelsea's had a really bad eight months, and I blame it on her co-workers."

"Not all of us are alike," Jake said, parroting what he'd told Chelsea.

Delaney's blue eyes were grim with doubt. "Men or firefighters?" she asked.

"Both."

"I'm not sure I can be unbiased with Derek."

"Of course you can," Chelsea said. "Laney, you're the best. And Derek needs the best."

Jake had a feeling about Delaney. Her impetuosity, her forthrightness, her I-don't-give-a-damn-what-I-say attitude might be just what Derek needed.

Or is this just another tie to the woman sitting across from you? an inner voice asked.

He took in Chelsea's tousled hair, black sleeveless knit top and white jeans. And his entire body hardened. He didn't need another tie to her. It was dangerous. It would be the best if Delaney didn't take on Derek.

Opening his mouth to retract his request, he was cut off by Dr. Delaney Shaw's sudden gesture. She stood up, smoothed her miniskirt and pronounced. "All right, I'll take him. Call my secretary and have her set up an appointment for this week. I'll tell her to make room." She glanced at Chelsea. "Let's go to lunch. I want to talk to you alone."

"Delaney, you're being rude."

"I don't care." She faced Jake. "My sister's sitting here looking like she went a couple rounds with Mike Tyson, and I want a chance to see how she's really doing."

Jake stared at her.

"I'll meet you in the parking lot." Chelsea stood and gave her sister a warning look. "I want to talk to Jake a minute."

"Sure." Delaney picked up her briefcase and swept out of the room.

Jake stood, too. "Well, your sister is an...interesting woman."

Chelsea smiled. "Don't be too hard on her. She's got a wonderful heart and she's brilliant with kids. She'll make headway with Derek, I know."

"The poor boy won't have any choice."

Thoughtfully, Chelsea stared after her sister. "We had a rough life growing up. She's the most affected by it. She's always felt this loyalty and...protectiveness toward me."

"It's easy to have those feelings for you."

Chelsea's eyes widened.

He raised his hand and brushed her unharmed cheek. "Way too easy."

Jake hadn't meant to say it; it slipped out. To preclude any more revelations, he turned and left her alone in the classroom.

THE DARKNESS swallowed him once again and spit him out, a giant monster transforming him. Nobody, not even those close to him, knew what he felt inside. Alone in his bedroom at home, staring into space, he tried to think through this whole thing.

What to do? Okay, so he felt like a hypocrite. He *was* a hypocrite in some ways. He was good at keeping his other side hidden; he'd joined in easily playing Galahad with the rest of them, hadn't he?

His hands fisted. Truth be told, that bruise on her face had thrown him. His father used to hit his mother and him; he hated that kind of violence. Whitmore's appearance had touched something inside him, and he'd played along for that reason.

But tonight, he was back to square one with her. She just didn't belong there. It would be best for her to get her out of there. Then she wouldn't be making guys like Billy mad enough to knock her around. Christ, she was thirty-six. She oughtta be home takin' care of babies.

He glanced at the doorway. Women needed to be put in their place by men who knew how to do it. It was for their own good. In a sense, it would be playing the knight in shining armor, sort of like the way they'd protected her at the academy today.

That did it. He'd known if he thought about it long enough, he'd figure out why he *had* to do this.

It'd be for her own good.

He'd take the first step right away.

CHAPTER NINE

IF JAKE SCARLATTA was upset by the fifty-foot tanker that sprawled across the expressway, spilling gasoline like water out of a hose, it wasn't obvious. Amidst the fine drizzle that had begun about seven and shrouded them in ominous gloom, he barked orders like the commander-in-chief of an army.

"Huff and Santori, the victim's yours." The pair leaped off the rig and headed toward the driver, who'd been thrown from his truck. "Diaz, get the foam ready. Whitmore, you're behind me on the hose." As he reached up and pulled the Nomex hood over his head, he asked, "Can you handle this one, Chelsea?"

"Yes, sir."

"All right, stay close. It could get dicey."

Sirens blared in the distance. Dimly they registered—the overturning of a tanker and its potential hazards would draw out all the brass, as well as several more fire trucks. But Chelsea was intent on getting her mask in place, adjusting the straps and making sure her gear was in working order. Fiery gasoline was a hungry monster that would bite anywhere it could.

Slowly, Jake approached it. At precisely the time he reached the spill, he activated the nozzle. "I've got foam," he yelled.

The hose grew heavy and bucked; Chelsea held on tight as Jake began the methodical, careful task of laying the foam blanket that would smother the fire. As he blew the foam, he followed its path through the lake of gasoline; she was right behind him.

Chelsea focused, blocking everything else out. Sweat dripped from her scalp under the hood and helmet and mask. In the center of the spill, the heat was an inferno. Every inch of her was sweltering.

Halfway through, she heard sirens and glanced up as more trucks, ambulances and official cars arrived. Bringing her attention to the hose, her gaze snagged on sparks. Behind her.

Oh, God, the gasoline had reignited.

And they were in the middle of it.

She grabbed Jake's arm and pulled hard. He turned and saw the fire, too. As cool as a guy watering his lawn, Jake backtracked and doused the flames. Chelsea blanked her mind, concentrated on the hose and followed Jake. It took a long time, but eventually they'd laid a twenty-foot foam blanket; the fire was out.

Mick came up and grabbed the line from them. "Goddamn, I thought you'd bought it," she heard him say as she yanked off her headgear.

Jake cocked his head. "Haven't you ever seen a foam blanket reignite?"

Mick shook his head.

Jake nodded to Chelsea. "You?"

"Never."

His eyes shone with appreciation. "Then you did good."

She smiled. "Thanks."

Two hours later they headed to the firehouse. They'd stayed and helped clean up the spill; when more backup arrived, the chief released them.

Chelsea ached everywhere from holding the hose. Tension had crept into her shoulders, and with the drop in adrenaline, exhaustion hit her like a sledgehammer.

They dumped their gear in the bay. Peter said, "Let's get coffee and see if that pie Whitmore made is as good as it smelled when we left." She'd been baking a pie that was just about done when they got the call.

"What kind is it this time, Whitmore?" Joey asked, tossing his bunker boots to the floor.

"Cherry." She smiled at Don, who let his turnout gear drop to his feet. "Don pitted the cherries."

"Just like home," he muttered good-naturedly as Jake led the way to the back of the firehouse. "I get all the grunt work."

Jake said, "But you're so good at it, Diaz. I think I'll—" He halted abruptly at the entrance to the kitchen. Chelsea, Peter and Joey bumped into each other. It would have been comical if they hadn't been so tired.

"What the…" Joey began.

"Peter, come up here." Jake's peremptory tone silenced them.

Chelsea scowled. Her first thought was that someone had broken into the firehouse. Just what they needed.

Quickly Peter threaded through them to meet Jake at the kitchen doorway.

"You're the gourmet. Is it just remnants of the spill I'm smelling, or is there gas in here?".

"It's gas." Peter swore. "From the friggin' stove."

Chelsea frowned.

Jake pivoted. "Chelsea, didn't you turn off the stove?"

"Of course I did. The call came two minutes before the timer was set to go off. I took out the pie and turned the stove off."

Peter scowled. "You sure?"

"I'm positive."

"All right," Jake said, entering the kitchen. "Let's air this place out."

Four firefighters opened windows as Jake crossed to the stove. Chelsea followed him.

He stiffened. Then he reached up and flipped the knob from on to off. When he faced her his gaze was stern. "It was on, Whitmore. The pilot light must have blown out again."

"I know I turned it off," she said, seeds of doubt sprouting inside her. "At least I thought I did." She threw up her hands. "God, Jake, I'm sorry. I can't believe I was so careless."

Mick came up behind her and rested a hand on her shoulder. "Hey, it's okay. We were in a hurry."

"No," Jake said, "it's not okay. But it's human. We all need to be careful with this damn thing until it's replaced." He sighed. "Okay. Let's drop it."

Chelsea stood staring at the stove as the guys got coffee. In her mind she replayed her actions. She'd been sitting at the table with Mick, razzing him about a sexist comment he'd made. The tone had sounded, and they'd both bolted up.

"Get the pie," Mick had ordered teasingly, then headed right. She remembered wondering where he was going, since the closest exit to the bay was left.

She'd opened the oven and taken out the pie. The steam had singed her wrist, and she'd yelped.

Joey had raced by her and asked if she was okay.

Don had come out of the bathroom and yelled for her to hurry.

She'd placed the pie on the burner. Then she'd reached up, turned off the stove and darted for the bay.

She'd bumped into Peter on his way into the kitchen for his gloves, which he'd been cleaning earlier.

Chelsea stared at the stove knob. Then she turned and watched her group gather around the table. What could have happened?

"WHY DOES HE stop crying with you?" Dylan asked as Jake picked up a squalling Timmy O'Roarke from the baby seat. The six-week-old bundle squirmed in Jake's arms until he held the child against his shoulder and cuddled him close. Just for good measure, Jake walked back and forth over the worn wood floor of the Dutch Towers main room. Painted a soft beige, the large common area housed tables and chairs, comfortable couches and a big-screen TV. Tonight it would be used for the first fire-department-sponsored physical fitness session, so all the furniture had been moved to the side.

"I don't know. Jessica was like that with Ben Cordaro. He was like a grandfather to her, you know."

Dylan watched from his chair at a small table in the corner. "Haven't forgotten how to do that, have ya, buddy."

Jake patted Timmy's back gently. "You never forget." What he *hadn't* remembered was the sense of peace a baby snuggling against him brought. "I wish I'd had more."

"It's not too late," Dylan said, leafing through *Firehouse* magazine looking for material for the latest trivia game. He and the baby had accompanied Beth, who'd volunteered to help Chelsea run the fitness classes at the senior's complex, but as usual Dylan brought along a pile of firemanics material. Guys had been teasing him about losing interest in the department since he got married, and he was trying to prove them wrong with the weekly trivia game. "You and Beth are the same age, and she just had the little monster."

Jake's gaze strayed to Beth, then to Chelsea in the front of the room. Damn, she looked good tonight. Though she wore a light warm-up jacket over her outfit, he could see a yellow T-shirt peeking out from the top; it drew his gaze like a red flag. Matching shorts revealed every inch of her long, shapely legs.

Dylan said, "Okay, here's one I could use. What's the highest award given by the NYFD?"

"Too easy," Jake responded, still staring at Chelsea. "It's the Gordon Bennett medal."

As she turned to write on the big chalkboard Jake had hauled in from another room, he found himself wondering if she wearing those red panties he'd caught a glimpse of two nights ago. He tried to distract himself by nuzzling the baby in his arms, but he couldn't stop the images....

He'd been waiting outside the showers for her to finish and had banged on the door after a few minutes. He knew she'd been in there a while. "Get a move on, Whitmore," he'd shouted, winking as Mick walked by. "This isn't Elizabeth Arden's."

"Stuff it, Scarlatta," she'd shouted back.

When at last she'd pulled open the door, he'd planned to check his watch and tap his foot, but his movements had been stilled by the sight of her. She wore gym shorts and the RFD T-shirt, traditional firehouse sleeping garb. Her skin glowed amidst the halo of steam surrounding her; greedily, he took in her peaches-and-cream cheeks, sparkling eyes. And her hair, damp from only being towel dried, reminded him of sex in the shower.

"For cripe's sake, man, I wasn't in there that long."

He swallowed hard. "Long enough." Even to his own ears, his voice was a come-to-bed invitation.

She'd sucked in a breath. He moved to his left, she to her right to defuse the moment, and the collision caused her to drop her toiletries. Falling to her knees, she scrambled to pick up toothbrush, shampoo and towel. Jake bent to retrieve a tube of lotion that had fallen open. Its scent was sexy as hell. He shoved it into her hand. When she stood, he noticed she'd inadvertently dropped a pair of panties, the tiniest scrap of scarlet lace he'd ever seen, on the scarred linoleum.

His hand gravitated to them. They were as sinfully soft as they looked. He held them a second, slithering the material between his fingers. Still squatting—he didn't dare stand up—he'd looked into her face. "You dropped these," he said huskily.

Her eyes were riveted to his big hand caressing the tiny panties. She said nothing, just stood statue-still.

He'd stayed half kneeling on the floor—like a slave at her feet. Then he'd thrust them at her. As if awakened from a spell, she'd snatched the panties and darted down the hall.

Sucking in a breath, he'd finally stood and gratefully headed for the shower....

"Oh, look at the baby." Mrs. Lowe came in, along with about ten other residents of Dutch Towers, and crossed directly to Jake. Her skin may have been old and wrinkled, but her eyes were young and sparkling.

Dylan said, "He looks just like me, doesn't he, Mrs. L?"

Adelaide Lowe smiled broadly at the proud papa. "Yes, he does." She focused on Jake. "Time's running out, young man. If you're going to have a son, you'd better get going."

"A daughter's all I need, Mrs. Lowe." He grinned. "You wanna hold Timmy?"

"No, I'm going to stretch before class starts." She patted Timmy's head and joined Mrs. MacKenzie and Mrs. Santori, who were up front near Chelsea and Beth.

"I'm gonna go talk to the guys." Jake bent to put a sleeping Timmy into his seat. "I said I'd help when I coaxed Mr. Steed, Mr. Olivo and Mr. Santori into being here."

"Okay, but before you go, here's another one," Dylan said. "What's the Scannel medal given for?"

"Rescue in an earthquake emergency. It was named

after the fire chief in the San Francisco earthquake at the time.'' Jake straightened and laughed. ''You're losing your touch, O'Roarke. Fatherhood's turned your brain to mush.''

When Jake reached the men, he was still chuckling. ''Ready to go for the burn, guys?''

Moses Santori, a burly, bald man whose rheumy eyes still gleamed with mischief at sixty-eight, patted his stomach. ''Josephine said if I don't lose some weight she's gonna stop sleeping with me.''

Sergio Olivo grinned. ''My Angie used to say that. It worked, too.''

Tall, trim and handsome, with a shock of silver hair falling into his eyes, gentlemanly Lawrence Steed smiled sedately. ''You should walk, like I do every morning.''

''If we could have your attention now,'' Chelsea told the group. ''Everyone come up front. We've got mats here to sit on, but I'd like you to take the chairs we've set out first.''

Jake smiled at her thoughtfulness. Older people couldn't get up and down on the mats easily.

''As you know,'' she continued, ''I'm Chelsea Whitmore, and I own the Weight Room, which is a couple of blocks away from here. Your local fire department is sponsoring this activity, which is why Jake and Dylan and Beth are helping out.'' All three waved. ''Tonight we're going to talk about fitness, see a video and walk some if it stays nice outside.'' She smiled. ''I hope you'll have a good idea if you want to continue on with us and might be able to convince some of your neighbors to join us next time.''

Chelsea turned to the TV. ''We'll start with a video made by a woman in her sixties when she began a fitness program. I'll let her tell you why.''

Jake watched the spry and attractive older woman who appeared on screen. The Dutch Towers residents were mesmerized as she told the story of witnessing her mother wither away because of lack of bone density and general physical fitness. As the older woman demonstrated her ability at sixty-five to leg-press one hundred eighty pounds, bench-press sixty, and do biceps curls with fifteen-pound free weights, he thought about Jessica. He was glad she kept in shape; he'd taken her to Chelsea's club last week....

"Oh, Dad, look at this equipment, it's state-of-the-art." Jessica had been effusive as Spike Lammon had walked them around the gym. It was impressive, with its extensive square footage, top-notch aerobic machines, mirrored walls and a large variety of weights. Its color scheme was gray and black, with a dark pink accent here and there.

Though he'd tried not to, Jake had kept scanning the area for Chelsea. She'd finally emerged from the back room. Her hair was damp, her skin glistening with perspiration. Wiping her face, she said, "Hi. Jeez, is it that late? I didn't realize."

More like a lover than an employee, Spike had ruffled her hair and said, "Been working out too hard, babe." He faced Jess. "She's competing in the local triathlon."

"What's that?"

As Spike led Jess to a poster on the wall, Chelsea looked at Jake. "I'm sorry, I lost track of time."

"You look whipped."

"I overdid it. But I can't get down some of the gymnastic moves that Spike choreographed."

Jake glanced at his daughter and the trainer. "How old is he?"

"Spike?"

"Yeah."

"Late twenties, I think."

Jake's gaze pinned her. "Are you involved with him?"

"*What?*"

"I asked if you were involved with him. He's… friendly."

The corners of her mouth quirked. "Me and Spike?"

Jamming his hands into his pockets, Jake felt foolish. "Well, I, um, asked because of how Jess is looking at him."

"How's that?"

"Like a woman."

"He's a good man. He wouldn't do anything to hurt her."

"You didn't answer the question."

"No, Jake, we're not involved."

The whole uncomfortable night had turned into a disaster when Jess happened upon the Help Wanted sign on the desk as they'd been leaving. Within minutes his daughter had sewed up a receptionist's job for the rest of the summer. He'd quelled his admiration at how Chelsea had treated Jess as an adult, the interest she took in her. Instead, he'd focused on the irritation this little move would cost him. He wouldn't let Jess drive alone in downtown Rockford at night, so Jake would be at Chelsea's gym often….

The spurt of fear he'd felt returned and brought him up short. He stared at the woman in the front of the room who was infiltrating his life and his thoughts too much.

These feelings for her were not acceptable. Physical attraction was inappropriate for a lieutenant to feel for someone in his charge. Moreover, he couldn't afford to lose his objectivity with one of his crew again.

He'd done it once, and look what had happened—to his personal life and his career.

As she smiled pleasantly at the group, Jake was stunned by the realization of what could happen if he didn't keep a check on his response to Firefighter Whitmore.

WHEN SHE LOOKED over the elderly participants, Chelsea caught Jake scowling at her from the back.

The Scarlatta scowl, Jess had called it. She smiled in spite of Jake's expression. Compared to her father, Jessica was an open book. Like Delaney, Jess said exactly what she thought, and in the three days she'd worked at the Weight Room, Chelsea had come to like the girl. She'd discovered that Jessica worshiped the ground her father walked on, worried about his monklike lifestyle and feared leaving him to go to college. Though technically she lived with her mother, she spent most of her time with Jake.

Chelsea wondered what the woman who had caught her elusive lieutenant was like. Did he prefer blondes or brunettes? Petite women or tall women? Smart or dumb?

It hit her suddenly and with stunning force. What the hell was she doing thinking about him that way? *Damn you, girl, don't you ever learn?*

Ruthlessly suppressing all thoughts of Jake Scarlatta's taste in women, she walked to the center of the room and smiled at the residents' faces. Some were twinkling with expectation, one or two revealed hesitancy.

"I hope the video affirmed that at any age, physical fitness is important." She pointed to the board. "What I have in mind is a threefold program. First, we'll work on your aerobic fitness by walking outside when the weather's good. We should find a way to get some machines in here for rainy days and winter."

"I got one of those bikes that don't go anywhere in my apartment," Sergio Oliva said. "Jake can bring that down for us."

"My son has a treadmill he's trying to get rid of," Lawrence Steed added.

Dylan contributed from the side, "Quint Twelve has one of each of those we can donate. We just got new ones." He thought for a moment. "We also have an old weight machine you can have."

Mrs. Santori said proudly, "My Joey can haul those over."

Chelsea continued, "That brings me to number two. Like the woman in the video, we'll be doing some light weights." At the buzz among them, Chelsea said, "Only what you can handle. It's a slow-starting program, but bone density is improved by weight lifting." She grinned at them. "Besides, you're all young enough to pump some iron."

"I like that girl, Jake," Moses Santori said. "Let's keep her around."

Jake's eyes flashed with pleasure.

Chelsea tried to ignore the warmth kindling inside her. When had just a look of approval from him been able to do that?

"The third area we'll cover is stretching. For all these, you'll need to wear loose or stretchy clothing."

Participants made a couple of jokes about octogenarians in spandex, and unobtrusively, Chelsea checked out Jake's khaki shorts. Then her gaze traveled hungrily to his black T-shirt with two tiny beige stripes bisecting his chest. His outfit complemented his dark coloring beautifully.

She shook off the awareness. "Now, who's up for a walk?"

With some coaxing, everybody agreed. They were heading out the back door when Jake fell into step beside her. "You're good with them," he said as they paraded outside. A warm breeze ruffled the chestnut strands of Jake's thick hair. "Thanks again for volunteering to do this. It means a lot to me."

"I know it does. But I want to help them, too."

"So you said."

"They really love you, Jake. It must be like having

twenty grandparents.'' Even to her ears, her tone was wistful.

''Don't you have family, Chels?''

''Just me and Delaney.''

''What happened?''

''When?''

''To your parents, for starters.''

They followed the sidewalk around the complex. ''My father died when I was five. My mother married Delaney's father a year later. It didn't help much, though.''

''Help?''

''Yeah, we were still on the road. My dad was a baseball player—minor league, but he made it to Triple A before he died in a car accident. Tom Shaw moved just as much as my father. He was always playing gigs with his band.''

''No aunts or uncles? Cousins?''

''No, our mother and both our fathers were only children. We never saw much of our grandparents before they died because we were always on the go. I do have a few of the woodworking pieces my grandpa made, though.''

Jake glanced at her. ''So you want stability for yourself now?''

''I never said that.''

''You did—indirectly.''

She shook her head in exasperation. ''How does our conversation always get back to me?''

''Beats me.''

''Let's talk about that captaincy exam,'' she said. ''The one I got the—''

''Oh, look, I think Sergio is limping. I'd better go make sure he's okay.'' Jake jogged off down the pavement.

''Coward,'' she yelled after him.

Chelsea had called Jake that on their last night shift, too, and for the same reason....

"What's this?" he'd asked as she'd handed him papers. He'd been on late watch, and she'd come out about three with a handful of documents.

"I was at headquarters today getting some insurance forms and I saw these on the counter."

Frowning, he'd scanned the papers. The bleakness in his eyes when he looked at her almost made her wish she hadn't gotten them. "I'm not taking the captaincy test."

"Why?"

"A lot of reasons."

"Give me one."

"I'd have to move if I made captain." Since every shift had a lieutenant but each house only had one captain and Ed Knight held the position in Quint 12, Jake would be forced to change houses. "I don't want to leave my group."

"It might be worth it."

He stared at her. "Maybe. But I'm not going to do it. I gave up those dreams a long time ago."

"Yeah, well, maybe that was a mistake." She sat on the desk and swung her feet.

He picked up his coffee and sipped it.

"You're the best officer I've ever worked under. You're only forty, Jake. You could still be battalion chief if you wanted to."

"I don't want to."

"You know what? I think you're a coward."

"What?"

"Afraid to risk."

"I take risks every day on the job."

"Not emotional ones. Go for the exam."

"Read my lips, Whitmore—I don't want this."

She shook her head. "A liar *and* a coward. Jeez, who would have thought...."

A HALF HOUR later, Chelsea was with Dylan and Beth in the common area of Dutch Towers watching Jake escort Mrs. Lowe to the elevator. The old woman reached up and gave him a big hug. Something shifted inside Chelsea at the sight; she turned away to distract herself.

Dylan lifted his nose from the book it had been buried in and asked, "How about this question. What's the NYFD training academy called?"

Beth rolled her eyes. "The Rock. That one's a snap. You're going soft on us, O'Roarke."

"All right, smarty. What did they call firefighters before the common usage of SCBA masks?"

"Even I know that," Chelsea said. "Leather lungs."

"Jeez, I can't score tonight."

"Well, let's go home and see what we can do about that, Boy Wonder."

Dylan glanced at the baby. "Oh, sure. As soon as we get comfy, hungry Tim will wake up."

"I just fed him. He's out for the count." Beth smiled at her son.

Chelsea checked her watch. "Hey, I've got an idea. It's only eight o'clock. Why don't I take Timmy home with me, and you guys go out on the town for a while? You can pick him up later."

Beth said, "Really?"

"Yeah, he'll be fine. France and I watched him when he was littler than this."

Dylan's eyes twinkled at Beth. "Maybe we can go dancing."

"Maybe."

"We can stop home first and change."

Beth shook her head. "If we stop home, we'll never get out of there."

Dylan pulled her close and whispered something in her ear that made his wife giggle.

"You sure you want to do this?" Beth asked Chelsea. "He can be a pain if he wakes up and won't go back to sleep."

"I think I can handle it."

"There's diapers and a bottle in there if he's hungry," Beth said, handing her a diaper bag. "We'll call you and let you know where we are."

Dylan kissed Beth's ear. "Maybe."

Chelsea pointed to the baby's carrier. "This is a car seat, too, isn't it?"

"Yeah," Dylan said. "Just strap him in the back."

"All right. Now get out of here."

The O'Roarkes beat a hasty retreat just as Jake came back. He glanced at the baby with raised brows. "They forgot their son."

Chelsea chuckled. "No, they didn't. I'm baby-sitting."

"You are?"

"Yeah, just for a few hours."

"Hmm." His look was intense. Chelsea feared he was going to ask to help. For a second she created a vivid fantasy of the two of them, cuddling up, watching the baby.

"Well, I'd best be going." She pretended to concentrate on collecting her belongings.

"You'll need help getting him to the car."

She looked up. His face was neutral. "Oh, okay."

After some fancy maneuvering, they managed to secure a still-sleeping Timmy into the back of Chelsea's Camaro. She glanced at Jake before she got into her car. "Thanks."

"Chelsea? Do you wa—"

"I've got to go. I appreciate the help."

Without waiting for a response, she slid into the front seat. She could see his legs tense as his hand grasped the top of the door. It seemed to take an eternity before he closed the door. When he did, she breathed a sigh of relief.

She stuck the key into the ignition and twisted it. Nothing. Damn, she'd been having trouble with the starter and had an appointment to get it fixed tomorrow. *Please, God, let it work tonight.*

She tried again.

Still nothing.

Cursing the fates, she dropped her head to the steering wheel.

CHELSEA OPENED the door to her house as Jake followed her, carrying the baby seat with a sleeping Timmy O'Roarke in it. Her hands shook at the intimacy of the scene—a man and a woman bringing a baby home. For a minute, some of her youthful dreams besieged her; she'd thought she wanted a good job, a good man and a baby or two. Damn, she wished this hadn't happened tonight!

Jake set the carrier on the floor in the center of the living room between the leather couches. Then he turned to her.

His face was cast in shadows, but it was nonetheless clear that some conflict was smoldering inside him. "Can I do anything before I go?"

"No, it's under—"

A piercing wail split the air. Jake gave a start, and Chelsea jumped; they both laughed. "The kid's awake," she said, circling Jake and bending to pick up Timmy.

Quickly she unsnapped him and scooped him up. "Shh, sweetheart, it's okay. Aunt Chelsea's here."

She began to walk him. The crying continued. Frowning, she started to croon. The crying got louder.

"I know he's just been fed. And Dylan changed him right before you came over." Jiggling him up and down, she whispered again, "Shh, baby, shh."

Timmy began to cry in earnest, then, and her heartbeat escalated. Could something be wrong? Oh, God, not with this baby, please. Dylan and Beth—

"Here, give him to me," Jake said. "Let me try." Jake reached for the baby and placed him against his shoulder; Timmy nuzzled into him. And stopped crying immediately.

Chelsea's mouth fell open. "What'd you do?"

He shrugged. "I don't know. He always reacts to me like this. I pick him up and he stops bawling."

"That's odd."

"Apparently not." He soothed Timmy's back with a big, strong hand. "When Jessica was a baby, she was the same way with Ben Cordaro." His face lightened, his gray eyes amused. "Once when I was on nights, she cried so hard Nancy got scared and called Ben to come over. Jess stopped crying right away for him."

"I've never heard of that."

He shrugged. "Some babies just have good taste, I guess." He glanced around the room. "So, what should we do?"

They both knew what he was asking. Being thrown together like this wasn't good. They were making a valiant attempt to avoid it—or at least they would as soon as things quieted down.

Chelsea suggested, "Well, why don't you rock him for a bit, then we'll try to put him down. You can leave when he's asleep."

"Sure, whatever you say." He scanned the living room impassively. "Where's the rocker?"

"Upstairs in the sitting room off my bedroom, remember?"

The impassive mask slipped. "I remember."

Quickly she turned. They proceeded upstairs and down the hall. Dusk pervaded the back room, enveloping them in a surrealistic glow. As Jake sought the white wicker rocker and sat down, Chelsea could see Timmy's little hands clutch the black T-shirt. Jake settled himself and brushed the baby's head with his lips. Chelsea's stomach flip-flopped.

"This brings back memories, I'll bet," she said.

"Yeah," he replied.

After dragging out the cradle her grandfather had made for her, Chelsea crossed to a trunk in the corner and drew out a soft blanket. She used that and a pillow to build a nest for the baby. Then she sat on the couch, her legs curled under her.

"Do you want to have kids?" he asked quietly.

"I did."

"Did?"

Running a hand through her hair, she blew out an exasperated breath. "This stuff with Billy has really soured me on men."

He frowned.

"I know, I know, they're not all alike." She touched her cheek. "But it's hard to forget how he turned on me, how I thought I could trust him and I couldn't. What if I really fell in love and the man did that to me?"

He nodded. "There's nothin' like somebody you care about turning on you."

She waited.

"When Danny turned on me, it felt like high treason. I couldn't handle it. I shut everybody out for a long time. Including my wife."

"Is that why you divorced?"

"Uh-huh." He stared into space. "I tried the same with my buddies. But Ben Cordaro wouldn't let me. I maintained some male friendships, but that was about it. And Jess, of course."

"No women?"

He shook his head.

"How long have you been divorced?"

"Eight years."

"I can't believe nobody's snagged you."

Something flared in his eyes, and she cursed her tongue. Occasionally the old Chelsea surfaced. She stood. "Well, let's try to put him down now."

He rose, walked to the cradle, eased Timmy away from his chest and placed him in the bed. The baby stirred, and Jake tipped the finely crafted wooden bed back and forth, soothing Timmy with his other hand. When he quieted, Jake kept up the motion for a moment, then straightened. All was silent. Jake smiled at Chelsea over the cradle. She smiled back.

The phone rang.

And Timmy began to cry.

Ten minutes later Jake was rocking him in the chair again. It had been Dylan on the phone, unabashedly telling Chelsea he and his wife could be reached at home; he asked if everything was okay and what time they should pick up the kid. After she hung up, she turned the Yankees game on low and offered Jake something to drink. They sipped from bottles of beer, looking at the screen.

"Think they got a chance for the pennant?" Chelsea asked, sitting on the floor and leaning against the couch.

"Yep. I'm hoping for another sweep like in ninety-eight."

"My father loved the Yankees. He always wanted to play for them."

"What was he like?"

"Young, handsome, not around much."

"Did you go to his games?"

"As many as I could. I had to go to school."

"Did he pitch?"

"Yeah." She focused on the TV. "Wow, look at that. Paul O'Neil caught it barehanded."

"Did he teach you to pitch?"

"Yep."

"Chels, I—"

"Look, isn't your arm getting tired? I could hold him."

She was trying to get rid of him, Jake thought. She didn't like the intimacy of the situation, the direction of the talk. And he shouldn't, either. Just as he shouldn't like watching the game with her or the fact that she was fun and interesting and bright.

He should go. He knew that. So he stood. "All right, let's give Pavarotti here another shot." Gently he placed Timmy in the cradle. This time, Timmy didn't need the phone to wake him. The motion did it.

Chelsea beat Jake to the cradle and picked the baby up. "I'll change him. That's probably it."

It wasn't.

"Should I try a bottle?"

"Go ahead, but didn't Beth just feed him?"

She rummaged through the diaper bag, found the bottle and tried to stick it in Timmy's mouth. He spit it out at her as if it was poison.

Exasperated, she looked at Jake. "I don't know what to do."

"Here, give him to me." He took Timmy and cuddled him. Of course the kid stopped crying. Jake had to smile. It felt kind of good.

"Jake, you can't hold him until eleven o'clock."

"Want me to leave you alone with a screaming baby?"

"God, no. I forgot kids could cry at that decibel level."

After another few minutes of rocking, Jake said, "I've got an idea. Lay a couple of blankets on the floor there." Chelsea did. "Now grab me a few pillows." Following his directions, she padded a six-by-six area. Jake dropped to his knees, then lay back against the pillows with the baby. He stayed that way for a few minutes, stretched out with Timmy on his chest, then eased the child to the floor very close to his body. Timmy could still feel and smell him. He placed a hand on Timmy's back and soothed him when he stirred.

Miraculously Timmy stayed asleep.

Chelsea breathed a sigh of relief.

"There, now I don't have to hold him. I'll just stay close."

Chelsea smiled, and Jake's insides clenched. "Grab me my beer, woman," he said gruffly.

She arched a brow.

"Hey, better do as you're told or I'll get up."

She laughed quietly and reached for the beer.

Jake and Chelsea watched the game like old buddies, sipping beer and talking intermittently. Jake felt his eyes grow heavy, and he sank into the pillows. It was the fourth inning, the Yankees were ahead and he'd had a beer. His eyes drifted shut.

"Jake."

He gripped the pillow. God, he was having this wonderful dream. He knew it was a dream, but he didn't want to let it go. Chelsea was dressed in the ice-blue negligée, but her body was burning with heat as he slid the shift off her creamy shoulders—

"Jake, wake up. It's almost eleven. Beth and Dylan will be here any minute."

He stirred but didn't open his eyes. Her hair shimmered around her bare shoulders, and his fingers went to it, buried themselves in the heavy mass. Hmm, so soft. He raised his thumb to her mouth and outlined her lips. Even softer.

He moaned.

Chelsea said, "Jake, please, wake up."

Reluctantly he opened his eyes. She was kneeling above him, like in the dream. But she was dressed in a yellow T-shirt and shorts instead of blue satin. He reached for her, anyway. "Chels?"

She swallowed hard. "You fell asleep."

He blinked. "For how long?"

"About an hour."

"Oh, jeez, I'm sorry." His hands were still on her. "I haven't been sleeping well at night." Fully awake, he glanced to the side. Timmy snuggled against him like Jess used to do on the bumper in the crib. "Did Paul Revere sleep, too?"

"Yep, the whole time."

He chuckled, and she tried to pull away. Sobering, his grip tightened, causing her to lean further over his chest. "I was dreaming."

She stared at him.

"About you."

"Jake, don't." She tried to draw back.

"Wait a second." One hand left her shoulder and traveled to her hair. His fingers threaded through it. In comparison, the dream had been a weak preview. The golden locks were silky and soft and unbelievably seductive.

"Jake…"

His other hand went to her mouth. "Shh, I know. Just for a minute." The pad of his thumb rubbed gently, thoroughly.

Her stiff shoulders softened. Their eyes locked. When his lowered, he could see her breasts beginning to rise and fall fast. His gaze traveled to her lips.

His hand tightened in her hair.

She leaned forward.

He came an inch off the pillows.

And then the doorbell rang.

And the baby started to wail.

CHAPTER TEN

LIKE A HEAD OF STATE leaving a peace conference, Local 601 union president Sammy Samuels strode out of the meeting with Jake, Chief Talbot and his two deputies and headed for the firehouse kitchen, where they would eat lunch with the crew. The long table had been set for twelve, and the spicy smell of oregano and tomato sauce wafted through the building.

Taking a seat, Sammy motioned for the others to sit near him. "Quick, before the ladies come. Listen to this one. A fireman came home one day and told his wife, 'We've implemented a new system at the fire station. Bell one rings, and we all put on our turnout gear. Bell two rings, and we head for the trucks. Bell three opens the bay door, and we're gone. So, from now on we're going to run this house the same way. When I say Bell One, I want you to strip naked. When I say Bell Two, I want you to jump into bed, and when I say Bell Three, we're going to make love all night.' The next day, he came home from work and yelled, 'Bell One.' His wife took off all her clothes. He then yelled, 'Bell Two,' and his wife jumped into bed. Then he yelled, 'Bell Three,' and they began to make love. After two minutes, his wife yelled, 'Bell Four!' The husband asked, 'What's Bell Four?' And the wife replied, 'More hose! You're nowhere near the fire!'"

Everybody laughed, and Jake relaxed. Though Chelsea and the chief's secretary weren't in the kitchen yet, he was wary of sexually explicit jokes in the firehouse; they could be a powder keg, depending on the circumstances. This story was cute, though, and harmless. Chelsea would have laughed.

Chelsea, whom he'd almost kissed two nights ago.

His hands curled into fists. How could he have been so stupid? The memory of what she felt like poised over him and where it might have led was still with him today and had kept him awake for two nights running. He'd tried to outdistance it by lifting weights and jogging, but exercise hadn't helped. Even dinner last night with Ben and Diana and Ben's parents, Gus and Grace, hadn't driven it from his mind. He wanted a woman, wanted Chelsea, but he couldn't allow himself to pursue her. Too much was at risk. As he took his seat at the table, he was glad for a good cause to distract him.

Though the reason they were having this big powwow was a hell of a thing to happen.

Peter called from the stove, "Get everybody, will you, Mick? We're about ready."

"And what did our own Julia Child make today?" Chief Talbot asked. Huff's cooking was legendary throughout the department.

Peter glanced over his shoulder. "Spaghetti and meatballs."

Jake was surprised by the meatballs. Once the guys had stopped ribbing Chelsea about not eating red meat, they'd cooked accordingly, substituting chicken for her portion, often choosing fish for all of them. Peter had been especially considerate. Oh, well, she could go without protein for one meal.

Damn, what the hell was he doing worrying about her diet?

As he listened to the official banter from the brass, he admitted to himself he knew the answer. He cared about Chelsea. In more ways than were good for either of them.

During this last bout of insomnia, he'd finally realized his feelings ran deep. It wasn't just that he was physically attracted to her, though she regularly set off fireworks in his body these days. It was that he liked being with her, sharing things with her and having her in his life at the firehouse—and outside of it.

As if conjured up by his thoughts, she appeared in the doorway; though she'd obviously just washed, her face was flushed and her T-shirt sweaty. Shrugging into the light blue dress shirt and buttoning it, she teased Don. "I won, Diaz. You do my cleanup all week."

"How the hell did you learn how to shoot hoops like that?"

"I'll never tell." She glanced around, frowning at the RFD officers and union members. Usually she was reserved around visitors, careful to stay in the background, like a student in class who didn't want to be called on.

"We having a department meeting here today?" Diaz joked.

"Nah, I met with these guys this morning," Jake told them. "I'll explain it over lunch. It concerns this firehouse."

"Chow's on." Huff stood back from the counter where he'd assembled the food.

They all headed for the serving line. Out of the corner of his eye, Jake saw Huff approach Chelsea. He said something in her ear, and she smiled broadly. Jake felt that smile zing all the way to his gut; he turned to the food.

Determinedly he didn't look at her again until she sat— at the other end of the table. They were avoiding each other and had been all morning except for the two calls they'd had where they were forced to work together. He glanced at her plate; it was filled with meatballs. Salad was the only other thing she'd taken.

Mick noticed, too. "You don't like pasta, Whitmore?"

"I love it."

"There's none on your dish."

"I'm only eating protein, vegetables and fruit this week."

"Why?"

She flushed. Jake opened his mouth to deflect her from the hot seat, but caught himself. What the hell was he doing?

"I'm competing in a triathlon Thursday night. So I'm bulking up."

"Really? I been thinking about doin' one of those myself." Joey was heavy into weight lifting and keeping in shape.

Chelsea's brows rose. "Yeah? If you want to talk about it later, find me."

"Okay."

Huff was the last to sit. "So," he said in typical policeman, no-nonsense manner, "why's the brass here?"

From the end of the table, Jake addressed his crew. "I asked them to come because I want to start a search to find a runaway teenager. Chief Talbot gave his approval this morning."

"I don't understand," Diaz said. "Why would we do that?"

"She's the daughter of a fellow firefighter in Illinois. I was at the union office yesterday when Rick Mayfield called to say his fourteen-year-old daughter, Suzy, ran away ten days ago. They got a tip that she was in Rockford. He and his wife are en route—" Jake glanced at the clock "—as we speak."

"Jeez, a fourteen-year-old's been gone ten days," Diaz commented. "My Katie's fourteen."

"What can we do for them?" Mick asked.

"First, we've set up a headquarters here in the back room of the fire station. Phones, a fax and a computer will be transferred there after lunch. On- and off-duty people will man it. Calls at night can be transferred to the watch room." He paused. "I'll oversee it."

"Sounds good to me," Joey said. "What do you need help with?"

"Well, we've got a sign-up sheet that's gonna go to all the stations today. Off-duty firefighters will canvass the streets with pictures, hand out leaflets for the next couple of days and man the phones here." He nodded to Mary Sokel, the chief's secretary. "Mary's been released from her duties today to do some phone work, like contacting the missing person's bureau and calling the newspaper and TV and radio stations to get coverage."

The guys all knew Mary. She often came over for lunch and was one of their favorite people.

The union leader said, "No one's required to participate, but I think it's good PR. It's also a way we can help out a brother. The local's putting both manpower and some benevolent money for copying, et cetera, behind this."

"Those poor parents," Chelsea said. Jake had avoided looking at her as he spoke, but he glanced over now and caught the sadness in her eyes. "Where are they going to stay?"

"We talked the Hyatt into putting them up free for a few nights, but that's only temporary."

"Francey's house has been empty since she got married," Chelsea told them. Jake saw Joey stiffen. "I'm sure she wouldn't mind if they stayed there."

Jake nodded.

"I'll take care of it," Chelsea said.

Talk continued through the meal. Huff had said almost nothing, which wasn't unusual; he was normally reticent. So Jake was surprised when he stood to get another helping of food and asked, "You guys like the meatballs?"

"Yeah," Diaz called. "Get me a few more."

"Bring the bowl," the chief said. "We'll pass 'em around."

Jake caught Chelsea's grin. He also noticed she took another portion. When everybody was chowing down like the meatballs were manna from heaven, Huff said, "Turkey's great, like you said, Whitmore."

"Mmm," she answered, busily chewing.

"Turkey?" Joey asked. "Whaddaya mean?"

All the men looked at their second helpings.

Huff announced, "Used ground turkey, instead of beef. Better for your arteries."

"Hell, my wife tried that once, and it tasted terrible." Diaz studied his plate. "I told her never to cook nothing like that again."

"I'll give her the recipe from *The Healthy Firehouse Cookbook*."

No one said anything, then Diaz quipped, "So long as we don't have stewed chickweed and acorns for lunch, it's cool with me."

Chelsea grinned as she sank her teeth into another meatball.

WHEN CHELSEA'S RELIEF arrived at the end of the day, she headed to the back room, a ten-by-ten square with a couple of windows, two desks and chairs and various machines humming away. It would function as the command post for Operation Suzy. Chelsea shuddered at the thought of a kid so young living on the streets. When she entered the room, Mary was hanging up the phone.

Her kind brown eyes smiled, belying her Attila the Hun reputation. She threaded graying hair off her face and said, "That's it. The flyers are done and the night shift is going to bundle them. We're circulating the sign-up to all the firehouses for volunteers to canvas the streets." She glanced at the clock, then her gaze swept Chelsea. "Are you going to be around a while?"

"For a little bit. Why?"

"Here are the lists of what I've done. Could you give them to Jake? My granddaughter has a dance recital in two hours, or I'd stick around."

"Sure."

The woman gave Chelsea a pat on the shoulder and hustled out of the room.

Chelsea sat and closed her eyes. *Give them to Jake.* Damn, she was trying not to *think* about Jake. But she could still see his face as he stared at her mouth and grasped her shoulders like a man who wanted to— She cut off the thought, just as she'd done for two full days— and nights—since she'd almost kissed him.

She'd almost kissed her lieutenant.

Smart move, Whitmore. Jumping from the pot to the fire. You blew it at your last house by getting involved with a fellow firefighter. Let's top that by picking the officer this time.

She sighed. She hadn't exactly *picked* Jake. It had just happened slowly over the past couple of months, like the way spring crept up on her, or dawn rose over the horizon. First she'd been impressed by his gentle but firm leadership. Then she'd been touched by his concern for her fitting in, his fairness in helping her do it. The night Billy attacked her and Jake had come to her sealed the deal. Along the way she'd noticed his world-class muscles and tall, lean length. Add to it how great he was with Jessica and Timmy, and she'd been caught by a web that had Jake Scarlatta's name on it.

Damn.

With more force than necessary, she punched out Delaney's number. Her sister answered on the first ring. "Delaney Shaw."

"Hi, Laney, it's me. I need a favor."

"Another one?"

Chelsea chuckled. "How's Derek doing?"

"He's a tough nut to crack. But he adores that lieutenant of yours, so he's giving me a fair shake. We're making progress."

That lieutenant of yours. "I owe you for that."

"No, I *want* to help. Besides, Scarlatta's payin' me big bucks for it."

"Oh."

Delaney laughed. "I offered to do it free, as a favor to you, but he absolutely refused."

"Jake's got his principles."

"So sis, what do you need?"

"Nothing big. The RFD's gotten involved in searching for a runaway who's been seen in Rockford. I thought maybe you could give us some pointers on what else we should do." Chelsea filled her in on the steps they'd already taken.

Delaney said, "That's easy. Got a fax there?"

"Yep." She gave her sister the number.

"I'll send over the names of organizations that offer shelter to runaways and a list of where kids on the street hang out. Will that help?"

"Yeah, a lot."

"Chels?"

"Hmm?"

"Is everything else okay? You sound funny."

"I just haven't slept well the last two nights."

"I thought that was getting better."

It was, before I almost kissed Jake.

"It comes and goes. Listen, you'll be at the triathlon Thursday night, won't you?"

"Wouldn't miss seeing my sister go for the gold."

"Thanks." Chelsea sighed. "I love you, Delaney." Her voice caught.

"Me, too. You sure you're okay?"

"Yeah, I'm fine. I'll look for the fax about helping Suzy."

"If there's anything else I can do, let me know."

When Chelsea hung up, she buried her face in her hands.

"You're not fine."

Startled, she swiveled in the seat.

Jake was leaning up against the doorjamb. "I overheard."

"Overheard?"

He came closer and stood above her. Tipping her chin, he said, "You look tired."

"Well, you heard me say I haven't been sleeping well." Chelsea searched the hard planes of his face. "You, neither, I can tell."

He swallowed. "Since the other night." The look he gave her seared her insides. She wanted to weep for what she felt. Dropping his hand, he nodded to the phone. "What's Delaney sending us?"

She told him.

His eyes glowed like coals burning low. "Really? You did that for us?"

She nodded. "Finding this girl means a lot to you, doesn't it?"

It was his turn to nod.

"Because of Jess?"

"Yeah, and Derek."

"Delaney's seen him."

Jake gave her a grin that made her stomach somersault. "He said she steamrollered right over his objections to seeing a shrink."

"She's good at what she does."

"Apparently. Of course the fact that Derek thinks she's drop-dead gorgeous doesn't hurt."

"Hey, whatever works." She looked away, gestured to the desk. "Mary left you some lists."

"Well, I'd better check them out."

"You'd better."

He crossed to the other side of the room. She said hesitantly, "I can help here for a while. I don't have a training session until six."

He cleared his throat and sat at the desk. His look was full of feeling. "Do me a favor."

"Of course."

"Leave."

She angled her head in surprise; then his reasoning hit her. He didn't want to risk being alone with her.

"All right." She glanced at the desk. "But I'm going to help with this search."

"That means a lot to me."

She stood. "It means a lot to me, too."

ON THURSDAY NIGHT, Jake pulled open the door to Our Lady of Mercy House, a popular haven in the city for teenage runaways, according to Delaney Shaw. Three stories high, the old brick building had been an elegant residence at one time. Jake preceded Ben Cordaro into the foyer and to the reception desk. There was a neat living room to the right, a hallway to the left, a staircase straight ahead. Though worn, the furnishings were tidy.

A tall, slender blonde looked at him. "May I help you?"

"Andrea?"

"Hi, Jake."

He stared at Mick Murphy's wife. "It's been a while."

"A few months."

"I didn't know you were working here."

She shook her head in dismay. "So Mick still hasn't told you guys I went back to work. I'd have thought with Chelsea Whitmore's influence, he'd be less Neanderthal at the firehouse these days."

"No, he hasn't told us." Jake turned to Ben. "Ben Cordaro, this is Murphy's wife, Andrea."

Offering his hand, Ben said, "Hi. I've seen you at functions, I think."

She nodded. "What brings you here, Jake?"

"Hasn't Mick told you about Operation Suzy?"

Andrea flushed. "Uh, no, Mick and I haven't...aren't...well we've been busy."

Jake frowned, picking up on the vibes that something was wrong between Mick and Andrea. But he said only, "Aren't we all." He explained their mission.

Ben handed her a photo. "Have you seen her?"

Immediately Andrea's big blue eyes widened. "Why, yes. She came here last night. But she was gone in the morning."

Jake's heartbeat escalated. "She say anything?"

"We talked a bit. She seemed upset. Her running away had something to do with her father."

Oh, God. Jake's immediate thought was abuse. Would they find this little girl only to send her back into a nightmare?

"It's not what you're thinking, Jake," Andrea said, as if reading his mind. "She seemed worried about her father, and her mother, who, I take it, drinks."

Surprised, Jake scowled.

"It was pretty dicey stuff, more than I could handle as a social worker. She needs psychological help."

"If we can find her." Ben's look was grim. All the firefighters with daughters were having trouble with this case. "Here." He handed Andrea the department's hotline number. "Keep this handy. Call us if you hear from her again."

"I will."

As they turned away, Andrea beckoned Jake back. "Is Mick all right? At work?"

"Yeah, fine, his usual cheerful self. Why?"

"Sometimes I worry about him. He's not happy I've gone back to work. It seems he thinks it reflects poorly on him as a breadwinner if his wife brings in an income."

"Mick's old-fashioned in a lot of ways."

"Yeah, I guess." Andrea smiled. "I'd like to meet this Chelsea Whitmore. Maybe she can lighten Mick up. She's doing a good job, from what I hear."

"She is," Jake said tightly.

Jake and Ben left the shelter. Outside, the hot July air enveloped them. A blanket of stars twinkled as they headed to their car to go to the next shelter on the list.

"So, Chelsea's working out all right?" Ben's tone was nonchalant, but underneath Jake caught fatherly concern and battalion chief worry.

As Jake made perfunctory remarks to Ben about Chelsea's performance, he saw her, in his mind, crawl through the pipe and face the guys haughtily; he pictured her tending to the gunshot victim like Florence Nightingale; he heard her voice over the radio warning about the newspapers in the old English teacher's house. "Yeah, she's a good firefighter."

"Jessica's crazy about her."

"I know."

She was in fact, at the triathlon competition right now. The one Jake refused to attend when Jess asked him to go with her. The place he'd rather be right now more than anywhere else in the world.

But he'd forced himself not to attend.

The disclosing of events in their lives had to stop. Then

the emotional connection would abate. Which would eventually stifle the physical thing that seethed between them like low flames waiting for enough oxygen to flare out of control. He intended to smother it.

It had to stop, because the consequences of pursuing a relationship that wasn't professional with Firefighter Whitmore were untenable. He knew from the past what could happen, and he'd be damned if he'd go down that road again. Especially because of the decision he'd finally made...

"Ben," he said carefully. "I've been thinking about taking the captaincy exam."

CHELSEA JOGGED into the arena of the Dome, a huge circular area surrounded by bleachers. She could almost feel the tension in the air as contestants, judges and fans prepared for the second event in the triathlon—the two-hundred-meter sprint.

She'd beaten out everybody on the weight lifting, but that was the easiest for her. The sprint, however, wouldn't be a piece of cake, she thought as she bent over one knee and stretched. Ditto for the gymnastics routine. In fact, she was most worried about that one.

Blank your mind, she told herself as she waited. *Don't think about winning. Just do your best.*

When the competitors were introduced, the fans roared, Delaney, Spike, Francey and Alex, Beth and Dylan and Jessica among them.

Jessica. Who'd shyly asked if she could come....

"I know I've only worked here a couple of weeks but I'd love to see you compete. If I wouldn't be imposing..." She had so many of Jake's mannerisms—the slight tilt of her chin when she was concerned, the casual way she shrugged off most annoyances, the gray eyes.

"I'd love you to be there, kiddo," Chelsea had said, wrapping an arm around Jessica's shoulder....

An announcer's voice came over the loudspeaker. "Ladies. Take your places."

Chelsea was in the first heat; she found her place and nudged her toe to the very edge of the starting line.

"Get on your mark, get set...go!"

Taking off like the wind, Chelsea reached top speed in seconds, her longs legs eating up the distance. Rounding the corner, she summoned more energy, like she did when she faced an unexpected turn in firefighting. She could see another entrant coming up on her left.

She pushed harder.

The finish line was just ahead. With one last Jesse Owens-like burst of speed, Chelsea broke the ribbon a split second ahead of her nearest competitor.

Sucking in air and letting it out in great whooshes, she glanced at the bleachers, where her personal cheering section was standing and clapping. She smiled and gave them a little wave. It was fun having them here, sharing this with them.

I wish Jake had come.

But she'd promised herself there would be no more confidences, no more sharing of their lives outside the fire station, no more closeness, physical or otherwise.

He'd found her before she left work today at the lockers. No one else was around. He'd stood a few feet away, as if afraid to come closer. Since the sparks between them seemed to ignite when they were in proximity, it was just as well.

"I wanted to wish you luck tonight," he said.

"Thanks."

He hadn't moved, just stood there and stared at her. Finally he said, "I can't go. I want to, but I can't."

She'd been shocked by his statement and the volatile

emotion on his face. So she tried to defuse them. "Oh, well, I don't expect you to." She gestured to encompass the rest of the firehouse. "It goes a little above and beyond the call of du—"

In a flash, he was next to her, his fingers against her mouth. "Don't."

She remained silent. His heat scorched her.

"We both know what's happening here," he whispered.

She stared at him. "Please don't say it aloud."

After a long moment, he stepped back. "All right. Knock 'em dead, Whitmore."

He'd left then, and she had felt a sting of tears as she watched him go...

Glancing at the stands again, she saw his daughter waving to her. She waved back and felt her eyes sting again.

AT TEN THAT NIGHT, Jake unlocked the door to his house, crossed to the kitchen and, juggling the mail, grabbed a beer and headed upstairs. It was cool and lonely inside, but it was late enough to come home now. Feeling like a kid who needed rules and regulations, he hadn't allowed himself to be alone until he was sure the triathlon was over.

Sinking onto his favorite leather chair by the window of the top floor of his house, he took a slug of beer and closed his eyes, remembering the last beer he'd drunk. He'd been stretched out on the floor of her sitting room, and she'd fetched him one like his own personal— He felt something plop in his lap. Hester Two. The kitten waited patiently every night for him to come home, then bothered the hell out of him until bedtime. She was a constant reminder of Chelsea.

He ran his hand down her velvety fur. "Hi, sweetheart, how ya doin' tonight?"

Hester pushed her head into his chin and purred madly. At almost four months old, she was still a runt.

"Think she won?" Jake asked the cat. "Think Spike is celebrating with her?"

What *would* she be doing afterward? He glanced at the clock. No, he wouldn't call her.

Settling Hester in his lap, he grabbed the mail. Bills. A form from Cornell. He read the letters carefully, then riffled through the catalogs. Jess got so much junk mail here he could hardly... What the hell?

The last catalog stared at him. Victoria's Secret.

On the cover was a lithe but shapely model. Long-limbed. Muscular. Blond. Wearing scarlet panties.

Ones he'd seen before. Ones he'd touched.

His hand went to the picture. Slowly, as if it were Chelsea, he outlined the lacy red band. He could almost feel her skin burn his fingertips. The smell of her lotion tinged the air, tantalizing him. Working its way down the page, his finger skimmed the juncture where leg met hip. He closed his eyes, imagining Chelsea hot and ready.

Swearing vilely, he bolted from the chair, dislodging the cat and sending the mail spilling to the floor.

"Son of a—"

The phone cut off his tirade. He crossed to it. "Scarlatta."

"Dad, it's me. Jess."

His heart started to pump fast. Suddenly he wanted very badly for Chelsea to have won, for all her hard work to have paid off.

"Hi, honey," he said casually. "How'd it go?"

"Oh, Daddy, it was great! Chelsea won!"

He let out a pent-up breath. "That's terrific."

"You should have seen her. She was awesome. What a body."

Oh, God.

"They invited me out to eat with them, but I couldn't go. I've got to get up…"

He missed the rest of Jess's words.

They? He had to know. "Oh, who went?"

"Francey and Alex after they dropped me off. Delaney and this really hunky guy. Dylan and Beth. And Chelsea and Spike."

"I see. Well, I'm glad you had a good time."

"Chelsea's so cool, Dad. I wish Mom was more like her."

Oh, Lord, he couldn't do this tonight. "Do you? Maybe we'll talk about that sometime." In a million years. "It's late. If you have to get up early, you'd better get to bed."

"Okay. See you tomorrow."

"Yeah."

"Daddy?"

"Hmm?"

"You okay? You sound…sad."

"Nope, I'm fine, pumpkin. Don't worry about me."

"I love you."

"I love you, too."

Jake hung up. He was fine. Just peachy. Couldn't be better.

Turning, he kicked the wastebasket halfway across the room.

STARS WINKED at her through the skylights as Chelsea entered her bathroom. She lit some candles, set a glass of wine on the edge of the tub and climbed into steaming water scented with Sinful Nights bath salts. Immediately she regretted her impulse. It was the fragrance Jake had used when he'd drawn her bath the night Billy attacked her. When he'd held her on this very floor.

Closing her eyes, she sighed as the hot water soothed

her tortured muscles. She felt like a gladiator after a battle. Maybe she was getting too old for grueling competition.

You do it to fill the emptiness in your life, Delaney had told her with all the subtlety of a train wreck.

Her sister was right. But at least Chelsea had won. If only she could choose her prize. She knew without thinking what it would be...

Jake behind her in the bathtub, her back against his hard chest, his big hands gliding down her arms, raising goose bumps on her skin. Then his hands sliding around her waist, moving up, touching her breasts, kneading them. One hand disappearing into the water, his fingers creating magic as they—

She was startled out of the fantasy by one of the cats batting open the door to the bathroom. She shooed Blaze away and reached for her wine. As she sipped, one tiny tear trembled on her eyelashes, then found its way down her cheek.

No use in crying about it, her mother had said when Chelsea would beg for them not to move again so she could stay in the same school.

She and Jake were not meant for each other, and she knew it.

Shake it off. Let it go. Get over it.

She climbed out of the tub and dried herself quickly. In her bedroom, she drew open a drawer in the dresser her grandfather had made, bypassed the ice-blue satin she'd worn the night Jake had been here. Enough reminders. Enough surrendering to memories.

Donning a yellow nightshirt Delaney had given her printed with First God created man, then He had a better idea, she slipped into bed and shut off the lights. She couldn't prevent one more renegade tear tracking down her cheek.

But she brushed it away and willed herself to sleep.

CHAPTER ELEVEN

CHELSEA WAS IN better spirits when she entered the fire station two days after the triathlon. She'd taken a couple of days off—she had a lot of furlough accumulated—and it had been just what she needed, time away from work and time to restore her body. She was happy that she'd won the event; she'd also won the internal battle to keep from calling or seeking out Jake Scarlatta for any personal reason.

"Drum roll, everybody." She heard the words as she walked into the kitchen at seven.

Trumpet blasts from a CD greeted her.

"Come right in, Ms. Triathlon Winner." Mick smiled at her from beside a chair, over which was draped some kind of robe and a crown from a local fast-food place.

"Can it, Murphy." She scanned the room. A newspaper picture of her after she'd won, hot, sweaty and elated, had been copied and was posted all over the kitchen. "Our heroine," one caption read; others were labeled, "Ms. Universe" and "Calendar Girl Material." Smiling secretly to herself—the affection under the teasing felt good—she got coffee and joined Joey and Don at the table.

Mick frowned at her. "Aw, come on, Chelsea, aren't you gonna sit on your throne?"

"You be Queen for a Day, Murphy."

From behind her, he plopped the crown on her head and hugged her. She shrugged him off but left the crown where it was.

Diaz said, "Nice shot of your legs in the paper, Whitmore." His tone was dry.

"Yeah, I think they got my good side." Remaining nonchalant was crucial, or these guys would eat her alive.

Joey raised his eyes from the newspaper. "Way to go, Whitmore."

"Thanks."

Jake hustled through the door, buttoning his shirt. "Sorry I'm late. I overslept." His gaze found hers immediately. He grinned at her crown. "Congratulations, Your Majesty."

She yanked off the paper hat, then gave him a brief nod. "Thanks." Hmm. He looked tired, for having overslept.

After a charged moment, he walked to the counter and poured himself some coffee. "It's gonna be a scorcher out there today." He angled his head to the window. "They're predicting ninety."

Diaz moaned. "Maybe we won't get any runs."

The crew made small talk, then Jake turned to her. "You're riding shotgun on the Midi with Adam Genier today."

"Adam?" She glanced around. "Where's Peter?"

"Took some sick time," Jake said. "Flu, I think."

"I've never known Huff to be sick a day in his life." Diaz frowned. "On the police force, they called him Iron Man, said he had the constitution of an ox."

"He's been acting weird since he cooked the turkey meatballs for the brass," Joey said.

Jake harumphed. "He's probably tired of listening to your complaining."

"You know what this means, don'tcha, Whitmore?" Mick asked.

Absently scanning the paper, she shook her head.

"You're low man on the totem."

She snapped the paper down and narrowed her eyes suspiciously. "I can't be."

"Yep, you are. Peter's new and got the least seniority, so he's always done the low-life stuff. But he's out."

Low man meant she'd have to do the rookie jobs like roll up the hoses, get wet if a hydrant broke—messy stuff.

"I'm older than Joey and Adam."

"We've got more years in the department than you, though, sweetheart." She was surprised by Joey's teasing endearment.

When she thought about it, she realized it was true. She hadn't entered the academy until she was twenty-seven. She swore, and the guys laughed.

"Looks like Ms. Universe is gonna get herself dirty." Joey was really getting into this.

"Any luck with Operation Suzy?" she asked to deflect more ribbing.

Jake shook his head. "We know she stayed in a shelter Wednesday night and hit another in town Thursday."

Chelsea saw Mick get up and go to the coffeepot even though he'd just filled his cup. Jake, it appeared, noticed this, too.

"Somebody over at Six's said she was spotted in Manhattan Square Park." Jake went on. "All the places Delaney told us to look."

Chelsea smiled. "I'm glad. I can help tonight."

"Good. There's a sign-up sheet in the back."

Adam came in from the bay. "Truck's checked out. Hi, Chelsea. Hear you're riding shotgun with me."

Chelsea nodded, resigned to her new lower status. When they broke for housework, Jake snagged her arm. She felt his touch curl through her like warm brandy.

"Hold on a second, Chels."

Her heartbeat accelerated. Not seeing him for two days had cooled the flames between them, but she knew the smallest thing could reignite her feelings for him. She worried about being near him, being alone with him.

He crossed his arms and leaned against the counter. "Jess said you were great the other night."

"Your daughter is a doll." *Just like you.*

"Yeah, she is." He grinned. "I'm proud of you."

"Thanks."

His expression sobered, and he studied her. His eyes asked what he wouldn't. *Can we do this? Do we really want to?*

Her return message was as clear. *I don't know.* Then she stared over his shoulder at nothing and said, "Well, I'd better go help clean up the bay."

He made no response.

The call came at noon just as they sat down to lunch. Swearing colorfully enough to make longshoremen proud, they dashed to the trucks. Though it was only a flooded basement, they took every call seriously. But in deference to the heat, they stayed in T-shirts and didn't don their turnout gear, but the equipment was on the truck in case it was needed.

Both engines pulled up to a narrow, two-story house on Meigs Street. A few children played in a neighbor's yard, but the stifling city heat had kept most people indoors with fans or air conditioners. Jake got out of the truck and scowled as Mick, Don and Joey dropped back to circle Chelsea. They were riding her like three big brothers.

"Get your wadin' boots out, girl. You're gonna be swimmin' today."

"Stuff it," she said, but a grin turned up the corners of her mouth.

It was good to see her so relaxed with the guys. She was still stretched like a tightrope with him, but if they could stay away from each other as they had the past two days, they might keep their heads above water.

Instead of drowning in each other.

Jake climbed the steps of a four-foot-square porch and knocked on the door. A small, obviously pregnant woman opened it.

"Fire department, ma'am."

"Oh, gracias à Dios. Mi sotano esta inundado."

"Do you speak English?"

"No Ingles."

"Don, get up here."

Diaz jogged up the steps.

"She doesn't speak English. Ask her what happened."

Diaz listened to the woman, then turned to Jake. "She said the kids were playing in the basement. Next thing she knew, it was flooded."

"Ask her if the gas and water into the house are turned off."

Diaz questioned the woman again. "She says no."

"Find out where the utilities are, and you and Mick turn them off." He crossed the threshold. "Come on, Whitmore."

Chelsea followed him through a tidy living room, Joey and Adam traipsing along to gloat. Shades were drawn, blocking out the hot noon sun. Sweat beaded everywhere on Jake's skin. In the kitchen they found two little boys sitting on worn chairs, as stiff as soldiers at attention. On impulse Jake said, "Adam, go tell Don to come in and ask the kids what happened."

Chelsea and Joey followed him down a creaky wooden staircase. They took six steps, hit a landing, then jogged down a few more. The smell of stale water and something foul assaulted them. "Lucky you," Jake said dryly.

She grunted.

They stopped about a foot before water hit the steps. Jake and Chelsea both shined flashlights into the cellar. All sorts of debris was floating on the surface. He angled his head. "Water's gushing from that pipe in the corner. You'll have to turn the valve off over there at the bottom if they don't shut it off from outside."

"I can't wait."

"Scoot, Whitmore. Get your boots and gloves on."

Sourly she said, "Yes, sir."

Passing Joey on the stairs, she scowled at him.

"Goin' for a dip?" he asked.

"Get outta my face, Santori."

As Jake stared at the basement, he had an ominous feeling, one he'd had before. "What did Diaz get from the kids?" he asked Joey.

"Nothin'. But the gas is off."

"Hmm."

"Why?"

Jake shrugged. "I don't know. Something doesn't feel right." He sniffed. "Smell anything funny?"

"It smells like the farm my grandfather used to own."

"Yeah. Tell Diaz to ask the woman if dogs or cats live down here." If there was animal dung, sanitary concerns meant they wouldn't be able to pump.

Again, Joey passed Chelsea on the stairs. "Don't go in until I get to watch."

She sidled in next to Jake. She was sweaty from the heat; her shirt was damp and clinging to her curves. He swallowed hard and forced himself to concentrate on the flooded basement.

This was routine. Nothing out of the ordinary.

But he still sensed that something was wrong.

She raised her foot to step down and he said, "Wait a second, Whitmore. Let's hear what the kids have to say first."

She glowered at him. "Oh, no, you don't, buster. You just want me to have an audience while I go wading through this shit and stick my hands in it."

Maybe that was it, he thought. But maybe not. He took two steps up backward. "No, really, Chels, wait."

She looked at him then, no doubt to see if he was serious. Apparently she decided he wasn't, for she turned her back on him.

When he saw her again raise her foot to step down, instinct propelled him forward. He reached her just before her boot hit the water and encircled her waist with one powerful arm. As he dragged her against his chest, she said, "What the hell?"

Simultaneously, there was clambering on the stairs. Joey yelled, "Jake, wait, don't let her go in. There's an electric space heater on down there."

And then the flashlight that was still in Chelsea's hand illuminated a cat floating on the water. A dead cat.

THE FLASHLIGHT crashed to the wooden stairs and tumbled into the contaminated, electrified water. Chelsea felt herself being dragged up the steps to the landing. Shouting and screaming could be heard overhead, but only one thought registered.

She'd been a step away from dying.

Her throat seized up at the knowledge. She closed her eyes, and spots swam before her. She was on a landing now, still supported by Jake's big arm around her waist.

"Can you stand?"

Was that Jake's strangled voice? "Uh, yeah." But her legs wobbled, and she sank against him. His other arm crossed her chest, and he held on. He felt so good, so solid. So alive.

"It's okay, Chels," he murmured. "You're safe." She could feel his heart pounding like a drum in his chest. Its rhythm matched hers.

"I know." Her voice was hoarse. She looked up.

Joey perched on a step above her. Mick behind him.

Diaz last. Their faces were ashen, their expressions stunned.

She swallowed hard and drew in a breath. She knew she had to be brave. Not to prove she was a good fire-fighter. Not to prove she was as strong as a man. But because her group was so obviously shaken. Summoning deep inner strength honed by years of taking care of herself, she said, "You look like you've seen a ghost. I guess I coulda been one, but I'm not." She smiled weakly.

In unison they deflated like balloons releasing air. Jake let go and, her insides whirling like a merry-go-round, she instantly missed his strength. Nevertheless she straightened.

Joey stepped forward first. He enveloped her in a hug. "You almost bought it, Whitmore."

She hugged him back. "Glad I didn't?"

"Yeah. I am."

Mick hugged her next, lifting her off the wooden steps. "God damn it, Chelsea…" When he drew back, his eyes were moist.

Diaz's face was stricken.

"I'm all right, Don," she said, accepting his embrace.

"Dios mio!" Then he added, *"Las mujeres fueron destinadas a ser protegidas."*

Chelsea translated the latter. *Women were meant to be protected.* She hugged him hard.

Jake blew out a heavy breath. "Okay, let's take care of this. Joey and Don, keep everybody upstairs. Mick and Adam, get the electric company out here."

When the group trudged up the steps, Jake waited a second, then grasped her arm and turned her to him. Gazing at her chalky face, he said nothing, just drew her to him. Her breasts were flattened against his chest, and her arms slid around his neck. One of his hands was at her waist and the other at her bare neck. He breathed in the scent of her.

She'd almost died.

Right there, amidst the cobwebs and dirt, he drew her so close that every possible inch of their bodies touched.

For one intense minute, his emotions bubbling up inside him like a hot spring, he allowed himself to bathe in his feelings for her. He'd almost lost her, *really* lost her.

Hearing voices from above, he let her go. And when she stepped back, he saw the same awareness—and an emotion so strong it almost leveled him—in her eyes.

AT EIGHT that night, Jake was sitting in his car in front of Chelsea's house. The sun was low in the western sky, but the temperature hadn't fallen. He'd showered, changed into jean shorts and an RFD T-shirt; they'd all cleaned up after their reliefs arrived, washing away the fear along with the grime of the day. Then they'd whisked Chelsea off to Pumpers for a beer.

Jake knew the syndrome. They'd needed to assure themselves she was all right. That each of them was all right. He noticed they touched her, and each other, more than usual.

Of course, the ribbing had been typical firefighter black humor. *You were almost toast, Chels. Wonder if her hair woulda curled. It's one way to get outta shit detail.* But underneath had been a relief so acute it was almost palpable. They'd discussed what had happened...

"Can you believe it?" Diaz said. "The two brats were havin' a contest to see who could stand the heat the best. Ninety degrees outside wasn't enough. They went to the basement while their mother was napping and turned on the electric heater somebody'd given their father." He scowled. "Man, I'd banish my kids to their rooms for a year if they did this."

"How'd the basement get flooded?" Mick asked. Of them all, he seemed the most upset.

"The heater was old and had something wrong with it, so it caught fire. An exposed water pipe was right there. The kids panicked and hit it with a hammer, hoping to crack it and douse the fire with the water. They did that, all right. They just didn't know how to stop it."

"Those kids are lucky they didn't get electrocuted," Jake said.

Joey shook his head. "Almost taken down by two punks, Whitmore."

She'd grinned, but Jake could see the strain around her mouth, knew she was still shaken. She sipped her beer and put up a brave front, but eventually she said, "I'm whipped. I've gotta go home." She found Jake's gaze. "I can't help canvas for Suzy tonight."

"Don't worry about it. We've got a lot of guys on." He'd squeezed her shoulder and wondered where he'd find the strength to let her go.

He hadn't. He'd called and canceled his stint at Operation Suzy to go keep vigil at Chelsea's house. Now that he was here, what would he do?

He scanned the quiet neighborhood from his open window. A lawn mower rattled down the street, and he could smell a barbecue cooking somewhere. She hadn't come home. He guessed she could have stopped at the gym. Or Delaney's. Did she go to Spike's?

Minutes later her sassy red Camaro sped down the road and pulled into the driveway. As she drove into the garage, he got out of his Bronco. Leaning against it, arms folded, he watched as she sat in her car for almost a minute. Then, unaware of his presence, she slid out and headed toward the door that led from the garage to the kitchen.

She wore a short denim skirt and a white camisole top that made his mouth water. At the bar, he'd noticed she

had no bra on. Not that she needed it. Her breasts were
perfectly shaped and firm, like the rest of her.

What would he do? She hadn't shut the garage door.

*If she looks my way, sees me, I'm going to her. If she
doesn't, I'll go home.* He felt like a teenage boy making
a deal with God.

Or the devil.

He saw her drop her keys. Was she still shaky? Her hair
falling to cover her eyes, she bent and retrieved the keys.
When she stood up again, she saw him. And froze.

In a flash he pushed away from the Bronco. Blocking
out the warning bells that went off in his head, he moved
up the driveway with long, purposeful strides. He was in
front of her in a minute.

She looked at him.

He looked at her.

Flicking his gaze to the wall, he reached out and pushed
a button; the garage door creaked down noisily, landing
with a heavy thud. Slants of light poured in from the four
tiny windows, bathing her in an ethereal glow.

And then he touched her.

"I WANT YOU."

His husky words warmed her like old Scotch. They
were just as intoxicating. His hand, cupping her cheek,
sent tingly shivers everywhere. His eyes searched hers for
a response.

She gave him the only one there was. "Yes."

Leaning forward, he grazed her earlobe with his mouth.
"No talking about it. Until after."

Her senses reeled with his nearness; she nodded, then
felt the brush of his lips on her skin. His hands came up,
skimming her bare arms from shoulder to elbow with a
feather-light touch. Passion and its potential simmered between them, like a fire about to rage out of control. But

he contained it, saying, at her temple, "I'm not going to hurry, honey. I've waited too long for this. I'm going to savor every—" he kissed her hair "—single—" then her forehead "—second."

A moan, low and lusty, escaped her throat.

Callused fingertips sought her neck and initiated a slow, sensual massage. Her stomach contracted.

"Tell me you want me, Chels," he whispered.

"I do…"

"Say it. Let me hear you say it."

"I want you," she said huskily.

He kissed her eyelids, her nose and then her mouth. At the very first taste of him, she inched as close as he'd allow and put her hands at the nape of his neck. His hair was incredibly soft, and his smell, clean and male, permeated her nostrils.

He touched her intimately, searing her. Still, he kept the flickers low, smoldering. "I've wondered what you'd feel like for so long.…"

She let her hands go on their own discovery, thrilled when his back muscles bunched, his buttocks clenched as she touched them.

"Chelsea," he gasped, drawing back, "I've got to have more."

She'd dropped the keys again, and he bent to retrieve them, then unlocked the door and urged her inside. They went through the kitchen, up the stairs to her bedroom.

He sat on the edge of the mattress and drew her to him, positioning her between his knees. Smiling with a deep inner joy, he undid each button of her camisole. His clever mouth traced every inch he bared.

Soon, her top fell to the floor. He gazed at her breasts, took them in his hands and said, "Watch," as he caressed her. After a long, delicious minute, he fumbled at the snap on her skirt. He slid it down her legs, then traced the band of her red panties. "These kept me up all night," he said as he ran his finger down the elastic to the notch where her leg and hip joined.

She murmured, "I've got a drawerful of them."

His finger sneaked under the band and felt her wetness. He moved it back and forth over the tiny nub exposed by his searching until she whimpered, "Jake, please…"

With trembling hands, he pushed the scrap of lace down her legs, leaned back and took her to the bed with him.

"No, your clothes," she said.

"You do it." His voice was husky, urgent.

He kept his eyes closed as he felt her ease back from him. He knew if he looked at her, kneeling there naked, the dynamite inside him would explode. He heard his zipper rasp, then felt her hands wander inside his clothes, searching, finding him. He came up off the pillow when she clasped him in her strong fingers and stroked his hard, aching length, and his moans toppled one over the other. Any minute, he thought, steam would pour from his body, and his skin would turn to cinders.

She slithered the shirt up his ribs and over his head, scraping him with her nails. Leaning forward, she explored his chest with her mouth; he struggled for breath.

Finally she dragged off his shorts and briefs. But she took a detour in coming back to him, brushing her lips on his shin bones, the underside of his knee, the inside of his thigh.

His restraint broke. He reached for her shoulders, flipped her onto her back, then covered her with his body. He felt like he was hurtling though space, his blood so heated it propelled him even against his will to take her now. Before passion consumed him, he reached for his pants, found one of the condoms he'd bought earlier and rolled it on.

"I want you so much," she said simply.

"Then here." He entered her in one swift stroke.

Her hips arched reflexively and they began to move, slowly at first, their rhythm matched like that of longtime lovers. His thrusts increased, deeper, faster...

Her eyes were closed, and he wanted to tell her to look at him when she came, but he couldn't talk, only feel. Then she tightened around him in the first spasms of her pleasure.

The inferno crept up on him, too. He thrust faster, spurred on by her moans, and the heat between them grew in intensity. When at last it exploded, they both cried out and surrendered to it.

TONIGHT THE DARKNESS taunted him. The Hyde in him told him he had to act again. The stove incident hadn't worked. He had to do something else. And soon. He had to save her.

She'd almost died. He needed to see that this didn't happen again. He rose from the bed and crossed to the window. Men and women had gone against nature, and now they were paying for it. He remembered seeing *The Handmaid's Tale* on TV not too long ago, and it had hit him then. Women needed to be taken in hand. They needed to be protected. They were too fragile, too soft, to be competing in a man's world. Those men were right to put women where they belonged, even though the movie tried to say otherwise.

He lit a cigarette and blew the smoke out the window. It calmed him, soothed his nerves.

Time for action. He'd made the plan last week. Now he'd implement it. It shouldn't take too long to get Chelsea Whitmore back where she belonged.

She was only one woman, but it was a start.

The good side of him—Jekyll—surfaced briefly and protested the unfairness of his plan.

Ruthlessly, he squelched Jekyll and let Hyde take over.

CHAPTER TWELVE

THEY PLAYED HOOKY for as long as they could, which turned out to be thirty-six hours. At nine that night, Jake slid into the bathtub behind her, fitted Chelsea to him and groaned when she shimmied back. The room was dimly lit by jasmine-scented candles burning on the vanity; the open windows allowed a cool August night breeze to waft around them.

He said, "Tell me about this again."

Water lapped her hips, kissed her stomach, flirted with her breasts. "I wished you'd been here the night after the triathlon. I *pictured* you here, what you would do...."

He brushed his lips over her ear and whispered, "Tell me."

When she did and he followed her fantasies to the letter, she twisted around and brought his mouth to hers. "It's so sexy," she whispered, her voice a silky rustle, "having you do to me what I imagined."

His grin was male and smug and gorgeous after he kissed her.

Submerging his hand in the water, he slid it between her legs. "I think I can take it from here."

"YOU'RE KIDDING, right?" Chelsea said late the following morning.

They'd shared coffee and kisses and confidences after awakening. Jake lay on the bed, both drained and renewed by their cataclysmic lovemaking of the night before. Linking his hands behind his neck, he said, "Nope, I want to see all that sexy underwear you said you had a drawerful of. I want to see you in it."

Grabbing a short white satin robe from the floor and slipping it on, she sashayed across the room to one of the dressers. She opened a drawer and pulled out panties and a matching bra. Slowly, her back to him, she slid on the panties underneath the robe, then dropped the robe to the floor and put on the bra. Then she turned.

He gasped. "Unbelievable. The gold lace goes great with your coloring," he said hoarsely. His gaze raked her from head to toe. "And I like what the underwire does to your breasts." He coughed, wondering how far he dare go. "Put on some heels with it."

Her brows arched, but she crossed to the closet and drew out backless three-inch black satin heels. As she headed to the bed, her hips swayed mercilessly and her breasts swelled above the scalloped lace. When she was close, he murmured, "Kneel on the bed."

She did.

By the time Jake had fulfilled every fantasy he had about her underwear, scraps of gold lace, teal satin with tiny bows, plush midnight black velvet and a naughty leopard print lay in a heap where he'd thrown them to the floor.

On the bed she made even more of his dreams come true.

BY SIX O'CLOCK that night it was pouring rain. From the sitting room floor where he rested his head in Chelsea's lap, Jake listened to it hitting the roof like tiny drumbeats. The room smelled of incense, which he'd discovered she was fond of burning. They both felt as contented as the two cats curled at their feet.

"Okay, read it to me," Jake told her.

At his request she'd agreed to read some bits of her diary. "May twenty-ninth—Jake was a doll today, and I was a bitch to him. He's so strong and solid, he makes me feel safe."

"Hey, I could be a golden retriever. Where's the good stuff?"

She chuckled. "There *is* one good part from that day." She read again. "Delaney met him at the game and says he's yummy."

"Yummy? I've never been called yummy in my life."

She gave him a quick peck on the cheek. "Well, you *are* yummy."

Angling his head up, he sipped his wine, a dry Chardonnay she'd had in her fridge. Wine was something neither of them usually drank, but they'd wanted to celebrate.

"Read some more."

She squinted at the pages. Found the night they'd given him the cat. "I wanted to be where that kitten was tonight, licking Jake's neck. I was astounded at the force of my feelings for him. Oh, God, he's my lieutenant."

Jake chuckled. "I tried like hell to get out of that kitchen so you wouldn't know how you affected me."

Her mouth dropped. "Really? I didn't see."

"I was in pain, lady."

After several more excerpts, each followed by increasingly hot kisses, she said, "Okay, last one."

"Make it good, babe."

"He's asleep on my floor. I'm staring at him right now, telling myself to leave him alone when I really want to go over and jump his bones. He was as tender as a son with Mrs. Lowe, a savior with Timmy. He's kind and strong, and…" She blinked hard. "I can't finish."

"And what? Tell me."

Her eyes got so bleak it took his breath away. Finally

she read "…and everything I've ever wanted in a man." She closed the diary.

He pulled her head down and kissed her passionately.

After a moment she drew away from him and said gravely, "But I also wrote that I knew I couldn't have you. It's wrong, Jake."

He stared at her, then eased up to lean against the couch and draw her into his lap. "All right, let's talk about it."

"It can't work between us. You're the officer on my group. It's unethical for us to be together like this. Not to mention our previous fiascos around being too close to a colleague."

"I know," he said. She cuddled into him. "Chels, I sent in my forms to take the captaincy exam."

"That's great!" Real pleasure shone in her eyes.

"Not for us."

"No, not for us." Her pleasure vanished. "You'll have to be unimpeachable now." She glanced around the room. "So we'll just have these few hours together."

Gently he pulled her to him. "I can't let you go, sweetheart."

"We have no choice."

"Yes, we do."

"What do you mean?"

"We'll keep it a secret."

"Sneak around?"

"No, we just won't tell anybody. Not Delaney, Francey or Beth. Not Reed or Ben. And there won't be a hint of our feelings at work."

She was silent.

He held her tighter. "I can't give you up. Let's take it a day at a time." When she started to protest, he said, "Honey, we both knew it shouldn't happen between us in the first place, and it did. How do you think we'll resist it now?"

"I can't go through what I did before, with Billy."

"I'll never turn on you like that, no matter what happens. I promise."

She nodded, said nothing for a minute, then looked at him. "If we do this, I'll do my part, too. I won't give you any reason to doubt my ability, to find fault with my firefighting."

"Of course you won't."

She pressed her fingers to his mouth. "Shh. Let me say it. If things *do* go wrong, I promise, I won't blame you like Danny blamed you. I won't turn on you, either."

His hand threaded her hair. "Then you'll try it my way?"

Chelsea braved a smile. "Yes, I'll try."

He kissed her searingly, then gave her a boyish grin. "Good, because now that I've gotten a good look, I'd really miss those undies."

THE BIG ninety-year-old, three-story brick house in one of the city's original neighborhoods had been built for a wealthy Rockford family but now was converted into apartments. A fire burned angrily inside, on the second floor where a flat roof addition jutted from the rest of the house. Already, Engine Four had laid hose to attack the fire, and Quint Six had followed with a second line to do search and rescue. Quint Eight had ventilated. On a second alarm, Jake's station had been called in for more help.

In the late-afternoon August heat Jake led his crew up the interior staircase to the seat of the fire. Clouds of gray smoke obscured everything; only the outline of the stairs was visible. The temperature jacked up big-time as he closed the distance to the fire; after just minutes inside, his body was covered with sweat and his clothes were sticking to him. He began to breathe faster and forced himself to be calm, to conserve air. He knew he was going to need it.

"They're worried about the ceilings," he'd told his crew as they'd tightened their turnout gear. "They're made of heavy-gauge metal and cement-based plaster. If they collapse, it'll be an avalanche. Be careful."

With Chelsea behind him on the hose and Mick and Don behind her with another line, they reached the doorway where four firefighters were knocking down the main body of the fire.

The smoke was lighter here, and it was easier to see but they received a blast of heat as they stepped inside. Halting, then squatting, Jake breathed deeply, gripped the hose and crawled to the other side of the room. Once there, he stood and, feeling Chelsea at his back, lifted the hose and pulled the lever.

A hot, heavy weight slammed into him from above; he fell forward. He saw Chelsea go down next to him. He hit the floor face first, and his mouth gear dug into his skin. He tried to move, but something pinned him from the shoulders down.

It took him a minute to figure out what had happened. The ceiling had fallen. There was no warning, no noise. It had dropped on them like a steel blanket, its weight pushing them to the floor.

Twisting his head to the side, his heart leaped into his mouth when he saw Chelsea facedown, her head and upper torso sticking out of the mountain of plaster and Sheetrock. Stricken by the sight, he tried to move but couldn't. Then she shifted, raised herself up on her arms, trying to free herself from the smothering wreckage. The relief he felt when he saw she'd survived the fall was intense. Had his men? He turned his head, checking for them. Through the smoke, he saw two firefighters who looked like Mick and Don crouched in the doorway to avoid the ceiling's descent. Two others had missed being buried by squeezing into the space made by recessed windows. Another quick scan told Jake two firefighters were pinned, only the hand of one and the helmet of the other visible.

Then he heard it. A beeping sound. Somebody's SCBA alarm, indicating low oxygen on their breathing tank. It couldn't be any of his group, because they'd only been in the building ten minutes.

He yelled, "Somebody's alarm—"

Off to the side, glass shattered and firefighters crashed through the window. They carried pikes, axes, a sledge-hammer, even a chain saw. As the fresh air fueled the flames, it got hotter.

Then Mick and Don were over them. Mick grabbed a pike from one of the men and began to pick at the plaster trapping Chelsea. She was freed in minutes and given over to Don, who dragged her to the window and handed her out to a firefighter in the bucket at the end of the aerial ladder. Jake watched her rescue, then dropped his head to the floor with a prayer of thanks.

He lay motionless. The weight of the plaster seemed to increase; brutal heat seeped into the back of his legs, so extreme it burned through his gear. He cringed with the pain. Steeled himself against it.

Dimly he was aware of the commotion over him. The weight lightened. Another minute. More weight gone. Two minutes. Finally the weight was completely lifted. Freed, he struggled to get up, felt strong arms on either side of him as he realized he was unable to stand on his own. Don and Mick flanked him; they pulled him to his feet, hooked his arms over each of their shoulders, dragged him to the window. His stomach roiled with the motion. He was yanked into the bucket by the strong, capable hands of RFD personnel. Once there, he collapsed onto the floor.

CHELSEA SANK onto one of the vinyl chairs of the Rockford Memorial Hospital's Emergency waiting room and willed her hands to stop shaking. Jake was going to be all right. The paramedics and then the doctor had told her that. And she was safe. Despite the fact that she'd been buried under a mound of hot plaster and her SCBA alarm went off, scaring her half to death, she'd survived without serious injury. The ambulance attendants had checked her out and found her with nothing more than a few first-degree burns; she'd refused any treatment.

"Chelsea, oh, God." Jessica Scarlatta stood like a fragile porcelain figurine in the doorway; then she bolted into the room. When Chelsea rose, Jess hurled herself into Chelsea's arms. Hugging Jake's child to her, Chelsea smoothed the girl's long blond hair, saying, "Shh, honey, he's all right."

Jess drew back, her face tearstained, her gray eyes stormy. "You wouldn't lie—he's really okay?"

"I'd never lie to you. Now let's sit and I'll explain his condition."

Jess turned. "Come on, Barb. Derek."

Chelsea hadn't noticed Barbara DeLuca behind Jess. Her face was furrowed with worry. Her son, Derek, a big, strapping boy with a man's shoulders and a street kid's eyes, held back. Keeping his fear for Jake at bay, Chelsea guessed. Afraid, like Jess, of losing a father.

Barb smiled weakly at Chelsea, then grabbed Derek's arm, and they all gathered at a small round table off to the side.

Chelsea took Jessica's hand in hers. "Your father has second-degree burns," she said in her best EMT voice. That she was talking about Jake made her stomach churn, but she didn't want to upset his daughter.

"What does that mean?" Jess asked.

"Burns are usually categorized by degrees. First is the

least severe. Second-degree means the outer layer of the
skin and the next layer are burned through, but there's no
damage to underlying tissue.''

Jess's eyes welled, and Chelsea watched Barbara slide
a motherly arm around her. ''Where's he burned?'' Jessica
asked.

''Only on the backs of his legs.'' She squeezed Jess's
hand. ''That's very good, honey. Face, hands and the groin
are much worse areas. The burns on the backs of his legs
will heal, probably with just ointment.'' She grinned to
ease Jessica's fears. ''He'll be a bear, though. There'll be
pain, swelling and blisters for forty-eight hours. He'll be
out of work a few days. But there won't be any scarring.''

Jess said, ''I don't care if he is a bear. I'll take care of
him. Just so he's all right.'' Jessica burst into sobs of relief. Barbara DeLuca took over as mother, putting her arm
around the girl, making soothing sounds.

Chelsea was startlingly jealous.

''Chelsea?''

Turning, Chelsea looked into the ashen face of her sister. ''Delaney? Who called you?''

Chelsea had telephoned Jess from the emergency department because she knew Jake had plans for dinner with
his daughter. She'd called no one else yet, though the battalion chief had come to the hospital and talked to her.
The rest of Jake's crew would arrive momentarily.

''I did.''

Stunned, Chelsea looked at the boy who'd been stone-
faced ever since he'd come in. Delaney put her hand on
Derek's shoulder. Her eyes were turbulent, but she was
summoning up the therapist. ''Are you all right?'' she
asked Chelsea.

''I'm fine. A few minor burns.''

''Jake?''

"He's okay, too. He'll be laid up a couple of days, but he's going to be fine."

Her sister's shoulders lost their cardboard stiffness; she bent, hugged Chelsea, then turned her attention to the stoic young man. "Wanna go get a Coke with me, buddy?"

Derek looked at her with an expression so nakedly needy it took Chelsea's breath away. He didn't speak, just nodded, rose and, towering over Delaney, walked down the corridor with her.

"She's working miracles with him," Barbara said, staring after them. "When Jess called us, the first thing Derek did was phone your sister. He wouldn't say a word to me, but I know he's terrified of something happ—" She broke off, realizing what she was saying in front of Jess.

A white-coated doctor approached the table. "Ms. Whitmore, is Lieutenant Scarlatta's family here yet?"

Barbara and Jessica stood. "We're here," they said in unison.

Chelsea fought the surge of need to be included. She wasn't Jake's family, no matter how close they'd gotten. And all that mattered was that he was okay.

"You can see him now." The doctor frowned. "Has Ms. Whitmore explained the situation?"

"About the burns." Jess's voice wobbled.

"We've got that under control. We're going to keep him overnight for observation. And he'll be going to X ray for his back and chest."

"X ray?" Jess asked, her hands wrapping around her waist.

"Yes, the plaster that fell on him was heavy. We want to rule out any internal damage." When Jess's eyes began to fill again, the doctor coughed. "There's no evidence of that," he told her. "It's all precautionary." Nodding to Barbara, he said, "Why don't you take your daughter in to see for herself?"

Chelsea swallowed her protest, and watched Jess and Barbara follow the doctor, feeling utterly bereft. Midway to the door, the doctor halted and turned. "Ms. Whitmore, you come, too. He's, ah, been asking about you. It would be best if he could see for himself you're all right."

Grateful, Chelsea rose; her legs were shaky, but she followed the group through the double doors and down a hallway. At the end of the corridor the doctor opened the door to a single room.

Jake lay on his back, half propped up by the hospital bed. His face was streaked with dirt. The too-small, faded hospital gown stretched across his shoulders. A sheet draped his lap. His legs were angled up like he was in traction, lightly covered with another sheet. His bare feet stuck out. In his arm was an IV.

"Daddy?" Jessica flew to the bed. She halted when she got there until he put out his arms, then she leaned over and hugged him, still sobbing.

"Shh, sweetheart," Jake murmured. "It's okay, I'm fine."

"I was so scared for you."

"I'm fine," he repeated.

Over Jess's back, his eyes locked with Chelsea's for a brief, burning moment. He opened his mouth to speak when Barbara stepped into their line of vision. Jake said, "Barb?"

"Hi, handsome."

Jess eased back, and as naturally as a wife to her husband, Barbara took Jess's place. Chelsea shifted and pretended to study the signs on the wall. She stuck her hands in her grungy uniform pants and fisted them. She could hear Jake murmur coaxing words, chuckle at something Barb said. The intimacy of the trio, and the exclusion Chelsea felt, made her eyes fill. She needed to leave the cozy family scene before she revealed something no one could know.

She reached for the door.

Just as it opened from outside.

Grim-faced, Mick, Joey, Peter and Don burst into the room. Though they'd hastily cleaned up and were in civilian clothes, they looked unkempt and thrown together. And worried.

Mick grabbed Chelsea's arms. "—Goddamn it, Whitmore, you sure you're okay?"

Blinking back the tears, she said, "I'm fine."

Peter came up behind Mick. "You should be admitted, Whitmore."

"No, I shouldn't." She straightened. "Don't rag on me, guys. Go see how Jake's doin'."

Immediately they turned to the bed, where Barb and Jess flanked Jake. Barb leaned into him; Jess held his hand. Jake said, "Jeez, don't I get the sympathy?"

The guys crowded around the bed, once more making Chelsea feel like odd man out. She reached for the door again.

"Whitmore, get over here. I wanna see for myself you're all right." Jake's voice was surprisingly strong.

Sucking in a deep breath, she bit her lip and pivoted. She crossed to the bed, where Mick and Don parted to make room. "Yes, sir."

His look was a caress. He examined her face, which she realized must be streaked with dirt like his. He scanned her chest, taking in the wrinkled, torn RFD shirt. He clasped her hands in his. Turned them over. They were grimy, too. He squeezed them, and if he held on a moment too long, no one seemed to notice. "You look like hell, but you aren't hurt, are you?"

She shook her head.

"I can see burns on your neck, Whitmore." This from Peter.

"First degree. The paramedics took care of them." She felt more in control after the connection with Jake. "I'm fine. It's your lieutenant who needs the coddling."

Joey sank onto a chair at the end of the bed. Lines of fatigue marred his brow. "He's just tryin' to get Barb to cook all his meals for him."

"I'll be glad to do that," Barbara said seriously, her petite hand drifting to Jake's shoulder. And staying there.

Jake's big hand came up and covered hers. "I won't be that laid up."

Mick asked, "They give ya anything for the pain?"

Briefly Jake glanced at Jess. "Yeah, a shot. I don't feel much yet."

"Chelsea said you'll be a bear for few days—with the swelling and blisters," Jess said, steadier. "But you'll be okay, Daddy."

Jake caught the youthful need to convince herself. He squeezed Jess's arm. "Chelsea said that, huh?"

"It'll be like the time you broke your leg," Mick teased. "Remember Nancy was chewin' nails until you went back to work."

Jake laughed.

All woman now, Jess said, "I'll take care of you. Barb can help."

Chelsea stepped back and sidled behind the guys. She saw Peter watching her. She needed to be careful of her reactions, but this homey little drama with Barbara De-Luca as a main actor was getting to her.

"Where ya' goin' Whitmore?" Jake asked.

"Um, nowhere. I need to sit down for a minute." She matched her actions to her words.

Peter crossed to her and tipped her chin. "You sure you're okay?"

"Just exhausted."

Joey said, "Man, that plaster had to weigh a ton. I'm surprised Chelsea—"

"Joe, let's not hash this out now." Jake's gaze flicked to Jessica.

"Oh, sure, time for a replay later."

Frowning, Jake said, "I just want to know whose SCBA alarm—"

The door opened, halting his question. Framed in it were a pale Derek, Delaney and Reed Macauley. Derek stared at Jake. Delaney said, "Hi, Jake. Derek wants to see you." She looked around the room and with her usual bull-in-a-china-shop lack of finesse announced, "Alone, if that's okay with Jessica."

Jess got the message. "Sure."

Reed said, "Jessica, why don't you and I go get some coffee? I checked with the doctor, and your dad's going to be admitted soon and taken to his room. We can help get him settled then."

Bending over, Jess kissed Jake's head, said, "I love you, Daddy," then crossed to Reed. "Okay. Let's go. She grabbed Derek's arm. "He's okay, Der."

Derek nodded.

Chelsea watched Barbara kiss Jake's cheek. "I'm staying, too. I'll be out in the waiting room until they admit you."

Delaney stood on tiptoe and said something to Derek. Then she turned. "Come on, Chelsea. You look like you're about to collapse. I'm taking you home."

All Chelsea wanted was a moment alone with Jake. Even thirty seconds. But she swallowed the need, remembering his words.

We just won't tell anyone. Not Delaney, Francey or Beth. Not Reed or Ben.

With Derek in the doorway, and Barb, Jess and Reed

out the door, the firefighters from Quint Twelve said goodbye to their injured lieutenant. Joey squeezed Jake's shoulder, Mick bent for an awkward hug, Don socked his arm,
Peter patted his hand. Chelsea rose to her feet. As the men
filed out, Jake said, "Come on, Whitmore, don't I rate
some TLC from you?"

On limbs shakier than when she'd run a marathon, she
crossed the room. Her gaze locked with his. She leaned
over the bed and closed her eyes to savor the solid, safe
feel of him. His hands came up to grasp her arms. He
whispered, "Easy, babe."

Swallowing hard, Chelsea nodded, turned away and let
Delaney escort her out of Jake's room. But what she
wanted more than anything else in the world was to stay
with the man she loved.

THE DARKNESS HOVERED around him, but in it he could
see specters from the day—Chelsea going down, then
Jake. He could hear the keening sound of her alarm.
They'd been rescued, but the effort could have taken several more minutes had the Quint Six guys not been so
prepared. Oh, God, what had he done? She could have
been killed.

He paced. He shouldn't have done something so drastic.
He'd have to make sure the next time wasn't life-
threatening. Goddamn it, he wasn't sure anybody had even
heard the alarm go off, so it could be all for nothing.

She could have been killed *for nothing*. When what he
wanted was her out of the department to make sure she'd
be safe.

Do you? the voice inside him asked. Hyde asked.

There was a knock on his door.

He swore vilely to himself; he didn't need interruption.
He needed to plan. It was even more important now that
he take care of her. After tonight.

IT FELT LIKE a thousand needles were pricking the backs of his legs. Once again, Jake shifted in the small bed, trying to ease some of the pain. Not much helped except the stuff they spiked his IV drip with every four hours. The latest dose, administered ten minutes ago by a nurse who was way too perky for six in the morning, should take effect soon.

In the dim twilight, the door to his room opened, a slash of light illuminating the interior. And his visitor.

"Well, maybe I'll get through the morning now." His voice was gravelly from interrupted sleep. Gruffer from seeing Chelsea.

"Hi." She stood by the foot of the bed, bathed in shadows. She looked tired. But so good he wanted to crush her to him and never let her go. Her hair was wild around her shoulders, incongruous with the fire department uniform she wore.

"Come here, love."

Slowly, like in a dream sequence in a movie, she came around to the side of the bed. She reached for the chair, never taking her eyes off him.

"Oh, no." He patted the mattress. "Right here."

She sank onto the bed. Some scent—outdoorsy, like a flower garden or maybe an apple orchard—surrounded her.

As if they'd been lovers for years, he reached up to enfold her in his arms as she leaned down and buried her face in his chest. Closing his eyes, he whispered, "When I saw you go down—" Though he couldn't finish, in his mind he pictured her toppling under the deadly weight and heat of the plaster.

"I saw you, too." Her words were muffled by his shirt. "You got hit worse than me."

No more needed to be said. As veteran firefighters, they both knew what could have happened.

Minutes passed. He savored her, rubbing her back tenderly. She kissed his neck, inching in as close as she could. Finally she drew back. Sat up. Reverently, she skimmed his cheek with her knuckles. He grabbed her hand and kissed it.

"I wanted you to stay last night." His voice was a dark-of-the-night whisper.

"It killed me to leave." Softly spoken, her words conveyed the hurt he'd seen on her face when everybody else had taken over the right to care for him.

"I asked Reed to call you."

"He did. I was in the bath. He got Delaney, instead."

Jake chuckled. "Fireworks again?"

"Not too bad. Actually they met in the ER last night and fell right into step to take care of Jess and Derek." She smiled. "He told Delaney you were out for the count." She leaned over and brushed his lips with hers. "Or else I would have sneaked in last night after my sister finally left me alone."

"I'm glad you came this morning." He ran the pad of his thumb over her lips.

"I figured nobody would be here before work. If they did come, I'd just say I was checking up on you."

"I'm sorry about the secrecy. That it hurt you last night."

She shook her head, belying the sadness in her eyes. "I'm just glad you're all right."

He studied her face. Took in the smudges beneath her eyes. The tight jaw. "Are you hurt? The truth, this time."

"A few minor burns. They kept me awake, but they're okay." She rubbed her shoulder. "I'm sore as hell."

He ran his hand down her arm. "You sure you should go to work?"

"What would *you* do, Lieutenant?"

"Touché." He shifted and winced.

"You're in a lot of pain, aren't you?"

He nodded. "I forgot it could be this bad. The painkiller will kick in soon."

She smoothed back his hair. Drank in his face.

"I want to tell you something," he said softly.

She smiled, so much feeling in those amber eyes he wanted to drown in them.

"I love you, Chels."

Her face paled. Her jaw slackened. Her breathing sped up. He expected surprise. But not the moisture that filled her eyes.

Wiping away a renegade drop with his finger, he formulated what to say next. He wasn't sorry he said he loved her; experiences like last night taught him he didn't have time to waste dissembling. But he didn't want to spook her.

So he said, "I know it's only been a couple of months. That we just made love a few days ago." He brushed back her hair. "But it's never been like this for me with anybody before."

Her tears multiplied.

His breathing accelerated. "Honey, it's okay if you don't feel this way yet. I know you care about me—I can see it in your eyes, feel it in the way you touch me, respond to me. The rest will come."

She shook her head, dropped her chin to her chest. She was crying hard. He tried to pull her to him, but she resisted. He edged toward panic.

Finally she lifted her head. Her eyes were bright with tears, her face glowing. "I love you, too, Jake. So much."

He hadn't realized what the declaration would mean to him. The sun coming out after a flood, winning the lottery or becoming chief couldn't have meant more to him.

She leaned into his chest again, and he held her. Kissed her hair. Locked his hand at her neck. "It'll work out, I promise. Nothing will come between us. If I take this captaincy exam—'' he hugged her tighter ''—who knows. All I'm sure of is that I need you. And I'll have you in my life.''

She nodded, but couldn't speak. She cried softly.

She was still crying, and he was still clasping her to his chest, when he heard a voice. ''Um, sorry to intrude. I didn't think you'd have visitors so early.''

Jake looked over Chelsea's shoulders to see Battalion Chief Ben Cordaro standing in the doorway.

CHAPTER THIRTEEN

BEN CORDARO stared after Chelsea, who with an embarrassed hello had left hurriedly. The knowing look on his face was something Jake had seen many times in the past. For a moment Jake was irrationally angry at having to keep something so important secret from somebody so significant in his life.

Facing him, Ben asked, "You okay, buddy?" He'd been out of town until late last night, Jake knew.

"My legs hurt like hell, but I'll live."

"Hot plaster." Ben cringed as he straddled the straight chair next to the bed. "I've been under it a time or two. Not pleasant."

Jake shook his head.

Again Ben glanced toward the door. "Chelsea okay? Francey's worried about her."

"She's overwrought, Ben. She was really shaken yesterday and broke down this morning when she got here."

The man who had been a father to Jake looked hard at him. Jake was reminded of the first man-to-man discussion he'd had with Ben about sex. "Want to talk about it, Jakey?" Ben asked, using the old childhood nickname.

Jake shook his head.

"As a friend, not a battalion chief?"

Still, Jake declined.

"All right." Ben scanned the room, as if searching for answers in the dim morning light. "You know, when Diana came back to town, I had some tough truths to face."

His gaze leveled on Jake. "Some things are more important than the Rockford Fire Department, Jake." He cleared his throat. "I'm grateful to have a second chance with her. But we lost more than twenty-five years together. Neither one of us will ever get over it."

Since Ben was usually reserved, Jake was surprised at his confession. "What are you saying, Ben?"

Ben stood. "I'm saying a son should learn from his father's mistakes." He smiled sadly. "Now I'm gonna go track down the nurses to see when I can spring you from this place."

"SON OF A BITCH." In the gray half-light of the bay, Chelsea stared at the dismantled air pack she held in her hands as if it were equipment from another planet.

"What's wrong, Whitmore?"

She whirled to find her crew—minus Ed Knight, Jake's replacement, who was in the office—standing behind her. Raising her chin, she faced them squarely. "My tank's empty."

"We know," Mick said softly, crossing his arms. "We heard it go off in the building yesterday."

"I thought the alarm malfunctioned." Chelsea kept her voice even.

"It didn't." This from Peter, who leaned against the rig.

She held his gaze. "I checked my air pack yesterday morning. The tank was full."

"We didn't use them before the fire," Diaz, hovering behind Mick, said.

"I know." She held their gazes unflinchingly. "But it was full."

Four doubting Thomases watched her.

"You don't believe me."

Mick shook his head. "Chelsea, we aren't upset about

this. Me and the guys talked about it over breakfast. We'll just forget it happened. It was one little mistake."

Over breakfast. "I wasn't invited to this little pow-wow?"

Mick hurried to explain. "We thought you'd be tired and want to sleep in."

She bit her lip and turned her back on them, ripping the mask from its hoses. "Yeah, sure."

Someone grasped her arm and pulled her around. Peter. "You can't blame us for worrying. You know as well as anybody a mistake like this could endanger the rest of us."

"I didn't make a mistake."

He shrugged. "Okay, so something's wrong with the tank."

"Yes, it is. I'll send it to maintenance and see what."

"Fine," Diaz said. Chelsea had learned that of all of them, Don liked conflict the least. "Let's drop it. We won't tell Jake."

"Oh, no," Chelsea said. "I'm reporting this to my officer."

"Why?" Mick asked.

"Because I did nothing wrong."

A few feet away, she saw something flare in Joey Santori's eyes, but he remained silent.

"Suit yourself," Huff said. "We're going over to see him after work."

"Am I invited to come along this time?" she asked sarcastically.

They nodded sheepishly. One by one, they headed for the kitchen to meet with Ed.

Facing the rig, she struggled for composure. The insidious feeling of exclusion, the fear of becoming a pariah with her crew, reared its head. She leaned against the truck, its metallic surface cool against her hot cheek.

What a morning. First Ben Cordaro, now this.

She'd been mortified when the battalion chief had walked in and found her and Jake in a compromising position. Though Jake had covered well, saying she was overwrought from yesterday, Ben's eyes had been knowing.

Forcefully Chelsea banished the image. Instead, she summoned Jake's hoarsely uttered words, a soothing balm to her soul. *I love you, Chels.*

"Whitmore?"

She pivoted to find Santori looming behind her. Another hurdle, she thought, very tired of running the same race over and over. "Yeah?"

He stuck his hands in his pockets. "For what it's worth, I told the guys to ask you to come for breakfast this morning."

"You did?"

"Yeah."

The look they exchanged was meaningful.

"Thanks."

"You're welcome." He smiled like a little boy, then reached for her arm. "Come on, Firefighter Whitmore. I'll buy you a cup of coffee."

THEY WERE DRIVING Jake crazy, now that he was home. Jess, Barb and even Ben had hovered over him like mother hens most of the day until he wanted to scream. He leaned back into the pillows on his sofa bed and sighed. A breeze drifted in from the open windows and skylights, but he felt hot and sticky in the August heat. He hated being laid up, being so dependent.

Liar. If Chelsea came and played nurse, you'd be just fine.

He couldn't help but smile. He could still see her eyes sparkling with tiny starlike tears as she told him she loved him. Years of loneliness, of self-imposed separation, had been washed away by three little words.

"Jake?" Barbara was framed in the arched doorway. Late-afternoon sunlight slanted in from the skylights. She looked tired and a little worried. "I'm leaving. Supper's in the oven for Jess to heat up before she goes to work at the gym tonight. Would you like me to come back?"

"No, Barb, I'm fine. You've done enough."

"Well, I'll be at home if you need me." She came farther into the room, leaned over and kissed him on the cheek. Then she gently caressed his face with her fingers. "I'm glad you're all right."

He grasped her hand. "Thanks for everything."

She started to say more, but stopped at a commotion on the stairs. It sounded like a buffalo run.

Jake grinned. "My group's arrived."

They'd called to say they'd be over right after work. Five uniformed Rockford firefighters traipsed into the room.

"Jeez, what is this, your own private getaway?" Mick, the first in, asked as he scanned the upper floor of Jake's house.

"How come we ain't never seen it?" Diaz wanted to know.

"Nice digs, Scarlatta," Peter commented.

"Hi, guys," Jake said dryly. He looked past Mick and Don, then Joey, to see Chelsea enter just before Huff.

Her eyes found his, and she gave him a private smile.

He scowled. Her face was drawn. Her mouth tight. Why?

After Barb bade them hello and goodbye, Peter and Don took the stuffed chairs; Joe and Mick pulled up straight-backed ones. He noticed Joey got a chair from the desk for Chelsea. "Sit down, Whitmore. We don't wanna have to give you mouth to mouth if you pass out."

She moved farther into the room. Before she sat, she went to Jake and gave him a hug. Brotherly. Like a colleague. Then she sank onto the chair.

"Not doin' good, Whitmore?"

"She shouldn't've come to work today," Don said, looking at the ceiling. "Women!"

"I'm fine. I just didn't sleep well." Her gaze focused on Jake. "How are you today, Lieutenant?"

"I had a great morning," he said mischievously, and watched her blush. "But the rest of the day's been downhill."

"Barb's babying you again?" Mick asked.

Chelsea lifted her brow. "Again?"

"Yeah," Mick teased. "Jake catches a little cold, and Barb's over here with chicken soup."

"Hmm," Chelsea said, her eyes narrowing on Jake.

He squirmed. "Tell me about today. What runs did we get?"

There was a brief silence. Jake felt the tension rise. Finally Joey cleared his throat. "Four calls, all EMS."

Jake waited.

Because she rarely spoke for the group, he was surprised when Chelsea said, "Jake, there's something you need to know. Yesterday my SCBA alarm went off just after the ceiling collapsed."

"That was yours?"

"Yes."

"I don't understand. We were only in the building ten minutes."

"I know. It malfunctioned."

Jake saw Peter turn away and study a picture on the wall. Mick shifted in his seat. Don looked at the floor. Joey watched Chelsea.

"Malfunctioned?" Jake asked. "That's pretty rare."

Chelsea's hands were linked in her lap. The sunlight

shining down on her made her face look even more drawn. "I know. Nonetheless, it did. I'm certain I checked it in the morning."

Ah, now he understood. He scanned his men. Okay. He needed to handle this as Chelsea's lieutenant. Not as her lover. In his mind he replayed the previous morning. Chelsea got to the station house later than usual. She'd gone right to the bay, but they'd had a call in minutes.

Focusing on her, he saw her bite her bottom lip. He struggled for objectivity. His men would be watching, too. What would he say to any of them? "You were later than normal, Whitmore."

"I went to the bay as soon as I came in."

"We got a call right away."

"I still had time to check my air pack and get my goods on the rig."

True, her gear was in place.

"You're positive you checked it?"

"Yes, sir."

He stared at her hard. He was about to drop the whole thing when he remembered something.

Chelsea, didn't you turn the stove off before we left?

Of course I did.

It was difficult for him, but he said, "A couple of weeks ago, you thought you turned the stove off, too."

Shock registered on her lovely features. And hurt. It pained him more than his legs. "I admitted I could have made a mistake with the stove, though quite frankly, I still remember turning it off. I *know* I checked my air tank."

The room was silent. He could hear clattering in the kitchen two stories below; larks chirped in the trees outside his window.

Jake thought for a minute. "Maybe we should discuss this privately."

"No," she said firmly. "I've already talked to the guys

about it.'' She enunciated clearly as she repeated, ''I checked the air tank. It was full.''

He surveyed his men. They looked conflicted. He realized they wanted to believe her. And, he knew in his heart, *he'd* believe one of them if he made the same claim. ''Fine. You say you did it, I believe you. Send the equipment to maintenance tomorrow for repair.''

''I sent it today,'' she said stiffly.

''Good.''

Discomfort hung like a rain cloud over them. He felt a responsibility to defuse it. ''Things like this happen,'' he told them. ''My Nomex hood got misplaced once, and I ended up in a fire without it.''

Catching on, Joey added, ''Remember the time my gloves fell off the truck? You were pissed off as hell.''

Jake smiled. Mick, Don and Peter chimed in with their own stories of mistakes, malfunctions, things that hadn't gone right. After ten minutes the tension was gone.

When the phone rang, Jake was chuckling at yet another story as he picked it up. ''Scarlatta.''

''Jake, this is Francey.'' She sounded upset. Or was it just excited?

''Hi, kiddo.''

''I'm at Our Lady of Mercy. I've got Suzy Mayfield.''

''*What?*''

''Jeez, Jake, Dylan and I were just patrolling and I saw her sneak in here. We followed her and cornered her in the foyer.''

Jake gripped the receiver. ''She's not alone, is she?''

''No, Dylan's charming her socks off.''

''Oh, God, this is great.'' He covered the mouthpiece. ''Dylan and Francey found Suzy.''

Cheers rang out.

He told Francey, ''I'll call the hot line, have them get in touch with her parents.''

Francey said, "I don't think that's the first thing she should do. She talked to me awhile. When she realized my father was a firefighter, she broke down. She ran away because she's afraid of losing her father. Of course, it doesn't help that her mother drinks because of his job."

"France, you okay with this?" he asked. "I'm thinking of what happened with *your* parents."

"Hell, yes. Dylan says fate had me find her. She and I talked for a long time about it. But I think she should see Reed before we bring in her parents. She's agreed."

"Wow. You guys are miracle workers." He sighed. "I wish I could come down."

"Tough luck, buddy. I'll call Reed, then let you know tonight what's happening."

"Thanks."

Jake's grin was broad when he hung up the phone. He told the crew the story. Chelsea, Mick, Don and Joey all talked at once about how great it was that the fire department had found her.

Beyond them, Peter sat, leafing through a magazine. He didn't appear to be listening.

Pictures flicked into focus. How silent Peter had been when they'd decided at lunch to do the search. His unusual absences in the days after. How he'd never once participated in Operation Suzy.

After a few minutes Mick glanced at his watch and got to his feet. "I gotta baby-sit tonight." He sounded disgruntled.

Don stood abruptly. "Oh, damn, me, too. I told Lucy I'd be home by six."

Joey rose, also. "*I* have a hot date, so I'm outta here."

From the bottom of the stairs, Jess yelled, "Chelsea, can you come down here a second? I can't figure out how long to heat Dad's supper."

In minutes he and Peter were alone. Huff had put down the magazine, crossed his arms and stared into space.

Jake said, "Wanna talk about it?"

"Not really." But his bleak expression said otherwise.

"It might help."

Huff swallowed hard. "Nothing helps this."

"Give me a shot, buddy."

A long silence. Then Peter sank back into the chair and sighed. "I left the police department four years ago because my partner was killed in an undercover operation." He didn't meet Jake's eyes. "I was in it with her."

"Her?"

"Yeah." He smiled. "Marla Mason. She was this gorgeous, stacked blonde. Married. Two kids, but she looked about sixteen." He closed his eyes. "I got involved with her. I tried not to, but it was too hard to spend all that time together and fight the attraction."

Jake understood Peter's dilemma all too well.

"What happened?"

"We were working in a bad section of the city." He stared at Jake. "She was posing as a runaway. Pimps preyed on the girls who hung out there. Got them into prostitution." He stood up and paced. "She took a bullet in the head from one of them when he realized she was undercover."

"God, Peter, I'm sorry."

"I witnessed it."

"Oh, no."

"I was posing as a caseworker at a shelter." He swallowed hard again. "They shot her right out front." His voice broke.

"I'm sorry." After a silence Jake asked, "Did you catch them?"

"Yeah. We broke up the whole ring." He shook his head. "I was offered a lieutenancy after that."

"Why'd you leave?"

"I went a little crazy. Marla died. I had a lot of contact with her husband and little boys and felt guilty for having had an affair with her." He went to the window to look out. "I decided I couldn't handle women in the department for a lot of reasons. I felt too protective of them, mostly." He faced Jake. "So I joined the RFD because there were only a handful of women here and I didn't think I'd have to deal with this issue."

"Surprise, huh?"

Peter jammed his hands into his pockets. "Whitmore's okay. But I have to stop myself from jumping in front of her in a fire, lifting things for her—that kind of thing." He shook his head. "She'd really appreciate that, wouldn't she?"

"She might understand if she knew the circumstances."

"No, I'd rather no one knew. I'm only telling you because…it's been plaguing me lately. Maybe because of this runaway thing."

"You could talk to Reed."

Peter shrugged. "Maybe."

"I'm glad you told me."

"I'm gonna go. I'm whipped." He smiled sadly. "The world just isn't what it used to be, is it?"

"No, I guess not." Jake was wondering about Peter's rather cryptic remark when Chelsea entered the room with Jess.

"See ya later," Peter said to them all as he crossed to the doorway. Jake heard his footsteps pounding down the stairs.

Jess said, "Chelsea's gonna stay and give you dinner. Is that okay?"

"Fine by me."

Jessica walked over and kissed him goodbye. "I'll be back in the morning."

"Jess, I don't need baby-sitting. I'll call you when I get up."

She looked hesitant; he looked stern.

"Okay. Talk to you then." She faced Chelsea. "Don't let him boss you around."

Chelsea smiled at his daughter. The smile died when Jess left and she faced him. Crossing her arms, she asked bluntly, "Were you and Peter talking about me?"

"No, but let's get this out now." He reached over and yanked her down to the bed. "Before it's blown out of proportion."

Chelsea was surprised at the temper she could see simmering in Jake's gray eyes. She tried to extinguish it. "I'm not upset or angry."

"I know." His voice was cold. "You look like you looked before, every time you talked about Milligan."

"No, I—"

He held up his palm. His other hand was still clamped around her wrist. "Damn it, I'm not Milligan. Do you understand that?"

Summoning her professional self-respect, she raised her chin. "Yes."

"Good. Now let's talk about the air pack. I handled you just as I would have handled Mick or Joey. You say you checked it, then you did."

"You don't know me as well as you know them."

His face softened. "I know enough. You laid foam and didn't blink an eye when the red devil reignited. You didn't panic in the ceiling collapse. You're an excellent firefighter."

She sucked in her breath. "Thank you."

"I want your trust, Chelsea."

"As an officer or as a man?"

His grip on her tightened fractionally. "Both."

"I'm trying."

That seemed to make it worse. "I'm not Milligan," he repeated. "That you'd lump me in with him is insulting."

Again she elevated her chin. "All right. I'll remember that."

He held her gaze, then said, "Are we done with this?"

"Yes. I'll let you know what maintenance says."

"Fine." He released the vise around her wrist. "Now go lock the door. And when you come back to this bed, come as a woman, not as a firefighter."

IT WAS SUPPOSED to be different, separate, but it wasn't. A hot tide of passion rose within Jake, muddying the roles. All he knew was that waves of desire were thrashing though him by the time she returned to the bed. He could tell from her eyes, which blazed amber fire, that she felt it, too.

"Take off the uniform." His voice was gruff with sexual need.

She didn't hesitate. In an instant boots were kicked off, shirt and trousers gone. She reached up and yanked the rubber band out of her hair; her glorious flaxen mane fell in wild waves around her shoulders.

She was a goddess, standing before him, strong, beautiful, mirroring the hues of the earth—honey-colored hair, tawny eyes, golden skin. Scraps of toffee silk bound her breasts and stretched across her hips.

"The underwear, too." His voice was hoarse.

She flicked open the front closure of the bra. Dragged down the panties. Again, like a goddess, she looked at him haughtily. "All right." Her words were husky, demanding. "Now you."

Chelsea watched as Jake flushed, darkening his tanned skin further. Everything about him was dark tonight—his gray eyes had turned charcoal; his hair looked sable against the beige pillowcases. A beard stubbled his taut jaw. She shivered involuntarily. He was dark—and dangerous.

And just what she wanted.

Roughly he ripped the T-shirt over his head. A little more carefully, given his burns, he shed the gym shorts. Her eyes searched his body with hungry need.

He reached out and hauled her to her knees beside him. Locking his hand at her neck, he took her mouth. Both were ravenous.

"Straddle me," he ordered.

She obeyed.

She was so sleek and so firm, he thought as he explored her with his hands. The suppleness under his fingers thrilled him; the muscles leaping in response to his sent hard shocks of desire through his body. He couldn't stem the passion within him to possess this woman, nor did he want to. And she obviously felt the same.

He flipped her onto her back, then covered her, mastered her with his body, his mouth.

"I love you," he said savagely against her swollen lips.

"I love *you*. Too much."

"I'll never hurt you, I promise."

"Jake, I—"

He took her then, before she could deny him, thrusting possessively into her. She arched to meet him, twisted to get closer.

"Say you trust me, Chelsea. Say it."

Helplessly, hopelessly under his control, she abandoned all caution, all self-protectiveness. "I do, I trust you. I need you."

Her words, and the violent orgasms that claimed them simultaneously, burned away the doubt and anxiety.

For now, at least.

CHAPTER FOURTEEN

IN WORKING ORDER. No repair needed.

Jake swore at the maintenance worker's scrawl on Chelsea's air pack. The damn problem wasn't over with, after all. It was back like flames missed in salvage and overhaul.

He sank down at his desk. He was alone at the firehouse for the first time. It was four o'clock, and his crew, headed by Ed Knight for one more day, was at a call. Jake had come in because he was going stir-crazy at home and wanted to check his mail, clean up his desk and get ready for his next shift.

He hadn't expected this. He thought it was done with. Leaning back in his chair, surrounded by an eerie quiet, he recalled the lovemaking with Chelsea, her telling him she trusted him; his body hardened at the thought. He'd had her in a way that bound them together irrevocably. And now this.

Unbidden, Danny's long-ago words haunted him like a bad dream....

Hell, no, Jake, I wasn't drinkin'.... I didn't leave the truck unattended.... I'd never disobey a direct order....

The recollection forced Jake to think like an officer. He fingered the maintenance report. Had Chelsea made a mistake? Had she lied? The answer to those questions was unequivocal. Neither was true. He'd stake his life on it. So he wouldn't think about Danny, and he'd treat the situation as he would for any of the men on his group.

His group. What would they do? How should he handle this?

Well, he'd listen to their views. But he was going to drop the whole thing, as long as it wouldn't cause World War Three.

He didn't think it would. Chelsea was getting along with them. They respected her firefighting skills; they liked her, too, shown in their teasing and their concern when she was endangered.

What wasn't to like? She was bright, quick, brave and funny.

And sexy as hell. He could still feel her under him, like she'd been last night and the night before, whispering she loved him, needed him, believed in him.

God, he'd never been happier.

Distracted from his thoughts by the bay door going up, he watched the rigs back in. Chelsea drove the Quint and edged it expertly into place. The crew bounded off the trucks, razzing each other. Mick called something to Chelsea. She rounded on him, grabbed him and brought his arm up behind his back. He yelped. Peter pulled her off and said something that made her laugh.

They were still laughing when they threw open the door and found him in the watch room. Ed Knight waved on his way past into the kitchen.

"Hey, Jake, welcome back." Peter's smile was his usual reserved one. But his eyes were uneasy. From their discussion the other night?

"Couldn't stay away, huh, Scarlatta?" Joey asked.

Jake smiled, made small talk.

Mick edged toward the desk. "I told Ed I'd fill out the incident report."

"Hang on a minute, will you?" Jake picked up the maintenance report. "Chelsea, look at this."

She took the paper, skimmed it. Raised troubled eyes to his. "I don't understand."

"What?" Joey asked.

Scowling, she passed him the paper. It went from him to Mick to Don to Peter.

Huff read it and crumpled it in his hand. "I'm sick of this. Chelsea said she checked the air pack, so she did. Let's bury it."

Nodding their assent, the other three firefighters looked to Jake.

He faced her and was heartened by the lack of wariness on her face. By the trust. "My sentiments exactly," he said with the confidence of a military leader who believed in his men.

In contrast, her smile was sweet. And soothing. His heart bumped in his chest.

"Let's go have coffee," Huff said. "Mick can tell Jake his sexist joke."

"Oh, please," Chelsea drawled.

"You can tell him your male-bashing one." Obviously the group had been trading barbs.

In the kitchen, they got coffee; Mick sank onto a chair. "Me first."

"No, me," Chelsea said, then faced Jake. "What do they call all that flesh around the penis?" She grinned. "A man."

Jake groaned. "Lame, Whitmore."

Mick asked, "Why do women fake orgasms?"

Jake sputtered into his coffee. "Isn't this getting a little chancy here, guys?"

"Nah, Chelsea's one of us." Mick's grin was broad. "Why?"

With feigned disgust, Jake shook his head.

"Because they think we care," Mick said.

Chelsea rolled up a newspaper and threw it at him. Jake

laughed and sat back in his chair. The firehouse was warm with the late summer afternoon air and the easy camaraderie.

Voices came from the hallway—Ed Knight's low rumbling and someone else's. It was too early for the next shift, so it must be a visitor.

A tall, broad-shouldered man filled the doorway. Familiar blue eyes zeroed in on Jake. Dark hair, once thick and a little too long, was cut short; it was receding a bit, and shot through with gray. Expensive clothes draped a frame that had more meat on it than the last time Jake had seen him.

Danny DeLuca said simply, "Hi, Jakey boy."

DANNY LEANED BACK in the padded booth at Pumpers and blew smoke in Jake's face. As he took another long drag on the Marlboro, Jake noticed the lines around Danny's mouth and eyes.

"I can't believe you're here," Jake said.

"Needed to check some things out."

So you said. Jake had been so stunned to see Danny, he hadn't heard all the explanation of why his old friend had returned after ten years, but he'd gotten the gist. The crew, who knew him back then, crowded around him, talked a bit and suggested they all go to Pumpers after work. They had, and now Jake and Danny were alone in a booth. The others were standing at the bar.

"How *are* you, Danny?" Jake asked.

The grin Danny gave him was silky. Jake had remembered his smile before as honest and sincere. "Never better." He signaled the waitress. "Hey, baby, get me another. Bring a shot of Corby's with it."

Obviously Danny still had a taste for alcohol. Even though his attitude and his personality seemed to have changed. "What are you doing down in Key West?"

"Sales." He raised his wrist. On it was a Rolex watch.

"Nice." Jake wasn't as impressed as Danny no doubt wanted.

"How about you, buddy? I thought you'd be chief by now."

Reflexively Jake's hands fisted under the table. "No, I'm not. Just the same as when you left."

"Well, some things have changed." He nodded to the bar. "I think she likes me."

"Who?"

"The fox."

Jake frowned. "The fox?"

"Firefighter Whitmore," Danny said in a singsong voice. He leered at her. Jake tried to ignore it. "She's been checkin' us out since we got here."

She's worried about me. Though he didn't like Danny's attitude, Jake hid his pique.

"She into kinky stuff?"

For a moment Jake panicked. He remembered how Danny had always known what girls Jake had been attracted to, the time or two he'd snuck out with someone else before he and Nancy got married. Danny had razzed Jake incessantly about being able to read his mind. Then, however, Jake hadn't worried about Danny using it against him.

"What do you mean?"

"Does she sleep with more than one of you at a time?"

Jake forced his shoulders to relax. "As far as I know, she doesn't sleep with any of the guys."

"Come on, everybody knows...." He grinned. "Never mind, I'll find out for myself."

Jake stared at the man who'd been like a brother to him for thirty years. He'd turned into a stranger. But Jake wasn't giving up on him. "Danny, why'd you come back?"

The salesman's mask slipped. Danny coughed. Shifted. "Derek called me."

Jake wasn't surprised. When Jake had been hurt, Derek had opened up more than usual, relating some of the things he and Delaney had explored in therapy. One of them was Derek's unresolved issues with his father.

As if confirming Jake's thoughts, Danny said, "Apparently he's seein' some shrink. She told him to call me. He asked me to come home for a visit."

"For Derek's sake, I'm glad you did. Have you seen him?"

"Nah. Barb said he was at work when I went by the diner." He shook his head. "She looks old."

"Don't we all?"

Danny examined Jake's face. "Actually you look pretty good. Must be gettin' laid a lot. Nancy still hot in the sack?"

"Nancy and I are divorced."

"Ah. Got a younger babe?"

Jake shook his head.

With narrowed eyes, Danny stared hard at him; again Jake was uncomfortable. This was not the same man he knew years ago. Glancing over Jake's shoulder, Danny lifted his beer in a salute.

"She's smilin' at me." Danny frowned. "You sure you ain't boffin' her?"

"No. I'm not boffin' her." Jake glanced at his watch. "Derek gets out of work at four, doesn't he?"

Snorting, Danny stood and threw a wad of bills on the table. "Yeah. Still the old nag, aren't ya, Jakey?"

Jake didn't respond. He rose, too. "How long you here for?"

"Who knows. My business is…seasonal. I got time." His gaze burned into Chelsea's back. "Let's see if I've still got the touch in this town."

He chugged the rest of his beer, then swaggered to where Chelsea sat on a stool, still sparring with the guys. Danny sidled between her and Mick.

Jake watched as gradually Danny angled his body near her. After a few minutes he inched closer. His arm slid around the back of her chair.

It was then that Chelsea caught on. He could see it in the stiffening of her shoulders. In her expression. She tried to swivel her stool away from him, but Danny's hand stopped it.

Finally she got to her feet. Jake prayed she didn't leave the bar; Danny would follow her, and Jake would be forced to intervene. Already on an emotional roller coaster at Danny's return, he wasn't sure he could disguise his feelings.

Instead, she headed for the women's room. Smart girl.

Jake sat in the booth. In minutes, she slid in across from him.

"You okay?" she asked.

He shook his head.

"I'm sorry he's here."

"Watch out for him, Chels. He's changed. He used to be a nice guy. Now he's.... I don't know, just watch out."

"Why's he back?"

"Seems your sister and Derek engineered it." Jake scowled. "I hope it's the best thing for Derek, but given how different Danny seems, I'm not sure it is. Poor Derek. He's got a lot of unresolved issues with Danny."

"He's not the only one."

"I know."

"Not a good time for the ghosts to return, is it?"

Jake shrugged.

"It makes our situation—"

"Don't say it. Don't compare us to him and me."

Spontaneously she reached over and squeezed his arm.

As she did, Danny appeared at their table. He stared at her hand on Jake. "Well, I'm off, Jakey boy." He scrutinized Chelsea for a minute, then reached out and pulled the tie from her hair; it spilled over her shoulders. He ran his hand down the thick mane. "I been dyin' to do that since I saw ya, darlin'. How about you and me gettin' together later?"

She yanked her head away. "No, thanks, lover boy. I got plans."

He looked at Jake's arm, from which she'd hastily withdrawn her hand. "I'll bet."

And then he was gone.

THE MID-AUGUST SUN beat down on the players. It was the big softball game between Quint/Midi Twelve and the fire academy. Chelsea was pitching. She took a practice throw and zinged the ball into Mick's glove. He tossed it back; she took two more practice throws and then the batter stepped up to the plate. It was the top of the ninth, Quint/Midi Twelve ahead by four. The batter was Ben Cordaro, looking more like forty-three than fifty-three. "Come on, girly," he growled. "Show your stuff."

She grinned. "Okay, old man."

From shortstop, her sister called, "Don't let the macho taunt get to you, sis."

Often friends and family members filled in for people who were on duty or sick. Chelsea liked having Delaney play on the team; she was good fun. Winding up, Chelsea whipped the ball to Ben.

He got a piece of it, and the ball grounded to her. Chelsea snagged it and threw it to Jake on first. He tagged Ben three feet in front of the base. Chelsea heard him say, "Not bad for a girl, huh, Ben?"

Ben grinned and trotted to the sidelines with a wave at Diana, who sat in the stands looking as fresh as a flower in a yellow sundress and hat—with a squirming Timmy O'Roarke on her lap.

Next up was Beth. Dylan had coerced her into joining the league. Despite her husband's protest, she played for the academy. From third base Dylan taunted, "Easy out, Chelsea. Lizzie Borden's no problem."

Beth ignored him, as usual, which increased his quips.

"She couldn't hit the broad side of a barn."

Beth let the first two pitches go, then swung at the third, sending it in a line drive to third base. Shocked, Dylan fumbled it. When she was safe on first, Beth cupped her hands and yelled, "Stick it, Boy Wonder."

Reed Macauley approached the plate. Chelsea suspected that Beth had gotten him to join the team along with her. He looked like he was having fun. Delaney, however, couldn't let him alone. She yelled, "This one's over the hill, Chels. No problemo."

Dressed in cutoffs and the green academy team shirt, Reed looked young and fit. He shook his head at Delaney's taunt and got two strikes. Then he hit a long drive down the first base line, past Jake, out to right field.

Joey scooped it up and threw it to Jake. Too high, the ball went over his head. Chelsea, who'd positioned herself about ten feet behind Jake, caught it and tossed it to him for an out. Beth, meanwhile, had made it to second. Jake jogged up to Chelsea and gave her a high five. "We make a good team, don't we, babe?"

The little devil in her that he always encouraged snuck out. In a lowered voice she said, "On the field *and* in bed."

"Shush," he told her, but chuckled.

"Great play, Jakey boy." Both she and Jake turned to the stands, where Danny sat with Derek.

Jake stiffened.

Chelsea trotted to the mound. *Jerk,* she thought. Jake

had been tense and worried since Danny had come to town three days ago. He'd tried to talk to Danny about the past, but Danny had sidestepped the discussion. She hoped Francey didn't invite him to the picnic at her house on the lake after the game, because she wanted Jake to have a good time.

Eric Scanlon, a captain on the Academy team, came up to bat next. Chelsea's first pitch was a strike. "Way to go," Delaney yelled. Minutes later, on a full count, Eric bunted and raced down the baseline. Jake came in and scooped up the ball just as Eric ran past him. Chelsea had run for first base, and Jake tossed the ball to her. She caught it only a split second before the runner touched the base.

"Out!" the umpire called.

The game was over. Quint/Midi Twelve had won six to two.

Jake jogged over to Chelsea and swatted her fanny. When she turned, indignant, he drawled, "All in good fun."

With an evil grin, she pretended to get in his face. "Underneath what you just tapped are the leopard panties."

His faced blanked, then he laughed. "Touché, Whitmore."

They joined their teammates and everyone hugged, including Chelsea and Jake. He lifted her and twirled her around, and as she laughed and clutched his shoulders, she caught sight of DeLuca staring at them. Then people crowded around, blocking him from view. Chelsea willed herself not to worry. It was a beautiful day, she was looking forward to the picnic, and she wasn't going to let Danny ruin anything for Jake and her.

As she and Delaney drove to Francey's, Delaney's idle comments about the few days Danny had been in town and how it had upset Derek made Chelsea's confidence waver.

"They're coming to Francey's," Delaney said. Chelsea pulled the car up behind a snazzy Corvette, and the women climbed out.

"Why?"

"I heard DeLuca wheedle an invitation from Alex."

"He's a jerk."

Delaney snorted. "Fathers! They can ruin things for a kid."

Chelsea grabbed Delaney's hand. "Was it so bad for you?"

"Sometimes. I'll never understand why Mom put up with it."

"Love."

Delaney snorted again. "All the more reason to avoid that trap."

They took the path that led behind the house to a beautiful sunny backyard. Cedar decks leveled off from each of the three stories of the Templeton house, which looked like something out of *Architectural Digest.* Umbrella tables spotted the lawn and decks. Several feet away the lake sparkled like jewels in the four o'clock sun.

Chelsea surveyed the group. Almost everybody from both teams was here. Ben sat to the side on a step. Diana perched on one above him, knees apart, rubbing his back. He chuckled at something she said.

The O'Roarkes were spread out on a blanket under a tree, Timmy asleep, Dylan with his head in Beth's lap. Utter peace shone from their faces as she read to him.

"Delaney?"

Chelsea looked into the pretty face of a woman she didn't recognize. She had blond-streaked hair and big blue eyes.

Delaney said, "Andrea. How nice to see you!"

The woman smiled. "What are you doing here?"

"Chelsea Whitmore's my sister. Chels, this is Andrea Murphy, a social worker from Mercy House. Chelsea's a firefighter."

"You're Mick's wife." Chelsea extended her hand.

"I never made the connection because of your different last names," Andrea said.

"Mick's been wonderful to me since day one." Chelsea smiled. "I really owe him."

A shadow crossed the pretty woman's face. "I'm glad. He's not so liberal with me and his daughter." The women made small talk until Andrea asked Delaney, "Can you and I talk shop for a minute?"

"Sure."

"I'll go meet your daughter," Chelsea said, and nodded to where Mick sat by a small blond child who swam in a kiddie pool the Templetons had set up. Chelsea had taken two steps when someone crashed into her.

"Watch where you're goin', doll."

She stared into the cold blue eyes of Danny DeLuca. "Sorry."

He touched her hair, and she backed away. "Did you wear it down for me?"

Chelsea took a deep breath. "Look, we don't know each other well enough for you to make those comments to me."

"I'd like to change that."

"I wouldn't."

He leaned closer; she got a whiff of something—pot? "Why not, baby? Why eat hamburger at home—" he nodded to where three of her group members stood, then patted his chest "—when you can have steak out?"

"I don't eat red meat at all, DeLuca."

She circled him and crossed to Mick. Sinking to the grass beside him, she said, "The creep."

"He's givin' our lieutenant a rough time," Mick told her. "He cornered Jake before you got here."

"He's a powder keg." She hoped Delaney knew what she was doing with him and Derek.

Mick frowned as he stared across the lawn. "What's your sister talking about to Andie?"

"Some case."

"Figures. My wife can't leave it alone."

Chelsea was shocked at the bitterness in his voice. "Mick?"

He sighed. "Don't mind me. I'm feelin' sorry for myself." His gaze surveyed the grounds. "Not a good day all around for our firehouse. Don's wife refused to come to the picnic."

"I wanted to meet her." When Mick was silent, she asked, "Is everything okay with them?"

"Don took a second job—they need the money. Lucy's not happy that he's gone so much."

"I'm sorry."

"Women!"

"Hey, watch it, buddy."

Leaning over, he splashed water with his daughter. "'Cept for you, huh, Casey?"

"She's beautiful."

Peter sauntered over.

"How come you've never got a woman on your arm?" Mick asked him.

Peter said, "All the good ones are taken."

Mick and Chelsea exchanged a glance.

"Anybody want a beer?" Peter asked.

"I'll have a soda until Andrea takes over watching the kid here."

Chelsea rose and accompanied Peter to the coolers set under the overhang of the deck. There she found Jake, talking with Francey and Alex.

Francey said, "Hey, here comes the arm."

Chelsea smiled and avoided looking at Jake. Peter snagged the drinks and left to go back to Mick.

"You two were certainly in sync today." Alex nodded to her as she got a beer and twisted off the top.

"Who, me and Jake?"

"Yeah."

"Got a good rhythm together," he said with a barely disguised sexual undertone.

The beer she'd just sipped sputtered all over. "Sorry." She wiped her mouth. "Yeah, I guess we do know where to put the ball."

His eyes sparked mischief. "And the glove."

Francey said, "Well, something went right."

"I like playing with Chelsea." Jake was obviously enjoying the double entendres.

She put the bottle to her lips and murmured, "You're not a bad guy to play with, either."

"France, come over here!" Dylan yelled.

"I'm comin', too." Alex followed her. "Maybe I'll get to hold Timmy." Alex and Francey left them alone.

Jake leaned against the cedar siding. He watched the calm blue lake and sipped his beer. Still without looking at her, he said, "Little girls who tease have to pay the price."

She pretended interest in the beer label. "Yeah?"

"Yeah."

"So what's the price?"

"You'll see. Later."

"Where? Your place or mine?"

Jake frowned. "I'll come to yours. I'm worried about Derek; I want to keep an eye on him for a while."

"I'm sorry."

He pushed away from the house. "You can kiss and make it better," he said, and walked away.

She watched him go, smiling.

"He's a great guy, isn't he?"

Chelsea turned. DeLuca again. "Yes, he is."

"Is he a good lieutenant?"

Chelsea couldn't resist. "The best."

"How's he in bed?"

"I wouldn't know."

"That's not what Jakey said."

She gave him a haughty look. "You're pathetic, De-Luca." Chelsea started to walk away.

He grabbed her arm roughly. "Listen, lady…"

She glanced pointedly at her arm. "Let go of me."

His grip tightened. She remembered Billy's violence, and her stomach clenched.

Joey appeared behind Danny. "Hey, Chels. I picked up the new car today. Wanna see it?" He said to Danny, "You don't mind if I take Chelsea for a minute?" Expertly he drew her away. Danny was forced to let go. Joey's face was full of thunderclouds as he escorted her to the side of the house. He stopped when they were out of sight of Danny.

She said, "No car?"

He shook his head. "Your arm's red."

She glanced down. Tiny marks were visible below the sleeve of her T-shirt. "Damn."

"Any man who treats a woman that way is an ass."

"Where does he get off?"

"I don't know."

"Thanks for helping me out."

"I thought you were gonna deck him. Not that you're not gorgeous, Whitmore, but I think he's doin' it to get Jake's goat."

She stiffened. "What do you mean?"

"Are you kidding? Jake's Sir Galahad. If he thinks

Danny's pushing you, he'll go after him. Danny's out to embarrass Jake."

"Why?"

"It's always been that way. Danny could never measure up to Jake—not in the fire department, not in high school. He blames Jake for all his problems when, really, he made Jake's life hell. Nobody's glad to see him back."

Chelsea smiled at him. "You're a nice guy, you know that, Santori?"

Joey chugged his beer. "Yeah, don't tell anybody." His eyes landed on Francey, and they lost their mirth.

Following his gaze, she asked, "Does it still hurt?"

"It'll always hurt," he said, and walked away.

Chelsea leaned against the wall and closed her eyes. An ominous feeling stole over her. She shivered with it. God, she hoped nothing worse happened today.

JAKE HAD FELT IT building all night, like a storm brewing over the lake. Maybe it was because he'd once known Danny so well. Maybe because he'd been the victim of Danny's anger and bitterness before. Maybe because he'd watched Danny all evening get progressively more stoned and more obnoxious. Regardless, it hurt to know what his friend had become.

So he wasn't surprised when he saw Danny heading toward where he stood on the edge of the lower deck with the five members of his group, along with Ben, Reed and Dylan.

One of the new academy trainers walked by as Danny approached. "How'd ya think it went this morning, Jake?"

Jake stiffened. "Ah, good. You?"

"Too tough for me. You probably aced it, though."

"Aced what?" Joey asked when Mike moved on. Danny stood in the background, listening.

Jake traded looks with Ben. Ben shrugged.

"I, uh, took the captaincy exam this morning."

Joey asked sharply, "Why didn't you tell us?"

"I didn't want to make a big deal out of it."

"If you make the grade, you can't be captain at Quint Twelve because Ed Knight already is," Mick observed. "You can only have one captain per station house."

"Ed Knight might be retiring this year. He just told me." Ben was trying to smooth ruffled feathers.

"You shoulda told us, Jake." Mick looked upset.

"I'm sorry, Mick. I just—"

"So, how'd you do?" Peter cut in. He seemed genuinely interested.

"Jakey boy probably got a hundred. He's perfect, don't you know that?" This came from Danny.

Diaz tried to joke. "Nah, we know his flaws."

"Do you?"

"Lay off, DeLuca," Joey said.

But Danny moved closer. He was unsteady on his feet, and his cigarette was within half an inch of burning Jake's arm. Jake didn't step away, however; he just stared at his old buddy. Guilt for his part in bringing Danny to this bumbling, drunken state flooded him. The sense of disappointment for what Danny had become was great.

"What's a matter, Jakey? They never seen your bad side?"

Ben said, "Danny, now isn't the time for this."

"No? Why not?"

Ben reached for his arm. "For one thing, your son is about ten feet behind you."

Pivoting, Danny scowled. Derek stood behind him with Jessica. "So what?" He faced Jake again. "Derek thinks you walk on water like the rest of them. It'll be good for him to hear the truth."

Reed stepped forward. "Danny, why don't we take a walk."

"Why don't you take a hike? And take that female shrink with you, away from my kid."

"Delaney's helping Derek. But let's go talk about it. She can come with us."

"No, I got something to say."

Ben opened his mouth to speak, but Jake intervened. He had to face this. Swallowing the hurt Danny's bitterness incited, Jake said, "All right, let's go inside. You can say whatever you want there."

"Wanna do it here. In front of everybody. I want them all to know." He indicated their little circle, and also Francey, Alex and Beth, who'd gathered around.

"Know what?"

"What kind of man you are."

"He's a decent man," someone said.

"Back off, DeLuca," somebody else said.

Jake was poleaxed by the vindictiveness on Danny's face.

"Y'all better listen to me," Danny said. "You could be next."

No one spoke.

"Do they know, Jakey, that you'll turn on them to cover your own ass?"

Jake stood silent.

"Does *she* know—" he angled his head to Chelsea "—not to get too close to you? That you'll pick on every little thing she does and make your faults hers?"

Jake remained stoic. He wouldn't defend himself. He wouldn't stoop to Danny's level.

Again, nobody spoke. Until Derek broke away from Delaney—Jake hadn't seen her come up to the boy—and elbowed his way to his father. "Don't, Dad."

Danny's eyes were glazed as they landed on Derek.

"He took you away, too." Derek's gaze snapped to Jake. "You took my job, my friends and even my son. Wouldn't be surprised if you were screwin' my wife." He threw a leering glance at Chelsea. "After you get through with her, that is."

Ben Cordaro stepped forward and put a hand on Danny's shoulder. "I've heard enough of this tripe. You're insulting my daughter's friends and ruining her party. Let's go, DeLuca."

Danny shrugged him off. "You're stickin' up for him. You always did."

Ben said, "He's always deserved it."

Reed came up on the other side of Danny. "Let's go."

Danny's gaze swung from Reed to Ben and back again. No doubt realizing he could never win a physical contest against the two, especially in his state, he said casually, "Sure, why not? I'm gonna blow this pop stand, anyway." He faced Derek. "You comin', son?"

Tears streamed down Derek's face. He stared at his father as if he didn't recognize him. Then he shook his head.

Danny deflated before their eyes. His shoulders sank, and he docilely let Reed and Ben lead him around the house.

Tension quivered in the air. Jake watched Derek, then stepped toward him. After a second Derek flung himself into Jake's arms. Jake's eyes stung for the boy Derek was, for the boy Danny used to be. Staring over Derek's shoulder, Jake saw a young Danny catching the football that Jake had passed him and scoring the winning touchdown.... Danny smiling as the best man in his wedding...Danny holding his hand the first time Jake had been badly burned. He closed his eyes to block out the current images of Danny—drunk and abusive. He clasped Derek to him. "Shh, son, it's all right. It's all right."

But he knew in his heart it wasn't. Would it ever be?

HIS BREATHING ESCALATED, and the darkness nipped at his heels as he paced. His strong side came out more now, *ruled* him, even in the daytime. He'd waited a week, like flames waiting to burst through in flashover. There would be no mistakes after this long. But it had to be tested.

Ever since the softball picnic he'd watched for signs. They didn't seem to treat each other differently. Maybe they were more comfortable with each other, but all of them felt at ease with Whitmore now.

He thought about spying on them, but it went against his grain. Instead, he'd test it, just as he'd tested the guys after DeLuca's spiel....

He's crazy, one of them said.

Jake's too smart for that, another put in.

Whitmore's not that kind of broad, somebody else said.

But they were uptight; the other accusation—that Jake wasn't a good leader, that he'd turned on one of his men once, that he'd made bad decisions—struck a chord.

So he'd kill two birds with one stone—see if the lieutenant favored Whitmore; it would show if he was, after all, a good leader *and* put one more nail in her coffin.

Jake would *have* to deal with what he had in mind.

CHAPTER FIFTEEN

FIRE RIPPED THROUGH several stores in a small strip mall in downtown Rockford. It reminded him of how, when he was a kid, he used to line up dry twigs, light them and watch them torch each other. The roof on one of the first buildings to ignite had been ventilated but was spongy now, so no one was allowed on it. Clouds of thick gray smoke billowed from several storefronts as the fire intensified; firefighters were barred from the inside.

He smiled to himself as he hefted the hose behind Jake. This was it. An exterior attack was perfect. He'd lucked out, which just went to show that his plan had been right. Judicious. Blessed. No one could get hurt if they weren't goin' into the building.

As he and Jake reached the side of one of the shops, he could see several aerials dumping water on the hungry flames that shot from windows and out the roof. The fire was a monster, needing to be appeased. Jake said, "Everybody's here," as he positioned the hose and lifted it. Whitmore would charge the hose, giving them water, back at the Midi, where she would also monitor the pressure. For a while. His conscience pricked him. His Jekyll side felt bad, but Hyde told him this was necessary.

"That's why we were called, Jakey baby," he said, rebounding as the pressure hit the nozzle and the hose pumped out gallons of water. "It's not our district." The blaze was so big and out of control, the battalion chief had asked for additional stations to come in and help.

Jake maneuvered the large, two-inch hand line in silence. It only took about five minutes for the water to recede. Jake shook the hose. "What the hell?" He turned. "You feel that?"

"Yeah."

Then the water stopped.

Battalion Chief Talbot came up behind them "What's going on, Jake?"

"We're out of water."

"What?"

"The water stopped." He could see the puzzlement on Jake's face. "I don't understand it."

"That's a hell of a deal." Talbot was irked. "Check the truck; see if you can fix it. We need all the water we can get."

Following Jake, his heartbeat escalated. This was it. Jake took long, angry strides toward his rig. When they reached the Midi, Jake went up to Whitmore. She had her head down, studying the gauges. "Whitmore? What's going on?"

Chelsea turned. Even in the darkness, broken only by generator lamps, he could see her face was pale. "I don't know. The gauges say we're out of water."

"That can't be. We can't have used more than two hundred gallons." He edged in front of her and checked the gauges. Then he turned. "It's empty. How is that possible, Whitmore?"

Her lips thinned and her eyes got as big as the moon above them. "I don't know."

"When you came in tonight, did you check the water level?"

"Yes, sir, I did."

"And?"

"It was filled. The truck wasn't used in a fire today, and the full gauge registered."

For long moments Jake stared at her. She stared back. Then he said, "I'll go see where Talbot wants us now."

Chelsea looked after him, then glanced at the gauges again. Shook her head. And walked off.

He sank back against the rig.

Whew. It was over. This was too public to let go. Jake couldn't possibly ignore it. All her other mistakes would start to add up, and there'd be action taken.

Would it be enough? He sure hoped so.

For her own good, he wanted her out of the RFD.

"I'D LIKE to see you in my office, Whitmore." Jake's voice was husky from fatigue and smoke inhalation. His linebacker shoulders were stiff with tension.

Her shoulders ached as if she'd carried a barbell on them all night. "Yes, sir."

Mick, Joey, Peter and Don stood behind her, openly listening. Peter stepped forward, as if to say something, but Jake turned his back, his message clear. This was between the lieutenant and one of his crew.

Jake trudged ahead of her; Chelsea kept her eyes averted, refusing to look at his safe solid back and those strong shoulders she thought she could lean on.

Stop it, she told herself. *This doesn't change things.*

Ever the gentleman, Jake opened the glass door to the watch office and held it for her to enter. It closed with a hiss in the still, silent firehouse. Chelsea could see the guys pass the office and traipse back to the kitchen.

"Sit."

She did, then he took a chair across from her. "What happened, Chelsea?" he asked simply.

"I don't know."

"I'm asking this in an official capacity. Did you check the water tank in the Midi when you came on duty?" His voice was toneless, but Chelsea could see the muscle leaping in his jaw. This wasn't easy for him. She respected the officer in front of her for carrying out a difficult task; simultaneously, her heart went out to the man she loved. God, what irony.

"Yes, I did. The tank was full."

"How do you account for its running out of water prematurely?"

"I can't."

"No malfunction?" Then he added, "Like your air tank."

She swallowed hard. "You said you believed me about that."

"I did. It's why I let it go. It was also only *one* thing, and I don't jump to conclusions."

He didn't mention the stove.

"What about now? Do you still believe me about the air pack?" This she hadn't expected. If he didn't believe her about that...

"It doesn't matter what I believe. What matters is that an entire operation could have been jeopardized by the loss of water. It wasn't, because so many rigs were there and we mounted an exterior attack. But if we'd been at a house fire, inside, and you made this mistake—"

"I know the danger of losing water, Jake." Her voice was cool; she straightened. "And I didn't make a mistake."

"Then how do you account for running out of water?"

"I can't."

He stared at her, his face blank. But his gray eyes rivaled the gloomiest of February mornings in Rockford. "I'm putting a memorandum in your file. Of reprimand."

Swallowing hard, she cinched her hands together in an effort not to react. "I see."

"For the record, I also put two commendations in there

after the foam blanket incident and the fire at the old man's
house.''

She nodded.

''I do that regularly for Santori, Huff, Diaz and Murphy.''

Again, she got the message. He was treating her like
he'd treat the guys. ''I understand.''

His officer persona slipped. ''Do you?'' he asked raggedly.

''Of course.'' She stood. ''Am I dismissed?''

He stared at her for a moment. ''Yes.''

A loud knock on the glass made them both jump. Her
relief waved to her. She gave him a weak greeting. Without another word she turned, opened the door and left.

JAKE SAT where he was as she disappeared into the locker
room. He took a deep breath and tried to blank his mind.
Instead, the ghosts came, specters from his past that were
never far away.

You turned on me, buddy. I'll never forgive you for that.
Danny's old taunt was accompanied by his newest. *Do
they know, Jakey, that you'll turn on them to cover your
own ass? Does she know not to get too close to you? That
you'll pick on every little thing she does and make your
faults hers?*

Don't think about it, he told himself. *Just do it.*

He turned to the computer. The memorandum took only
five minutes to type. Five minutes to destroy months of
trust building. No, he wouldn't think about it. He couldn't
confuse the roles. Not again.

As he printed the indictment, the office door opened and
his men entered. They came in silently, took seats or
leaned against the wall and closed the door. Were they
vigilantes today or the cavalry coming over the hill?

''What'd you do?'' Peter asked.

"I questioned Firefighter Whitmore and am putting this—" he held up the memo he'd just finished "—in her file."

Peter nodded.

"We don't have no say in it this time?" Mick asked. "'Cause if we do, I think you should drop it."

"He can't drop it," Joey said. "Not after the stove and the air pack."

"You don't want him to?" Mick's tone was accusing.

Joey scowled. "I don't know what I want."

Diaz said nothing, Jake noted. His face was sad.

"None of this matters. As your lieutenant, I've made the decision. It's done."

Out of the corner of his eye, Jake saw Chelsea exit the locker room, her bag looped over her shoulder. She hadn't showered. She'd removed her dress shirt and wore only the RFD T-shirt and pants. Her hair bounced around her shoulders like a golden halo as she walked. Coming even with them, she looked up.

Damn. He could imagine the tableau they created, gathered in the office without her. She scanned the men, her face showing confusion first, then the hurt that betrayal causes. Jake knew the look intimately. This was the second time in his life he felt like Judas. She watched them only a moment, then turned and headed out of the bay.

The room was uncomfortably silent. Firefighters from the day shift began to filter in. O'Roarke threw open the door. "Scarlatta and Santori, you're sprung."

The men nodded. Joey stood and, without saying anything more, left. So did Diaz.

Mick had a parting shot. "I think this stinks."

After they left, Jake leaned back in his chair and watched Peter, who, as he'd done the day Jake had questioned Chelsea about her air pack, had stayed behind.

"I haven't been a firefighter as long as you guys," Peter told him. "But I was a cop for twenty years."

"Yeah?"

"Something isn't right here."

Jake cocked his head.

"This doesn't fit with her MO."

A glimmer of hope sparked inside him. "I know."

"She's too good a firefighter."

"I know," Jake repeated. "But the stove and the air pack and now the water thing, Peter. They can't be ignored."

"I didn't say you should ignore them. I just said it doesn't add up." He stood. "This could cause problems."

As Jake watched Peter go, he thought, *You don't know the half of it.*

BETH O'ROARKE sat in the dining alcove of her kitchen, breastfeeding Timmy. But her expression was one of a Spanish inquisitor rather than a Madonna. "It doesn't make sense. Something else is going on here." Her no-nonsense tone calmed Chelsea, whose hands were still shaking from telling her story.

She'd come to the O'Roarkes' right from work. Dylan was at the firehouse, and Beth had taken one look at Chelsea and called Francey, who arrived within the hour. Chelsea had told them as quickly as possible what had happened.

Pouring coffee for the three of them, Francey took a seat across from Chelsea. "What are you saying, Beth?"

Beth's big brown eyes widened, and Chelsea remembered how she used to give that incredulous look to the recruits. "It's simple. Either someone else did these things, or Chelsea's losing her mind."

"I'm not losing my mind."

"Then…"

"Do you honestly believe she's being sabotaged?"

"I know it sounds cloak-and-dagger, but the stove was on, the air tank empty and the water in the truck low. Chelsea remembers turning the stove off, she's sure she checked her air tank and she's positive the Midi was full. Somebody else did it."

"Jeez." Francey stood when Beth drew back from her son to burp him. She eased Timmy from Beth and held the baby against her shoulder. Rubbing his back, she said, "That means it's somebody from Chelsea's group."

"Not necessarily." Beth stirred her coffee and stretched her legs out in front of her. "Other people have access to the bays. To the firehouse when the trucks are out."

"Who?" Chelsea asked.

Beth thought. "Maintenance people?"

Francey said, "Some."

"Officers?"

"A chief would do this?" Chelsea couldn't believe it.

"If he was out to get you." Beth frowned. "You make any official enemies lately, Chels?"

Chelsea froze at the nickname. *I love you, Chels.*

"Chelsea?" Beth asked.

"No, no enemies among the officers. At least not that I know of."

Beth thought for a minute. "Maybe Francey's right. Maybe it's a crew member."

Chelsea thought of Joey. *For what it's worth, I told the guys to ask you to come to breakfast this morning.*

She remembered Don's horrified look when she almost stepped into the basement water.

There were Peter's comments at the gunshot site—*You did a good job, Whitmore* and then at the old man's house—*I told you it was good to know you could handle him. I meant it.*

Finally Mick—his consistent, unflappable support. Could one of them really have done this to her?

She buried her head in her hands. "I can't believe it."

Leaning over, Beth rubbed Chelsea's back while Francey put Timmy into a Portacrib by the window. With the shades drawn, it was cool and dim there.

"Chelsea, don't go emotional on us now," Beth said gently. "We've got to think this through."

Raising her head, Chelsea said, "All right."

Francey came to the table with a pad and pencil she'd scrounged from a nearby drawer. "Let's go through each of the crew. For motive and opportunity."

Chelsea stirred her coffee as she told them about Mick, Don, Joey and Peter all being near the stove after she'd left.

Francey wrote it down. "And the Midi was open game for the whole day."

"They all had access to the air tank when I went to the hospital," Chelsea replied.

"Except Jake." Beth's tone was sober.

Abruptly Francey dropped her pencil, and Chelsea's spoon clattered to the table.

"What?" Chelsea was incredulous.

"You can't be serious." Francey said. "Jake?"

"Look, I know he's close to you."

"He's a *brother* to me."

"Even people we love are capable of hurting us. Especially if they think it's for our own good." Beth shook her head. "Anyway, since there's no way Jake could've had access to your air pack, he's ruled out."

Chelsea's head was starting to throb.

"So everybody had opportunity," Francey continued. "Who has motive?"

"Joey." Beth was thoughtful. "He's still raw over losing you, France."

"Are you sure?"

Chelsea said, "*I'm* sure. He told me at your picnic."

Francey's face fell. "He hates you because you're my friend and tries to hurt you? Oh, God, this is awful."

"A vendetta against all women?" Beth said. "Maybe."

"How about the other guys?"

Regretfully Chelsea thought of something else. "I know Don and Mick are both having marital problems."

"That could do it," Beth and Francey said simultaneously.

Chelsea smiled in spite of the circumstances. "Oh, as if you two have experience with that."

"Alex and I fight. Still. Over my job."

"Dylan's better about risks, but I yell at him at least once a month for doing something stupid." A pause, then Beth added, "No relationship's perfect."

After a moment's quiet Francey asked, "What about Huff? He's pretty closemouthed. I wonder what baggage he's carrying."

"I don't know." Chelsea pictured Peter's inscrutable face. "The quiet hides a sadness, I think."

"Maybe over a woman?"

"Maybe." Chelsea stood. "Look, this is so farfetched. Because Mick's wife went back to work and he didn't want her to doesn't mean he's mentally unbalanced. Diaz's wife being miffed because he's never home doesn't prove a mental defect in the guy."

"No, they're just clues to who might want to hurt you."

"But what good is this doing?" Chelsea asked.

Timmy began to wail from the crib. Chelsea crossed to the window and picked him up. Holding him to her chest, she paced as she talked. "Now we know everybody—except Jake—has the motive and means to hurt me. That doesn't help us at all."

"Yes, it does." Beth stood and poured more coffee. "It

reinforces that you've got to protect yourself, be suspicious of everybody. Watch your back. Somebody's out to get you.''

Chelsea pictured her crew and wanted to bawl like Timmy.

''He'd have to be a Jekyll and Hyde, then,'' she said forcefully.

Beth frowned. ''Some men are, honey.''

Clutching Timmy to her, Chelsea thought, *Some men, but not all. Certainly not Jake.*

JAKE SAT in his car in front of her house, trying to quell the hundred tiny voices in his head that chanted, *You blew it.* Damn. Where *was* she?

Since the shift ended, at seven this morning, he'd been looking for her. As soon as he left work, he'd driven to her house, telling himself she'd go home so he could meet her there and talk. She hadn't. Then he'd checked out his house, hoping she'd call or come to him. He'd taken a shower, drunk some coffee, waited. The demons had taunted him too much, so after more phone calls, he'd headed to the gym. Jess was working; surreptitiously— which he realized he was getting tired of—he'd found out Chelsea wasn't there, hadn't been there and hadn't called in. That worried him even more. He'd driven to Francey's, figuring he could make excuses for seeing his surrogate sister; no one had been home.

Now, at two o'clock, he was at Chelsea's place again, dressed and ready for work. He had to be at the firehouse in a couple of hours, but he sure as hell didn't want to see her then for the first time. They needed to talk, so he waited for her, as he had after the basement incident. Purposefully he summoned that day—the kisses in the garage, the promises in her bed.

He heard his own vow. *I'll never turn on you, no matter what happens.*

And her reply. *If things do go wrong, I promise, I won't blame you like Danny did. I won't turn on you, either.*

Did she mean it? She had to. He'd trusted her with his heart; he'd taken a risk he thought he'd never take again.

Just then her red Camaro sped down the street and swerved into the driveway, then into the garage. She got out and went to the house without seeing him.

Hell. He stomped out of his car and strode to the door. She'd given him a key, but he rang the bell, anyway.

She pulled it open. Her face was drawn, her eyes bloodshot. She'd untucked the T-shirt from her cutoffs and kicked off her shoes. Her hair was wild.

There was surprise on her face. Anger kindled, licked at him, like just-beginning flames. Could she honestly think he wouldn't come? "Where have you been?" he asked, trying to quell the cauldron of emotion bubbling inside him.

"Excuse me?"

"I've been looking for you all day."

She stared at him.

"I was worried."

"I'm sorry."

"Are you?"

"Yes. I didn't think you'd... I didn't expect..." She shrugged. "I guess I wasn't thinking."

About me. That hurt.

He leaned against the doorjamb. "Can I come in?"

"Of course." Stepping aside, she let him into the living room. He was reminded of the night Billy had come after her. Of what had started here. He'd be damned if he'd let her go without a fight.

Plowing his hand through already disheveled hair, he

sank onto a couch. She perched on the footstool, out of touching distance.

"We need to discuss this." His tone was no-nonsense.

"What's there to discuss, Jake?"

"I'm not turning on you, Chels."

She clutched her hands together until they were white. "I know that."

"Do you?"

"Yes."

"Then why didn't you come to me today?"

"I needed to think."

"Where did you go?" If she said, "To Spike," he didn't know what he'd do.

"To Beth and Francey."

Even that hurt. "All day?"

"Yes. We talked through the morning, had lunch. I showered and tried to take a nap at Beth's."

"Why didn't you come to me?" he asked again.

She looked at him, exasperation crossing her face. "Jake, you're part of this. You're part of what I'm trying to deal with. I can't talk to you about it."

"I hate hearing that." Edging off the couch, he came to his knees in front of her. "I'm not turning on you," he repeated.

As she grasped his hand, the struggle was evident in every line of her lovely face. "I know. I believe that." Her eyes were bright. "It's just hard to deal with."

"We'll deal with it together."

"How?"

"By weathering it. By letting it run its course."

She looked unconvinced.

He said raggedly, "Tell me you trust me on this. I need to hear it."

She waited a long moment. "I trust you." He knew that was probably the hardest thing she'd ever said to him.

Relief flooded him; he reached into his pocket and pulled out the soft cloth bag he'd taken from his dresser at home. "I've got something for you. I was going to wait until your birthday, next month, and wrap it up pretty. But I want you to have it now."

Her hands were shaking, which was all right because his were, too. She emptied the pouch in her palm.

Looking up at him, she cocked her head. "What are these?"

"They're medals I found in a fire fighter's catalogue." He reached down and picked up the smaller, more delicate twenty-four-carat chain. On the end of it was half a medal with half of a Maltese cross etched in it. "This is yours. The bigger chain's mine." He picked the second medal up and fitted one half of the cross to the other. "It reads, 'May God watch over you when we're apart.'" He coughed, cleared his throat, rocked by the same emotion that had overcome him when he ordered the medals. "When the medal's together, it's whole. When it's apart, it's incomplete." He threaded his hand through her hair, and their gazes locked. "Just like us."

Her eyes swam with tears.

"I want you to wear this and not take it off until we can be together openly." He took her gold chain and slipped it over her head.

And he waited.

In seconds she took his, longer and heavier, and reverently roped it around his neck.

"I love you, Chels. I want to be with you for the rest of our lives. I'm like this medal, not whole without you."

"I love you, too."

He touched his forehead to hers. When he drew back, he stood and held out his hand. "I know we don't have much time, but come to bed with me. I need you."

His heart was full at the watery smile she gave him. Then she placed her hand in his.

CHELSEA SHOWED UP for work at four-thirty, just on time. Still raw about the water problem, she'd decided to follow Beth's advice and observe her co-workers on the next two nights. Was one of them a Jekyll and Hyde? The idea made her stomach churn.

Her thoughts turned to Jake; he'd beaten her here by only minutes, as they'd left her bed with just enough time to shower and dress. He was in the office as she walked by and gave her a casual salute through the glass barrier. She nodded, staring at him, remembering how only an hour before his body had driven into hers with almost frightening possessiveness. He'd showed her, physically, that she was his. Fingering the chain barely visible around her neck, she tore her gaze away and headed for the kitchen.

Joey, Mick, Don and Peter were sitting at the table, each reading. Briefly she wondered if they'd gotten together today, too, to discuss her. She felt tiny pinpricks of pain at the thought.

"Whitmore, get some coffee and come over here. I need help." Peter was surrounded by books; he looked like a scholarly professor with glasses perched on his nose. She grabbed a mug and took a seat next to him.

"What's this?" she asked casually, as if her world wasn't caving in around her.

"Cookbooks. I'm chef tonight and need help finding a good recipe for this fish." He rolled his eyes. "One *Mick* will like."

"I'm not a fish man," Mick said, his eyes glued to his book. Then he laughed at what he read.

Joey grunted, reading the paper.

Don snorted. "You're too picky. Lucy would never put up with that."

Chelsea couldn't ignore the comment. Come to think of it, he—and Mick—had made a lot of those remarks in the past few weeks. *Was* there trouble in their marriages? Or was she looking at things with a magnifying glass?

Chelsea glanced at Peter's books. *The New Healthy Firehouse Cookbook, The Firefighter's Low Fat Cookbook* and *The Fit Firefighter's Recipe Book.* "Where'd you get these?" she asked.

"I bought 'em. Thought we needed new ones."

She smiled. Mick laughed again.

"What are you readin'?" Joey asked him.

"Something I brought in for Whitmore. I'll tell ya in a minute."

As Mick continued to read, Chelsea and Peter paged through the cookbooks. Chelsea found a possibility and pointed it out to Peter.

"You like orange flavoring, Mick?" Peter asked.

He raised his eyes. "I like orange Popsicles. That count?"

She and Peter decided it counted, and chose orange-glazed halibut.

After another burst of laughter from Mick, Joey said, "What the hell you got there, Murphy?"

"It's a book of firefighter jokes."

"God, those are awful. I read some before, and they were stupid."

Mick's eyes twinkled. "These are different. They're all female-firefighter jokes. Andrea found it at a bookstore a while ago. I was savin' it for a special occasion, but…" His voice trailed off. Though last night stood between them like a brick wall, Mick's comment was the closest anybody had come to mentioning it and the strain between them.

Chelsea gave Mick a warm smile. He always came through for her, though she recognized Peter's intention with the cookbooks was to include her, too.

"Okay, shoot." She made her voice firm. "But I warn you, if they're sexist, I got a whole locker full of male-bashing jokes that Delaney got off the internet. I'll get 'em out."

Don, Joey and Peter groaned loudly.

"Nah, you'll love these." Mick lowered his eyes. "What do you call a firefighter's wife who knows where her husband is every night?"

She shrugged.

"A widow."

Chelsea laughed. The rest of the men grunted.

"A firefighter had a conversation with God. He asked, 'Why'd you make woman so beautiful?' God, said, 'So you'd love her.' The firefighter said, 'Why'd you make her so dumb? God replied, 'So she'd love you.'"

Again Chelsea laughed. Three jokes later, Peter said, "Murphy, gimme a break."

Jake came in and threw a paper on the table. "This week's trivia from O'Roarke. They're tough."

Don picked it up. Peter stood and went to the fridge. Joey buried his face in the newspaper.

"Here's a good one," Mick said. "How many sensitive, interesting, liberated men in the fire department would it take to clean the firehouse?"

Everybody shook their heads.

"Both of them."

Jake came to the table. "What's all this about?"

"A book his wife found," Chelsea explained. "It's dedicated to female firefighters."

"Just what we need." He winked at her, though. She smiled. "We're doing some training after dinner," he told the crew. "The last of the confined-space program."

"Dinner's at six," Peter informed them.

"Let's do the training first," Joey said. "There's something I want Chelsea to help me with later."

Everybody agreed, but Mick said, "One more, then I'll put this away. A female smoke eater told her colleagues that her boyfriend was like a snowstorm. She said, 'You don't know when he's coming or how many inches you'll get or how long it'll stay.'"

"Enough!" Jake roared. But everybody laughed, and the tension was suitably broken. Once again, Mick was a lifesaver.

After the training and dinner, Chelsea headed for the exercise room. She was exhausted from no sleep last night and hoped working out would tire her enough to make her zonk tonight. She was still tense and upset, but at least she and Jake had found a way to deal with this so far, and things at the firehouse were okay, too. Like bad food, she shoved away thoughts of sabotage. They were impossible to digest.

Joey found her on the treadmill after a half hour. He carried a newspaper with him. He'd folded it open to an ad and put it in her line of vision. "There's a triathlon for men just before Christmas."

Lightly jogging, Chelsea nodded. "I know, my gym manager is thinking about entering."

"Grip's Gym might sponsor me. That's where I work out."

"It's a good place, but they're hurting for trainers."

"Yeah, they are."

When he didn't say any more, Chelsea asked, "Do you want some help from me, Joe?"

"I'd pay you."

"Don't be silly. I don't want your money."

Folding his arms, he watched her for a minute. "Then how about my friendship?"

Slowing, she cocked her head.

"I haven't been the best since you came on board."

"You've been okay lately." *Everybody has. Could it possibly be one of you?*

"Can I do somethin'?" He motioned to include the firehouse. "You know, about this stuff with the air pack and water tank?"

She felt her eyes sting. "No, you can't, but thanks." She got off the treadmill and wiped her face with a towel. "Give me the paper and get a pad. Let's outline what you should start with. You don't have a lot of time."

He grinned, said, "Thanks," and headed for the door.

"Santori?"

He turned.

"Thank *you*."

Just before bed, Don found her in the common room leafing though *Firehouse* magazine. In his hand he had a paper. "Hey, Chelsea, wanna go in on the trivia game with me this week? I always feel like I'm back in grade school on this and thought if I had some help…"

Recognizing the gesture, she smiled. "Sure."

Taking a pencil from behind his ear, he sat on the couch. "It's hard."

She read the questions aloud. "Name the country with the following fire-suppression regulations." She looked at Don. "You sure you want to do this?"

"I already know three," he said proudly. "Japan's the place where a person can be imprisoned for causing a fire because of negligence. Sweden trains chimney sweeps to inspect fireplaces and furnaces. And France pays only partial insurance to landlords to decrease the possibility of arson on their parts."

"How do you know those things?"

"My kid has books on firefighting. Lots of stories in

them about those countries. I figure we got a shot if I know three."

"I only know one. Delaney went to England last year. They spend a million dollars a year on fire-safety commercials."

He grinned. "Two to go, kid."

"I have no idea what place has fire marshals in its apartment buildings."

"Hong Kong." Chelsea looked up to see Jake smiling from the doorway. He shrugged. "It's the only one I know, so I'm not playin' this week."

"Hot damn." Don punched his fist in the air.

"That leaves the one that has building codes and insurance laws that require every room to have two exits."

Jake shook his head. "Sorry. Don't know it."

"Me, neither," Chelsea said.

Don stood. "Joey's father's in insurance. Maybe he'll call him. This'll be a real team effort." Don squeezed her shoulder as he left; Chelsea patted his hand.

"You okay?" Jake sank into a chair, looking tired and tense. She wanted to touch him, to rub his back, to curl up in his arms and take the tension away.

"Yeah." She glanced at the door. "They're something else."

"They're trying with you, Chels."

"I know. They did good tonight."

"How about me?" he asked boyishly.

"You're doing good, too."

"You look exhausted."

"I am."

"Me, too." He ran a hand through his hair. "I hope you sleep tonight."

"You, too."

"Too bad we—"

She stood abruptly. "Don't say it, Lieutenant. We're at

work.'' On her way past him, she touched his arm. Feeling better than she thought she would, she headed for the showers.

UNDER THE COVERS in the black-as-night bunk room, the man checked the lighted dial of his watch. Three. He hadn't been able to fall asleep.

Damn. It hadn't worked. Everybody'd been nicer to her, including Jake. All that came out of it was a goddamned letter in her file.

And she looks like shit.

Well, that couldn't be helped. He'd thought the guys would ostracize her, and he'd be the hero by being nice to her.

Again, his plan hadn't worked.

He grasped the sheet tightly. He'd have to do something else. And soon. Hyde wouldn't let him rest until he did. He couldn't sleep, thinking about it.

Neither could they. First she'd crept out of the bunk room about one. Jake had followed a half hour later. That wasn't unusual. Both of them were insomniacs. He'd found them out in the kitchen talking on many night shifts.

Hmm. Insomnia. No sleep.

He turned over. That gave him an idea. A really good idea, one he wouldn't have to wait long to implement. Maybe he could even do it tomorrow night.

Jeez, it was a biggie. Did he dare?

Jekyll didn't.

But maybe Hyde would.

CHAPTER SIXTEEN

ON THE LAST EVENING of their night shift, Jake couldn't sleep. He was exhausted, but the demons would not be kept at bay. He lay in his bunk, all that had happened in the past few days running through his mind.

As a show of faith, Chelsea had come to his house this morning right after work. He'd fixed breakfast, they'd talked about superficial stuff, then they'd made love. Once again, like the afternoon before, it was a tender, bittersweet union; it had been partly an effort to cement their bond, partly to heal the wounds caused by doubt. They slept briefly, but each had commitments—she at the gym, and he shopping for college with Jess—so they were both running on empty when they reported for work that afternoon. With three days off coming up, he hoped to catch up on his sleep—with her.

She'd looked spent tonight when she got to the firehouse. So much so that the guys had surreptitiously taken care of her. Jake smiled into the darkness, thinking of the men who slept around him. First, Peter cooked dinner—they hadn't eaten until eight because of some calls—and then he served up her plate himself and got her iced tea to drink. Later Jake watched Mick fetch her after-dinner coffee; then Don refilled her cup as they chatted around the table. Joey had poured her milk with dessert. They were tripping over themselves to coddle her. Obviously they were all worried about her. So was he.

Jake checked his watch dial. One. She was on first

watch tonight; he hoped she'd catch some sleep when she was relieved at two. Maybe he'd get up and go—

The tone sounded, and the lights in the bunk room came on. "Heart attack victim, seventy-year-old female at Dutch Towers. Midi Twelve go into service."

As he whipped off the sheet, Jake's heart thudded in his chest like a runner's. Though Peter and Chelsea were on the Midi—the other guys rolled over and went back to sleep—Jake bounded out of bed, dragged on his pants and boots and headed to the bay. A cold stab of fear in his chest reminded him that Mrs. Lowe was seventy.

Peter was right behind him. "Why didn't she come in?" he asked, buttoning his pants.

Jake didn't know what Peter meant. Then he realized that Chelsea hadn't come to the bunk room, the traditional watch behavior. Before he had time to react, he reached the office to get the computer printout.

He froze at the sight that greeted him. Chelsea was hunched over in her chair, her head pillowed in her arms. For a minute, he panicked, thinking she was ill or... He raced to her as Peter stopped in the doorway.

Grasping her shoulder, he shook her. "Chelsea."

Nothing.

"Chelsea."

"Jake, the Midi has to go." Peter's reminder startled him.

Chelsea raised her head. He eyes were glazed and groggy. "What..." she muttered drowsily.

She'd fallen asleep! Jake stared openmouthed at her; then, without a word, he turned and hurried after Peter to the Midi, taking Chelsea's place on shotgun.

In the cab he operated on automatic, ignoring the cold knot in his stomach. They'd lost a precious minute, maybe two. Because a firefighter had fallen asleep on watch. Jake blanked his mind, read the computer printout and talked to the dispatcher.

A tinny voice told him, "CPR is being given by a fellow resident, who phoned nine-one-one after the victim called her with chest pains. The victim's lost consciousness and maybe pulse. An ambulance is on the way. Over."

"You had the Red Cross teach the CPR course out at Dutch Towers," Peter observed.

"Maybe it'll help." Jake said in the radio, "Who's the victim?"

The dispatcher came over the line again. "We don't know. Just a seventy-year-old woman."

Sirens blaring, lights flashing, the truck skidded to a halt; Jake and Peter bounded out of the Midi. Peter took the ALS bag, and Jake went around to get the oxygen.

Inside the front door, they were met by Sergio Olivo and Moses Santori.

"It's Addie," Moses said. "Apartment—"

Jake knew the number. Choking back the raw emotion in his throat, he raced down the hall. *Please God, please, don't let her die.*

The door to her apartment was open. They hurried in. Adelaide Lowe lay on her back in a flowered nightgown looking as tiny as a child. Another resident of Dutch Towers, Katherine MacKenzie, knelt over her and compressed her chest. When they reached the woman, Jake could see that Mrs. Lowe's skin was pasty and her lips were blue.

Peter said, "Mrs. M, you're doing a great job. When I give you the signal, I want you to stop so I can check for a pulse. Now, stop compressions."

Mrs. MacKenzie stopped. Peter palpated the carotid artery, then took over the chest compression. "No pulse."

With robotic movements, Jake got out the oxygen tank,

broke the seal and fitted the mask over Mrs. Lowe's mouth.

The ambulance sirens sounded close, and in moments paramedics dashed into the apartment. Jake and Peter stepped back as the attendants took over CPR and set up the defibrillator equipment.

"Stand back," one called.

In the chill black silence, broken only by the obscene buzz of the electric shocks, Jake watched the team deliver treatment to the small, fragile chest. He cringed, hoping the pressure didn't break brittle bones. Holding his breath, he prayed hard for the life of the old woman he'd come to love.

CHELSEA LEANED against the counter sipping coffee as Jake and Peter trudged into the kitchen. Still woozy, she blinked hard and tried to calm the fear that coiled in her stomach like a poisonous snake. "Is she all right?" Chelsea asked them.

Passing her to get coffee, Peter patted her arm. "We don't know yet. The paramedics got her heart started and rushed her to the hospital. We're not sure how she is."

"Who was it?"

"Mrs. Lowe."

Chelsea's whole body tensed as a painful knot of remorse lodged in her throat. "Oh, Jake, I'm sorry."

He hadn't looked at her. Now he did. She shrank from what she saw there—blame.

"Come into the back office with me, Chelsea." His voice was like a coroner's announcing a death.

With grim resignation, she followed him down the hall. The station house was quiet again. Mick was on watch; Peter had gone to find him. In a few hours everybody would know.

The back room still held desks and a phone from Operation Suzy. Quietly Jake shut the door, leaned against the desk and pinched the bridge of his nose. Then he looked at her. "What happened?"

"I don't know."

He drew in a deep breath. "You were out cold."

A heaviness in her chest almost kept her from answering. "I know. I'm just not sure why."

"You were exhausted. You haven't slept for days."

"I've had catnaps. In any case, I've stayed awake on watch before without rest."

"I found you asleep myself, damn it."

She arched her eyebrows; her pulse escalated at the spark of anger flaring out of him. "I know. And quite frankly, I still feel groggy."

He threw his hands up. "That doesn't help."

Determined, she crossed her arms. "Jake, I feel like I feel after I take a sleeping pill."

"People usually do when awakened from a sound sleep."

Damn, he wasn't getting it; she had to say it out loud. "I feel drugged, Jake."

"Drugged?" His face was incredulous. *"Drugged?"*

"Yes."

He stared hard at her. Like a stranger. Like *she* was a stranger. "What are you saying?"

Deep in her heart, she knew she had to go for broke. She only wished she'd told him before. Then this wouldn't sound like such an excuse. "When I went to Beth's two days ago, we discussed something I didn't tell you about."

"You wouldn't tell me anything then."

"I was wrong. I should have approached you as my officer."

He arched a brow, waiting.

"Jake, none of this fits. Too many things have gone wrong in the last few weeks. Either I'm the most incompetent firefighter in the department, or something else is happening.''

She noticed he didn't deny her incompetence.

So she raised her chin, remembering her childhood lesson. *You only have yourself to rely on, Chelsea.* Feeling utterly alone, she said, ''Well, I'm not incompetent. What's more, I'm not careless. And I'm certainly not negligent enough to fall asleep on watch. I've had hundreds of watches where I was more tired or upset than I am now, and I've never even dozed off. Besides, I had two cups of coffee, and tea at supper, then more coffee on watch tonight.''

As if in slow motion, she pictured Peter getting her iced tea from the fridge. Mick and Don taking turns refilling her coffee. Joey serving her milk.

''What are you saying, Chelsea?'' His voice was like cut glass.

''I'm saying I turned off the stove a few weeks ago. I'm saying I checked both my air tank and the Midi water.'' She drew in a steadying breath. ''I'm saying several people had access to what I drank tonight.''

The shock on Jake's face cut like a scalpel. It twisted in her gut when she saw the doubt follow it. ''Are you saying…are you accusing one of my men of…'' It was like he couldn't get the words out. Finally he finished, ''Sabotaging you?''

It sounded stark and melodramatic.

Yet it had to be true. Beth was right. There was no other explanation.

''I should have told you earlier about my suspicions.''

''I…I can't believe it.''

''You mean, you can't believe *me*.''

''Chelsea, do you know what you're saying? Who you're accusing? One of the guys, here, in our group. I've worked with them for years. I've trusted them with my life."

Swallowing hard, she tried to close the door on the hurt. But it kept pushing, trying to get out. "All I know is I'm not incompetent, careless or negligent. And my body tells me right now that something isn't right inside."

His face was blank. "I don't know what to say."

"It's obvious what you think."

"What?"

"You don't believe me."

"Chelsea, I—"

"Well, do you?"

He stared at her. Finally he said, "I don't know what to believe."

Chelsea wasn't sure what she expected, but it wasn't the wrenching pain that ambushed her, taking her down unexpectedly. The best she could do now was protect herself. "Never mind what you believe. What will you *do?*"

"I have to report this to the battalion chief."

"I expected that."

"You'll be brought up on charges. Suspended."

She cleared her throat. "It doesn't matter." Nothing did, in the face of his disbelief. His distrust. Staring at his stunned face, she remembered his words. *Say you trust me, Chels.* She swallowed hard, blinked back tears. She had to be strong. A brittle silence stretched between them.

He broke it. "What do you want me to tell them?"

"Just the facts."

"Will you tell them…what you suspect?"

"I don't know." What did it really matter, anyway? She was finished. With the fire department. With a lot of things. She told him, "I'll wait here, if you don't mind. Chief Talbot will probably come right over."

Looking stricken, Jake nodded. He straightened and approached the door. She turned her back to him.

After a moment he said, "Chels?"

She pivoted.

His face was a mask of agony. Because she loved him she whispered, "Go make your call, Jake. I know you don't have any choice." It wasn't much, but it was the best she could do.

She turned before he could say more. Then she heard the soft swish of the door opening and closing. Sinking onto the chair, she told herself to be strong, to think clearly, to ignore the immobilizing fear kindling inside her. She needed all her wits about her to get through the next few hours—alone.

THE NEWS of Chelsea's suspension spread through the Rockford Fire Department like wildfire in a drought. Jake knew that Ben Cordaro would have heard about it already as he approached the chief's office at five that night.

What a day, Jake thought as he climbed the academy stairs. First there had been the painful witnessing of Chelsea's meeting with Battalion Chief Talbot. She'd remained stoic through the whole thing and left the office and the firehouse without looking at Jake. He hadn't gone to find her after his relief arrived. Instead, he'd spent hours at the hospital, waiting for news on Mrs. Lowe. By three, when he was able to see the old woman in intensive care, it looked as though she was going to make it.

She'd grasped Jake's hand in her thin papery one and said, "That CPR course you had the Red Cross teach us saved my life. You're a good firefighter, Jake Scarlatta."

He didn't feel like a good firefighter. He felt like the worst kind of traitor. All day long, he'd berated himself for betraying the woman he loved in the only way she'd asked him not to. All she'd wanted was for him to trust her. And he didn't. He could still see those brandy-colored eyes muddy with pain and disappointment. When he wasn't thinking about how he hurt her, he pondered her words. Could someone on his crew be sabotaging her? It was almost unthinkable.

But he had to think about it and he needed help doing that.

Ben's door was ajar; Jake knocked lightly. "Come in," Ben said, then waved Jake to sit down. He mumbled into the phone, "I've got company now. I can't talk anymore." He scowled. "I'll make you pay for that one, Mrs. Cordaro, when I get home." He glanced at his watch. "I'll be leaving soon. Try to behave yourself until I get there."

After he hung up he grinned at Jake sheepishly. He looked like a young suitor. "My wife thinks we're sixteen again."

Jake was amused by Ben's affectionate gruffness. And jealous. His heart clenched as he remembered how he'd wanted that kind of bond with Chelsea.

"What's wrong?" Ben asked, studying him carefully. "Is it the thing with Chelsea?"

"Yeah."

Ben grimaced. "Francey's all up in arms."

"I need to talk to you about this, Ben."

Sober, Ben rose, closed the door and took a chair across from Jake. "Shoot."

"First, let me say I abided by protocol in handling this."

"I never thought otherwise."

"You might."

"Why?"

Briefly Jake described the stove, air pack and Midi water incidents.

"I've got no problem with how you handled them," Ben told him. "It's what I would have done." He watched Jake. "What else is going on here, Jake?"

"Two things. The first is that Chelsea swears she wasn't negligent in any of these cases."

"You found her asleep."

"She says she was drugged."

"*What?*"

Jake outlined Chelsea's claims.

"That's unbelievable."

"At first I thought it was crazy. But the thing is, she's got a point. She's an exceptional firefighter. Having so many things happen, so close together, *is* suspicious."

"You said two things. What's the other?"

Jake held Ben's gaze unflinchingly. "I'm in love with her."

At first Ben didn't react. Then he nodded. "Well, that's a handful."

"Because of what happened with Danny," Jake said raggedly, "I know this doesn't look good for me. I think I handled everything objectively, but who knows?" He stood and began pacing. "But more's at stake here than just that. My group's integrity is in question."

Ben said, "I think we should call Reed in on this. Tell him Chelsea's suspicions, and yours. Then we'll decide where to go with it."

"All right."

Thoughtful, Ben added, "We don't have to tell him about your feelings for Chelsea."

"No, I'd like him to know everything." Jake ran a hand through his hair. "I'm sick of this secrecy."

"Maybe you'll feel differently when you see this." Scooping a paper off his desk, Ben handed it to him. "The results of the captaincy exam."

Jake scanned the memo. "I came in first."

"Yes. And, off the record, Ed Knight *is* retiring in January. So there's an opening in your own station house."

"Wow."

"Does this change what you want to do now?"

Shaking his head, Jake said, "No."

"Then let's take this one step at a time."

An hour later Reed Macauley scanned his notes, every inch the professional. "This is incredible."

"I think now that she might be right, Reed," Jake said.

"Me, too. For several reasons. First off, it's too much of a coincidence that these mistakes would happen all at once." He frowned at the papers. "And the opportunities that each of the men had to execute each incident are certainly here.

"Mostly, though, it's the guys' personal situations that worry me. Don and Mick's marital problems, Peter's experience with his ex-partner and Joey's long-standing anger over Francey give them reason to want women out of the department—in their place, so to speak."

Ben shook his head. "I can't believe it's Joey."

Jake stood again. "I can't believe it's any of them. I've worked with these guys for years. They're like brothers to me. I've eaten, slept and played with them. It's so hard to believe...."

"Is it easier to believe Chelsea's incompetent? And foolish?" Reed asked.

Jake thought, *No, but that's how she probably sees it.* For the first time he realized the import of his disbelief. Oh, he knew he'd betrayed her. But he hadn't realized just how badly. And there, facing Ben and Reed, Jake knew in his heart it couldn't be fixed.

Grimly he remembered her words that first weekend together. *I couldn't bear to go through what I did with Billy again.*

You won't, he'd said. *I promise.*

But she was.

Because of him.

THOUGH HE WAS exhausted, Jake didn't go home. Instead, he drove to the firehouse. Both the Quint and the Midi were out on a call. He strode into the deserted bay, feeling like the walls were closing in on him. His chest was tight with loss. He hadn't handled this right, hadn't tried to understand her side of it.

He headed for the locker room. He didn't know why until he got there. Sitting down in front of the row of lockers that were his group's, he looked at the name tags. Whitmore. Scarlatta. Murphy. Huff. Santori. Diaz. Staring at them, he saw images of each of them with her—Huff cooking turkey meatballs for her, Joey's sheepish thanks for the apple pie, Diaz and his silly prank with the bedspread, Murphy's stand, *'Cause if we do have a say, I vote to forget it.*

Feeling more conflicted than he ever had with Danny, Jake sighed deeply, and his gaze dropped to the floor. In between the vinyl and the wall, below Murphy's and Diaz's lockers, he noticed something. He leaned over and tried to pry it out of the crack. When it wouldn't budge, he reached into his jeans pocket, pulled out the pocket-knife Derek had given him for Father's Day and used it to flick the item out.

His heart hammered in his chest. The little blue pill nestled obscenely in his palm. He turned it over with the knife and recognized the over-the-counter sleeping pill trademark. He closed his eyes.

Oh, my God.

Fear, along with profound regret lodged in him like a dead weight. Zombielike, he stood and walked to the kitchen. Slowly he pulled open the drawer, took out a plastic bag and, à la *NYPD Blue,* placed the evidence in it. He zipped it tight, all the while assaulted by a damning litany. *You didn't believe her. You didn't believe her. You didn't believe her.*

The phone jarred him out of his daze. "Quint Twelve. Lieutenant Scarlatta speaking."

"Oh, good, Jake, you *are* on. This is Andrea Murphy. Can I speak to Mick?"

"Mick? Andrea, we're off for three days."

"Oh." She coughed. "When you answered, I thought...."

"Andie, why don't you know that?"

Silence. Then sniffles. "Oh, Jake, Mick and I have been separated for weeks now."

"What?"

"I moved out...for a lot of reasons." She began to cry in earnest.

"Listen, where are you? I'll come over."

"I'm at work. But you could come to Mercy House. It's quiet here tonight."

"I'll be right there."

HE LIT CANDLES to breach the darkness. It was so quiet here now. He almost couldn't stand it. Maybe some light would help. He poured another shot of whiskey from the bottle that Hyde had told him to buy on the way home. In the dim light, the quart looked half empty. Had he drunk that much? It didn't matter. He sipped the booze as he watched the flames flicker.

It was done.

It was for the best.

Adamantly he blocked out the pain in Whitmore's face. It was for the best. Now she'd take her rightful place....

The doorbell rang. Who could that be? Maybe it was... He rose quickly, bounded for the door like a boy at Christmas, hoping... He yanked it open.

"Jake. Hello."

"Hi, Mick."

Mick squared his shoulders, summoned Jekyll and squelched Hyde. "Come on in, buddy."

With heavy steps Jake walked into the room, then stopped abruptly. "What are you doing, Mick?"

"Havin' a little drink."

"Candles?"

Jesus, he'd forgotten. He crossed to the votive offerings and doused them. Then he flicked on a light. "Ah, sometimes I get carried away when Andie's workin'. Feel maudlin. You know how it is."

"Yes, Mick, I do."

Mick went cold inside, like he did when he was afraid he'd revealed a glimpse of his dark side.

"Want a drink?"

"No, thanks. But I'll sit." Jake dropped into a chair. Mick wished he'd stop looking at him like that.

"Feelin' bad about Whitmore?" Mick asked. *The best defense…*

"Yeah, I am."

"Shit, who'd've thought?"

"I never would've, Mick."

"You know, though, it's for the best. I liked her enough, Jakey, but women… You really think they can cut it in our job?"

"Don't you?"

"Nah." He took another belt. "This women's lib stuff…"

He got up and poured more whiskey. He'd lost track of how much he'd had. At the counter, he kept his back to Jake.

After a long silence Jake asked, "Is that why you did it, Mick? To protect her?"

He whirled around, grasping the edge of the counter for balance. "Did what?"

Jake pulled a plastic bag out of his pants pocket. Mick

stared at it. Jake said, "I spent an hour with Andrea tonight. She's worried about your behavior lately, your black moods, your isolation. She's especially worried since she took your daughter and moved out."

Mick's throat closed up, but he raised his chin like a little boy caught shoplifting. "So now you know."

"Yeah, now I know, Mick," Jake said softly.

CHELSEA JOLTED UPRIGHT in bed. Both Blaze and Hotstuff were snoozing at the foot of the mattress, and she focused on them for grounding. Some kind of ringing had awakened her. She looked at the phone. It was silent. Then she recognized the sound as the doorbell. She glanced at the clock. One in the morning.

Terror tripped her pulse. No, it couldn't be Billy. She'd heard only last week that he'd left town for a while.

Whoever it was persisted. She crept out of bed, not bothering with a robe to cover her baby-doll pajamas; she had no intention of opening the three locks on the door. She'd just see who it was.

Downstairs, she looked through the peephole.

Jake.

She leaned her forehead against the door. After the confrontation with Talbot, Chelsea had come home and shut herself off, like she had when she was a child, a teenager, and needed to make sense of her world. She'd locked herself inside her house and not answered any calls. During those desolate hours, she'd made decisions; many had to do with the man outside the door.

As if he sensed her presence, he knocked hard on the wood. "Chelsea, it's me, Jake. Let me in."

Rattled by the events of the day, she couldn't block the refrain. *Let me in. Trust me. I promise....*

"I know you're there," he said. "I'm not going away."

Slowly she undid the locks and opened the door. He

stood before her in jeans and a black T-shirt. He looked haggard, pale.

But his eyes did her in. They were tormented. "I'm not going away," he repeated. "We have to talk."

She guessed it didn't matter when they talked. What she had to say would always cut like glass slivers into tender flesh. Without a word she stepped aside and Jake strode in and over to the couch, a man with a purpose. Jamming his hands in his pockets, he swallowed hard and stared at her. "I have two things to tell you. First, officially, you *were* sabotaged."

A quick right to her jaw couldn't have stunned her more. *"What?"*

"You were sabotaged. I have a full confession from Mick."

"What?"

He reached out and squeezed her arm. "Yes, it was Mick, honey."

Mick? *Mick?* Oh, no, no, not him. Like previews from a movie, images flashed before her—Mick welcoming her the first day, Mick telling her stupid jokes, Mick overwrought when she was almost killed.

It was too much to bear. She backed up until her legs hit the couch, and she sank onto it.

Jake squatted before her and grasped her hands as he told her the details. She almost couldn't take them in—a childhood with parents who sparred regularly over his mother's role in the family, an obsessive need to be the man of the house in his adult life, a wife who wanted a measure of independence. Jake thought Mick did it to protect her. Andrea had told Jake that Mick had been treated for a mental disorder, but they'd kept it from the fire department for fear he'd lose his job.

Tears trickled down Chelsea's cheeks, as he finished the dismal story. She said only, "Poor Mick."

Jake wiped away her tears with his thumb and smiled sadly. "You're something else."

He took a seat across from her on the footstool without letting go of her hands. "The department will provide medical and psychological help, but he's finished as a firefighter."

She nodded, still numb, as if she'd spent hours in a cold lake. Jake went on. "There'll be an official apology to you from the RFD. Chief Talbot wants to meet with you as soon as you're up to it. He said to tell you you can have as much time off as you need." Jake cleared his throat. "He's upset about how the department has treated you."

Chelsea shook her head. "I'm not going back to the department."

Jake's jaw tensed. "Why?"

"I'll never belong there, Jake. This is the second station where I didn't fit. I'll always be an outsider. I'm done with this. I don't want to be a firefighter anymore."

His gaze seemed to bore into her soul. "What about me? Are you done with me, too?"

She stood then, unable to weather his penetrating gaze. She crossed to the window and looked out. Night closed in on her, and she found it hard to breathe. Wrapping her arms around her waist, she said, "Yes, I am."

"Because I didn't believe you."

"Yes. When you stood there and told me you didn't know what to believe, it felt like the guys at Engine Four turning on me all over again. I'm not sure I can ever forget that. Ever trust you again."

"I know it hurt. I wish I could take it back." He came up behind her and rubbed her arms gently. "Can't we work this out?" His voice was a low, tortured whisper.

"No." She turned. "Look, not one single person knows what's happened between us. You can come out of this unscathed."

"I want to come out of this with *you*."

"That's not going to happen."

Jake stared at her. "After what we've shared, do you think I'm going to simply accept this decision?"

She raised her chin. "Yes. I expect you to honor my wishes."

He could feel his face flush. "I want you to marry me. We'll work everything out," he repeated.

"You made that promise to me before. You couldn't keep it."

Reaching over, he cupped her cheek. "Chels, I can't believe you mean this."

"I mean it."

"What if I won't accept it?"

"You have no choice. I want nothing to do with the fire department ever again. That includes you, Jake."

"So, we're a package deal? Get rid of me and the fire department in one fell swoop?"

"I can't separate the two."

"Well, I guess that shows me how important I am to you."

Her face paled. "It's for the best."

Looking hard at the woman he loved, he stepped back. Anger boiled within him. It felt good, for it knocked out some of the pain. He clenched his hands. He could beg. Try to convince her to change her mind. He could defend himself, tell her he'd been caught off guard, that she should have shared her suspicions with him before. He could explain he'd been overwrought by Mrs. Lowe's condition. He could remind her that the whole incident brought back so many ghosts of Danny.

But he said none of those things. It would be too much like asking somebody to love you more than they did. To love you enough. The pain blindsided him, making him speechless. He watched as she reached up and grasped the chain around her neck. Slowly she removed it and placed the medal in his hand.

He thought he might die.

But he swallowed hard and, with the edges of the medal digging into his closed fist, he leaned over and kissed her forehead. In a voice like granite he said, ''I love you enough to work it out, Chels. I'm sorry you don't feel the same way.''

Then he turned and walked out of her house, quietly shutting the door for the last time.

A WEEK LATER, Chelsea pulled her Camaro into the Quint/ Midi Twelve parking lot. She sat unmoving for a moment, then drew a deep breath. So many homes she'd had and lost. This was just another one. In the rearview mirror, she saw Beth's Accord and Delaney's Miata draw up behind her. Shaking her head, Chelsea got out of the car. ''What's this—reinforcements?''

A long white dress swishing around her ankles, Delaney exited her car and descended on Chelsea like an avenging angel. ''Yep,'' she answered, and kissed Chelsea's cheek. ''You didn't think I'd let you face the enemy alone, did you?''

''They're not the enemy, but I appreciate the gesture.''

Delaney snorted and turned as Beth and Francey approached.

''Hi. Ready to bite the bullet?'' Beth asked.

''Yes.'' Chelsea frowned. ''You didn't have to come. I don't need an entourage to sign a few papers.''

It was Francey's turn to frown. ''You need support, Chels.''

Chels.

''What I need is to get this over with.'' Chelsea scanned the parking lot and winced. ''They're not gone. All their cars are here.''

"Who?"

"My group. I mean, Group Three."

"Dylan came in for the next shift," Beth said. She slid an arm around Chelsea's shoulders. "Your group must have waited to say goodbye, honey."

Feeling the familiar whirlpool of emotions well inside her, Chelsea said only, "They're entitled, I guess."

"They're not entitled to anything," Delaney snapped.

"Let's go," Chelsea said to forestall that discussion. All she needed was a scene.

The women entered the station house in force. Expecting the usual hustle of the firehouse shift change, Chelsea was surprised to see the bay empty. The trucks were out.

As if on cue, a line of uniformed men exited the station. First came Chief Talbot. Then Ben Cordaro. Finally Reed Macauley. They looked liked they were headed to the gallows.

"What's he doing here?" Delaney asked, nodding to Reed.

"Dad didn't say he'd be here, either," Francey commented.

Beth edged them forward. "Well, let's stop being shrinking female violets and ask."

They met the men head-on. "Hi," Chelsea said. "Is something happening I don't know about?"

Chief Talbot told her, "No. Cordaro and Macauley came for moral support."

She caught Ben's gaze and read the steady fatherly message in it. He and Reed had come for Jake. Chelsea was glad.

Talbot looked at her. "You sure you won't reconsider, Firefighter Whitmore? We could talk about a staff or academy job."

Reconsider? She'd had some second thoughts about resigning and about Jake's actions and why he'd done them.

But she'd pushed them aside. She didn't want to think about any of that.

"No, those aren't options. This is best. Thank you for offering, though."

"Shall we do this in the watch office?"

"Yes." She scanned the bay. "And fast, if you don't mind."

Chelsea went into the watch room. Images arose like dreams she couldn't control. Jake the first day. *I can understand why you're cautious. But for the record, I find your attitude unnecessarily defensive.* The night she'd given him the captaincy exam papers. *You know what? I think you're a coward.* Even Catwoman…so many memories. Her eyes misted.

Talbot was efficient. Within minutes, she'd signed away her past for an uncertain future. He said, "I'm sorry about all this, Chelsea."

She fought back the emotion. "Yeah, me, too."

Barely able to shake hands, she turned and left the office.

In the bay she stopped short. Don, Peter and Joey were just outside the door, soldiers standing at attention. A few feet away, Ben and Reed flanked Jake.

He looked sad. He looked tired. He looked so good she wanted to throw herself into his arms. Instead, she approached her crew. "I didn't think you'd be here."

"You thought wrong, Whitmore." This from Huff. His features were taut. "About a lot of things."

"Jeez, Chelsea, don't do this." Don's face was grim.

Joey stared at her.

"It's done." She smiled. "I'm gonna miss you guys."

She started with Peter. Reaching up, she gave him a big hug. "Stay cool, buddy."

"Always," he said, and held on for a minute.

Don's embrace was warm. *"Vaya con Dios,"* he said.

When she came to Joey, he pushed away from the wall and picked her up and hugged her. "This sucks big-time," he whispered.

"Hey, I'm gonna see you. At the gym."

Putting her down, he nodded.

Drained from the emotional encounter, she turned. She knew she had to face Jake. She just wished they didn't have an audience. She felt like she was on stage. What could he be thinking to have made his goodbye so public?

Jake watched her approach and felt his gut clench at the look on her face. He had to smile, though. She wore a white islet curve-hugging sundress that set off her tan. And strappy sandals. Feminine, frilly, so unlike the firefighter she was.

She shook hands with Reed and hugged Ben.

Then she stood before him. She extended her hand.

"I don't think so," he said gruffly, and encircled her with his arms. She felt so right, so much *his* he wanted to toss her over his shoulder like a caveman and drag her out of the bay. Instead, he held on, kissed the top of her head, then let her go. When she drew back, her eyes were watery and she didn't speak. Instead, she turned and walked away from him.

He let her get halfway across the bay before he called, "Hey, Whitmore?"

She froze, and her hands balled into fists.

"Turn around, love."

She did. Slowly.

Surer than he'd ever been in his life, Jake crossed his arms and said loudly, "You can leave if you want, but it's not over."

Her mouth opened. "Jake..."

"I know, I know. You think nobody should know about this. But you're wrong." He made sure he projected his voice.

There was a stirring among the women behind her, and the crew mumbled. He felt Talbot shift uneasily beside him.

"I want everybody to know about us. I'm done hiding it. I love you, Chels. I'm not letting you go without a fight." Hell, he'd do battle with the devil before he'd surrender.

She closed her eyes as he crossed the distance between them. Gently he grasped her arms. "You told me once I don't take emotional risks. How's this one?"

Looking at him with tear-spiked lashes, she said, "It's crazy."

"Good, because *I'm* crazy. About you." He rubbed his hands up and down her bare arms. "I'm not letting you go, babe. I know I let you down. And I'm sorry. I overreacted, plain and simple. I should have listened to you. I should have trusted you more. But I was so stuck on what happened with Danny, I didn't see it." He grasped her forearms. "Please, Chels. Forgive me for that. For being so stupid." He swallowed hard. "Say you'll try it again, between us. Say you love me enough to do that."

Her lips trembled. Fat tears formed in her eyes. "All right." She leaned into him. "I'll try again. I love you, too. I'm not sure I can live without you. I've been so miserable."

He smiled then. So did she.

"That's my girl." He reached into his pocket, took out her medal and looped it around her neck. Intimately, he tucked it into her dress. And then, in front of the amazed eyes of the Rockford Fire Department, he bent his head and kissed her.

EPILOGUE

"TEN, nine, eight, seven, six, five, four, three, two, one…" On the large TV screen, the announcer made the traditional count as the lighted ball dropped in Times Square over the crowd on Forty-Second Street.

When the clock struck twelve, Chelsea received a kiss from her husband of three and a half months.

"Happy New Year, love," he whispered.

She hugged him close. "Happy New Year. I love you."

He squeezed her. "I'll never get used to hearing that."

A Cheshire-cat smile crossed her face; after another brief hug, they turned to greet their guests. All off-duty personnel from the station house, along with some friends and family, had gathered in Jake and Chelsea's house to bring in the new year—the new millennium.

Chelsea's mouth dropped as she glanced toward her sister in the corner. Delaney had been sequestered almost the entire evening in the small alcove off the living room—with Reed Macauley. Like opposing lawyers, they'd been gesturing wildly, sometimes raising their voices, always shooting daggers at each other. Which was why Chelsea was shocked to see Reed lean forward, lock his hand around Delaney's neck and take her mouth in a long, sensual kiss. When Delaney pulled back, she stared at him, then rose abruptly and left the room. Reed went after her.

"What's that all about?" Jake asked, following Chelsea's line of vision.

"I have no idea."

Before they could speculate, the O'Roarkes approached them. Dylan looked spiffy in the slate blue sweater and shirt Chelsea had helped Beth pick out for him. Beth, svelte and sophisticated in a green velour pantsuit, hugged both Jake and Chelsea.

"Happy New Year, Captain Scarlatta." Dylan smiled broadly at Jake and shook his hand.

"Same to you, buddy. And congratulations, both of you, on your first wedding anniversary."

Beth and Dylan hugged. Then Dylan whipped out a paper. "This is my swan song for the trivia game. Since you're such a hotshot in the department now, I'm turning it over to you."

Grinning like he'd been given a birthday present, Jake grabbed Dylan's paper. "My pleasure."

"Dylan," Beth said, "maybe Chelsea won't—"

Chelsea interrupted, "I'm fine with it. I love having the guys here." She nodded to Joey and Don and Peter, who'd gathered in a sitting area across the room. Lucy had come with Don—things were working out for them—and Joey had a gorgeous redhead in tow, but Peter was alone. "As a matter of fact, I've got some news."

Francey and Alex, looking like ads from a fitness magazine in their matching Ralph Lauren burgundy warm-up suits that Alex had gotten them for Christmas, came up behind the O'Roarkes and caught the tail end of her sentence. Francey scowled. "News? Don't tell me you're pregnant. Alex will never let me alone about having a baby if you are."

Alex took her shoulders in a gentle grasp and kissed her hair. "You know you loved having Timmy when Dylan and Beth went to Jamaica after Christmas."

To celebrate their first anniversary, the O'Roarkes had taken a belated honeymoon—"Where it all started," Dylan had said, referring to his encounter with Beth at the

Templeton's wedding. Francey and Alex had watched Timmy while they were gone. Chelsea grinned as she thought about the three phone calls they'd made to Jake, frantic when the baby wouldn't stop crying. Jake had come to the rescue, like a knight in shining armor, and calmed Timmy.

He'd make a good father. Someday.

Jake had gone still at Francey's question and watched his wife. She was a vision tonight in a black velvet jumpsuit with gold trim; he didn't have a clue what she was going to say.

"No, I'm not pregnant." She gave him a private grin that said, *Not yet, anyway*. "But I do have something to tell you."

Diana and Ben breezed through the doorway, bearing trays of champagne. Chelsea's news was tabled while Ben stopped and offered champagne to them all.

"It's about time," Jake said to Ben. "You two went out to the kitchen way before midnight to get the bubbly."

Ben's face held not a hint of embarrassment. "Yep, we were neckin' out there." He kissed Francey's cheek. "I hope you're all as happy as *we* are."

The three couples smiled.

When everybody had champagne, Jake raised his glass. "I'd like to welcome in the new year and the new century with a toast to my wife, who's made me happier than anyone or anything in the world."

"Even the fire department?" Chelsea asked pointedly.

"Even that." He leaned over and kissed her, surprised she'd bring up the fire department in front of everybody.

At first, contact with the guys, official events and even the softball games had been hard for her. But eventually Chelsea had begun to feel at home with the RFD again, to forget the nightmare of Mick, who'd been hospitalized for a few months and was putting his life back together.

"It's my turn," she said, then raised her glass.

Dylan groaned. "Oh, God, now she's gonna toast him. You guys are so schmaltzy. You act like lovesick teenagers."

Beth and Francey said together, "You should talk."

"Nope," Chelsea told him. "My toast is different." She nodded to her group. "To the Rockford Fire Department, which," she said smoothly, "is very lucky to get me back, starting next week."

Jake nearly dropped his glass. "Really?" he said.

She smiled. "Yep. You're not the only one who loves the fire department, Captain."

His gaze flew to Ben. Jake and Chelsea had discussed her return to the department at length; he'd offered to move to another group to accommodate her if and when she decided to return. But nothing had been definite, or so he thought.

"No, you're not moving," Ben said, reading his mind. "And Chelsea's not going anywhere else but home to Group Three. The brass decided you two handled your issues like pros before you were married, and there's no reason to think there'll be problems now."

Joey said, "Yeah, over at Quint Six there's a married couple on the same shift."

"No one's worried," Ben added. "Besides, it's worth a try. If it causes personal or professional problems, we'll rearrange your assignments."

Jake hadn't thought anything could make him happier than he'd been at midnight. But this latest news... Not only did it show the department's faith in him, but also Chelsea's unconditional trust.

He felt like somebody had given him a million bucks.

But, hugging Chelsea to him, he glanced around the room at his group, his best friends, Ben and Diana. A million bucks was no match for the special people in his life.

He raised his champagne glass again and smiled broadly. "To all of us," he said.

* * * *

Look out for The Fire Within, *the final book in Kathryn Shay's exciting* CITY HEAT *series— on the shelves in February 2004.*

SILHOUETTE® SUPERROMANCE™

AVAILABLE FROM 16TH JANUARY 2004

SUBSTITUTE FATHER Bonnie K Winn

After their disastrous blind date, Luke Duncan never expects to see Kealey Fitzpatrick again. Then Kealey turns up as the social worker for the three kids Luke's adopted. But can they accept their differences and acknowledge they're right for each other—as a ready-made family?

THE NOTORIOUS MRS WRIGHT
Fay Robinson

Susan Wright lives a quiet life with her son Tom and owns a successful restaurant called Illusions—but is she the same woman as Emma Webster, who ran away as a teenager leaving a trail of deception and false identities? It's PI Whit Lewis's job to find out...*no*t to fall in love.

THE FIRE WITHIN Kathryn Shay

City Heat

Past pain is preventing former firefighter, now counsellor, Reed Macauley from letting anyone get too close. But Delaney Shaw isn't just anyone—she's the woman who loves him and she needs to help Reed overcome his past if there's any chance of a future for them...together.

SHOOTING THE MOON Brenda Novak

When her sister died, Lauren Worthington was left to bring up Audra's baby son, Brandon, alone. But when Brandon's father turns up wanting to get to know his son, Lauren doesn't know what to do. She'd always been told he was trouble—except he looks so good in that leather jacket...

AVAILABLE FROM 16TH JANUARY 2004

 **SILHOUETTE®**

Sensation™

Passionate, dramatic, thrilling romances

ONE OF THESE NIGHTS Justine Davis
MOMENT OF TRUTH Maggie Price
BENEATH THE SILK Wendy Rosnau
PRIVATE MANOEUVRES Catherine Mann
THE QUIET STORM RaeAnne Thayne
HONKY-TONK CINDERELLA Karen Templeton

Special Edition™

Vivid, satisfying romances full of family, life and love

MICHAEL'S DISCOVERY Sherryl Woods
HER HEALING TOUCH Lindsay McKenna
TAKING OVER THE TYCOON Cathy Gillen Thacker
BABY 101 Marisa Carroll
THE WEDDING BARGAIN Lisette Belisle
THE MISSING HEIR Jane Toombs

Intrigue™

Danger, deception and suspense

DADDY TO THE RESCUE Susan Kearney
PHANTOM LOVER Rebecca York
FAKE ID WIFE Patricia Rosemoor
UNDER LOCK AND KEY Sylvie Kurtz

Desire™ 2-in-1

Two intense, sensual love stories in one volume

LIONHEARTED Diana Palmer
INSTINCTIVE MALE Cait London

KISS ME, COWBOY! Maureen Child
THE TYCOON'S LADY Katherine Garbera

CINDERELLA & THE PLAYBOY Laura Wright
QUADE: THE IRRESISTIBLE ONE Bronwyn Jameson

 SILHOUETTE®

turning
point

SHARON SALA

Paula Detmer Riggs

Peggy Moreland

Three mysterious bouquets of red roses lead to three brand-new romances

On sale 16th January 2004

*Available at most branches of WH Smith,
Tesco, Martins, Borders, Eason, Sainsbury's
and all good paperback bookshops.*

0204/055/SH67

SILHOUETTE®
SPECIAL EDITION™

proudly presents

a brand-new series from
GINA WILKINS

THE McCLOUDS
OF MISSISSIPPI

*Three siblings find their way back
to family — and love.*

THE FAMILY PLAN
January 2004

CONFLICT OF INTEREST
March 2004

FAITH, HOPE AND FAMILY
May 2004

0104/SH/LC81